Sailing into a Storm

by

Laura Freeman

Sailing into a Storm

COPYRIGHT © 2024 by Laura E. Freeman

Cover Art by *Lisa Dawn MacDonald*

The Wild Rose Press, Inc.
PO Box 708
Adams Basin, NY 14410-0708
Visit us at www.thewildrosepress.com

Publishing History
First Edition, 2025
Trade Paperback ISBN 978-1-5092-5944-1
Digital ISBN 978-1-5092-5945-8

Published in the United States of America

Dedication

To my ancestors who bravely sailed across the Atlantic and settled in the fledgling colonies of America.

Chapter One

Lady Meg Culbertson entered the great hall of Whittington Manor. The cold winds of February chilled the large room, and she gathered her wool shawl tighter around her shoulders. The female servants had informed her a messenger had arrived from London and her father wished to speak to her. An hour ago.

She stood before the raised dais. "You summoned me?"

Lord John Culbertson, Earl of Whittington, gripped the lion heads carved into the arms of the ornate chair where he conducted business. "You took your time responding." His words were slurred. He was drunk, as usual, and his clothes were wrinkled as if he had slept in them.

Owen O'Leary spread a document on the table to her left next to a glass inkwell and quill. Thin and hard like a sliver of flint, he was the eldest of the earl's illegitimate children and now served as his steward. "The betrothal agreement has arrived from the colonies. The Honorable Eliot Richmond has signed the agreement as well as his father, Lord Dudlee. All that is required are your signature and Lord Whittington's."

She had paid little attention to the visits from Isaac Richmond, the second Baron of Dudlee. His family had accumulated wealth importing and exporting with the American colonies. She had thought he was loaning money to her father.

"If you had bothered to consult me, I would have informed you that I will not agree to marry someone I have never met," Meg said.

Her father stood with the aid of a servant and stepped toward the table. "It is not your decision but mine, and I have given my word."

She stared at the document that would seal her fate. If her mother, Katherine, had not been killed in a tragic accident two years ago, she would have fought this agreement. "I don't think the countess of Whittington would have approved." Meg crossed her arms. "I refuse to sign."

"I warned you she would resist," Owen said. "She would rather see you thrown in debtor's prison."

Her mother had taught her the skills of managing a large estate. She visited the tenants, making sure they had essentials for the ongoing winter months. She examined the inventory in the storage sheds and asked about the animals who would have to wait for warmer weather to graze. Although she had made mistakes initially, the estate seemed to be prospering, and Owen's dire prediction appeared false. How could the estate be failing with last year's harvest one of the best in years and the price of wool so high? It didn't make sense.

"You are the steward," Meg said. "Are your skills so lacking that you have driven this estate into ruin? Why don't you let me examine the ledgers?"

Owen's pale skin reddened, clashing with his strawberry-blond hair. He clenched his fists at his sides and jerked his body away to address the earl. "She dares defy your authority, Lord Whittington. You have been too lenient with her since her mother's death. She needs to be reminded who is her lord and master. You need to teach your daughter her place."

"I will be twenty-one in July," she said. "I will choose my husband then and not before."

"It will be too late." Owen's screech echoed off the stone walls. "I have paid the collectors the minimum to keep them at bay, but they want more. She has shown no interest in finding a husband. You have done your duty as a father to arrange this beneficial match."

"Sign, Margaret Katherine." Her father pointed at the document. "Or you leave me no choice."

Meg refused to budge. "I am the one with no choice."

Her father signaled to a servant who returned with a leather whip on a silver platter as if it were a meal.

She had witnessed this punishment upon others and thought it barbaric. "You would beat me? This is 1774, not the Middle Ages."

"Then sign." Her father removed the whip from the tray and snapped the grip with his wrist to crack the strip of leather in the air. The earl preferred to deliver justice in person and commanded obedience through fear.

Her knees went weak, but she fought the terror rising in her throat. She needed to remove her gown before it was ripped from her body. She handed her shawl to her half sister standing behind her. "Help me undress, Lilibet."

Lilibet shook her head so fiercely scarlet curls fell from her cap. "Please sign, Lady Meg," she whispered as tears glistened in her green eyes.

"I won't." She untied the stomacher from the bodice. "This is my favorite gown, and I don't want it ruined."

Lilibet assisted with shaking hands and took the garments. She turned to another maid. "Tell my mother what is happening."

Meg's chemise, linen corset, and petticoat offered a remnant of modesty. Some of the men in the hall turned their backs, but none of them stepped forward to stop the punishment by the earl.

A daughter shouldn't hate her father, but she despised him and his brutal choices. He had never learned to curb his appetite for drink, gambling, or women. He expected others to obey his every whim and suffer punishment when they disobeyed. All because he had been fortunate to be firstborn in a privileged line of noble aristocrats. He wouldn't respect her if she gave in to his demands without a fight. Others had endured a lashing. She could do the same.

Owen escorted her toward the whipping post in the center of the hall, a sneer on his face. "I'm going to enjoy this," he whispered in her ear.

A servant bound her left wrist in a leather strap and buckled it tight. The attached band was threaded through a metal ring behind the support column and buckled around her right wrist. The ring was suspended from a rope that could be raised and lowered on a pulley attached to the crossbeam that spanned the width of the room. The servant raised the ring so her arms were fully extended above her head.

A sob escaped her lips, and dread overcame her. What had she done? She twisted around and saw her father approach. Mercy was absent from his face.

"The sting of the lash should teach her to obey," Owen said. "One for every year of her rebellious life."

Twenty? Was he insane? The first strike against her

bare back sucked the breath from her lungs, the pain cutting so deeply she was too shocked to make a sound. The burning of the wound pulsated long after the leather strap left her body. She did not remain silent. Meg's screams echoed in the great hall, reverberating off the stone walls after each lash of the whip slashed her bare flesh. Her throat ached from the cries of anguish in response to the torture.

She struggled to balance on her toes, but the weight of her body caused the leather bindings to tighten. Her hands were already numb, and her body jerked in anticipation of the next pulse of agony.

The earl had previously wielded the lash with skill acquired from countless years of practice, but his strokes were flawed in his current drunken state. Instead of bruising her flesh, the lash cut deep, and blood flowed with every pulse of her heart.

Meg should have known better than to refuse the betrothal agreement, but she had never met Eliot and thought it foolish to marry a stranger. What if he turned out to be a man like her father? A whipping was better than a lifetime of bullying, or was it? No one could be as evil as the man wielding the whip against his own flesh and blood.

Owen came in a close second for immoral wickedness as he counted the lash strokes, his voice more excited with each number.

She considered herself brave but not foolish. Even if she held out for the full count, the result would be the same. She would marry Eliot. Why suffer longer than she already had? Any argument she had thought to make fell on heartless souls.

Owen had counted seven lashes.

"I'll sign," she cried out as the whip stung her slim back and cut a ribbon of flesh. The warm blood trickled down her cold skin.

"She agreed!" Lilibet interrupted before another lash could be delivered.

Lilibet's mother, Erin Dugan, placed a cold poultice on her bloody, battered back.

Meg allowed a sigh of relief to escape her sore throat and shivered, her naked flesh prickling with goose bumps as the compress absorbed the biting stings crisscrossing her back.

A servant released the ring that had held her arms aloft. Erin unhooked the straps around her bruised wrists.

Meg fell to her knees as every muscle in her body turned liquid.

Lilibet knelt beside her. Another by-blow of their father, she had been born nine months after Meg's younger brother Micah's birth. Celebrating the birth of his heir apparent, the drunken earl had forced himself on young Erin who worked in the kitchen.

Only Meg and Micah could claim to be born within marriage. It was not a privilege. They legally belonged to their father and were his property to dispose of as he wished. Someday Micah would inherit the title and what was left of the estate. For now, he was safely away at the University of Cambridge.

Lilibet offered a handkerchief, and Meg dried her tears. The more her father bullied, the more her defiance grew. But she could concede a battle in order to win the war. Her mother had taught her to use strategy when facing brute force. How could she have forgotten that all-important lesson?

Meg remained kneeling on the floor. She needed

time to recover and thought of her mother. When she was nineteen, they had traveled to London and stayed with her aunt Felicity for her introduction into society and the marriage market with the hopes of making a love match. While others judged the gentlemen on their titles and annual income, they researched each prospective bridegroom, looking for the flaws her father had hidden before marriage and flaunted afterward. Did the man gamble? Did he owe money? Did he drink to excess? Did he have a mistress? Did he mistreat his servants?

Future dreams filled with promise and happiness were shattered when her mother was struck by a runaway wagon and died the next day. Meg returned to the country manor in mourning. Her father barely acknowledged his loss, but the household mourned Lady Whittington. Meg assumed her mother's duties and avoided her father and Owen as much as possible. Too much. The announcement of the betrothal had taken her unprepared. She had remained out of their business and stupidly expected them to stay out of hers.

The earl handed the bloody whip to a servant and rubbed his hands. He extended one toward her.

She refused his help and rose to her feet with the assistance of Lilibet. Meg took a tentative step. The movement took her breath away as her body ached from the unnatural posture endured for the lashing, but she reached the table on her own.

Owen dipped the quill and handed it to her. "Here." He pointed to the area for her name.

The signatures of Eliot Richmond and Lord Dudlee were already on the parchment. She scrawled her name on the page.

Owen offered the quill to the earl. "Your signature

is needed, Lord Whittington."

He scratched his name and title on the document. His face had turned red with the exertion of acquiring her obedience, but he had what he wanted. "You made me do this." He emptied the glass a servant offered.

Meg stared at the man who had sired her. His lifestyle had aged him with sagging jowls, deep wrinkles around his eyes and mouth, and a softness to his body. A persistent cough hinted of health problems more pressing than obesity.

"Your bad investments and gambling made this marriage necessary." Courage returned and gave her voice. "But instead of taking responsibility for your actions and retrenching your extravagances, you use me to solve your problems."

"You are my daughter, a drain on my resources. You serve my bidding and will do as I say." His voice rose with each statement, and he pounded the table. "I own you."

She pointed at the parchment guarded in Owen's hands. "Not anymore. I belong to the Honorable Eliot Richmond." She grimaced as the poultice slipped from her shoulders. "If he will accept damaged goods."

Her father strode to her side. "Let me see."

Erin lifted the poultice. Meg's skin burned with its absence, and she sighed when it was returned.

He looked from Erin to Meg. "How did this happen?"

Did he forget he was the one wielding the whip? "It's your handiwork."

"I know how to handle a whip."

"When sober."

He raised his arm as if to strike her.

She was beyond caring. "Do you plan to mar my face as well?"

He lowered his trembling hand. "You try my patience, child."

"By the time she reaches the colonies, the scars will be healed," Owen said.

Her father rubbed his face and spoke with a slur. "When does the ship sail?"

"Lord Dudlee said the captain who brought the agreement will return to Riverside in late March."

"So soon?" She failed to hide her fear. Less than two months would hardly be time to say good-bye to family and friends. She couldn't leave England without seeing Micah.

"We must not wait too long." Owen exchanged a worried look with the earl.

Meg schooled her body not to react. What was the urgency? What secret were they hiding? Lord Dudlee might reveal the reason for a rushed marriage, but he was in London. So was her aunt, Viscountess Rudnack. Felicity was sometimes vain and frivolous, but she knew all the gossip and wouldn't hesitate to share it.

Now that her fate was sealed, she needed to bargain as much as possible. "I can't go to the colonies without a proper trousseau. I need to travel to London. Aunt Felicity will help me prepare for the trip."

"It's a trick," Owen said. "The viscountess will help her escape."

"Then we'll travel to London with her," her father replied as if she weren't present.

"You'll have to stay elsewhere," Meg said. "Aunt Felicity won't allow you under her roof."

He scowled. "I have my own townhouse in St.

James."

Her mother had refused to occupy his residence. While in London they stayed with Aunt Felicity, and most knew the women of Whittington Manor occupied a separate wing in the country house. It was a scandal no one bothered to hide. Lord Whittington's dissipated reputation was well known but overlooked by the gentry.

Owen whispered something in his ear.

Her father waved his finger in her direction. "You signed the agreement. I expect you to honor it. You will not attend any social gatherings unless you give your word you won't try to elope."

The thought of eloping to escape this forced marriage had not crossed her mind. Yet. She doubted she would find anyone brave enough to defy her father with such a scandalous solution and the ability to succeed.

"I always uphold the family honor." Which was no honor if measured against her father's word. She wanted to see her brother, and she could arrange a meeting in London. "I won't elope. I look forward to traveling to the colonies and putting an ocean between us."

She turned toward the doorway and stumbled.

"I'll have someone carry you." Her father was being kind now that he had what he wanted.

She turned to face him. "No man is allowed in the East Wing. That rule will continue after I'm gone." She didn't wait for a rebuttal. She leaned on Lilibet, and Erin kept the poultice in place as they walked into the foyer and headed past the staircase to the rooms on the eastern side of the mansion. Built in the mid-sixteen hundreds, the addition could only be accessed through a single doorway. Now the entrance was guarded by two mastiffs and provided a safe haven for the women living under

Lord Whittington's roof.

Her mother had protected those weaker, and Meg had followed her example. During the day, the women worked in pairs. If the earl or his boisterous friends sought female companionship, they found it outside the walls of the manor. Her experience with men had left her cynical. Eliot wouldn't have to be much of a man to exceed her expectations.

Meg had taken over her mother's former room, keeping it the same as she had left it. Erin removed the poultice and eased her onto a stool. She gave orders to strip the covers off the bed with only a sheet covering the grass-filled mattress. Lilibet placed Meg's clothing on a chair and helped the maid remove her blood-splattered undergarments.

Besides cooking, Erin was familiar with healing herbs. She held a cup to Meg's lips. "Drink this. It will dull the pain."

Meg whimpered when Lilibet pulled her long hair from a gash.

"I'm sorry," Lilibet said. "Your hair came free during the beating and is caught in the wounds from the lash."

"Cut it." Meg considered her thick curly hair one of her strongest assets. The dirty-blonde tresses lightened to a shade of wheat during the summer months and softened her strong features. Too tall and toned to compete with delicate blondes in the marriage mart, she had learned to value intelligence and wit, and her mind served her well. Most of the time.

Erin retrieved a razor from her medical bag. "Are you sure? Your betrothed may object."

"If he does not object to the scars on my back, he

will not refuse to marry me because my hair is not to my waist."

Chapter Two

Captain Banner Youngblood stood on the deck of his ship, the *Gabriella*, as barrels and crates were loaded into the hold. Twice a year he sailed to England with native foods and fish along with raw goods from the colonies and brought back manufactured items, sugar, coffee, tea, and spices to sell for a profit.

He wished his friend Eliot had a backbone and had journeyed to London with him, but they were both victims of primogeniture. His older brother, Wilbur, had inherited the title, lands, and wealth of their father and had produced two sons. Banner's options had been to join the military or clergy for an income above the allowance granted by the estate. He'd chosen the Royal Navy and had fallen in love with the sea but not the violent atrocities officers inflicted on sailors. Three years ago he had left British naval service at the age of twenty-five and purchased the majority share of a merchant ship.

Banner had concluded business during the past weeks, and his men would continue to load his cargo and the portion belonging to Lord Dudlee for the journey across the Atlantic. He would collect the betrothed bride of Eliot when he was ready to sail. He prayed his friend would make the necessary preparations for his future wife before his return. The man had been reluctant to vacate his mistress and child from his home.

Banner made a point to visit his older brother when

in port and hired a hackney coach for the trip from the crowded docks on the Thames River to the elegant London townhouse inherited by Wilbur Youngblood, the Earl of Stonebrooke.

Wilbur greeted him and ordered the servant to take Banner's bag upstairs.

The three-story building boasted high ornate ceilings, marble and wooden floors covered in imported woven rugs, and walls decorated with large family portraits of previous earls all the way back to the first earl of Stonebrooke in the twelfth century. He had been proud of his family heritage, and yet he had been cast aside. But in order to maintain an aristocracy, membership had to be limited and wealth concentrated in the primogeniture system. He was an unnecessary spare.

"Come join me for a drink."

Banner followed his brother to his study overlooking the gardens behind the house. Wilbur took his father's former seat behind a massive desk, and Banner sat opposite. He had faced his father's stern visage from this same perspective. An authoritarian, his father had barked orders and expected them to be obeyed without question. The strict control had prepared Banner for life at sea and in his role as captain. But he remembered the commands had been tempered by patience. His father had loved him, but Banner hadn't learned the extent of his generosity until after his death two years ago.

Wilbur was his only family, and yet he wasn't a part of it. Wilbur's wife and children were his priority. Banner visited enough times not to be forgotten completely.

"Did you receive my message?" Banner asked.

"Yes, and I have obtained an invitation for you to attend the ball tonight."

"Will Lady Meg Culbertson be there?"

"My wife has assurance from the hostess that Lady Meg and her aunt will be attending."

A servant silently entered, poured two drinks, and served them on a silver tray.

Banner kept his attention on his brother while enjoying the wine. Wilbur was eight years his senior, and he had idolized him and had accepted the special treatment bestowed on an heir for being firstborn. He had learned from an early age to accept his lower ranking in the family. They were as close as brothers could be with so many years between them. Wilbur had settled into his role as title patriarch and a member of the House of Lords, but Banner was still seeking his destiny. Even though he loved the sea, something was missing from his life.

"Why are you wearing a wig at home?" Banner remarked as Wilbur scratched at his forehead.

"They shaved my head to fit the linen base, and my hair looks like bristles on a pig." He removed the wig to prove his point. A shadow of short hairs sprouted from Wilbur's head.

"Why don't you let it grow out and stop wearing a wig?"

He replaced the fake head covering and tugged it into place. "The gentry must project nobility to the public, and my hair is thinning, unlike yours."

Wilbur favored their father with his thin brown hair while Banner had his mother's raven curls.

Wigs were worn by most gentlemen, but many men

in the colonies were discarding the fake hairpieces. The wig made his brother appear older than thirty-six, and he tried to soothe his vanity. "It's only hair."

"You can say that. The ladies will want to run their fingers through your thick locks."

Banner labored for every coin and was keenly aware he could lose it all with a sunken ship or bad investment. "I doubt their fingers will linger once they learn I have no title or lands in England." The ladies of London were not impressed by the title of sea captain.

"On your last visit you spoke of buying land and building a house," Wilbur said. "Are you giving up the life of a merchant?"

"Someday, but land is abundant, and I'm tired of living above a tailor's shop when I'm not at sea. I hired some men to clear the land and plan to lay the foundation when I return."

"Then you have no thoughts of purchasing a house in London?"

London's upper class barely acknowledged him, but he was highly respected by the untitled businessmen in Riverside Village in Connecticut. "Riverside is my home now."

"I hope it's a peaceful town." Wilbur removed snuff from an ornate box, inhaled, and offered the finely crushed tobacco leaves. "Everyone is talking about how the British Army had trouble with some rabble-rousers in Boston last December. Is that close to Connecticut?"

Banner declined the snuff. He had sailed less than a week after the destruction of the tea incident and had heard both sides. "We pass Boston on our way to and from port at Riverside."

"Why would they ruin perfectly good tea by tossing

it in the sea instead of paying for it?"

"The merchants of Boston didn't want to save the East India Tea Company from bankruptcy," Banner said. "They felt the owners should pay for their own financial mistakes. The colonists couldn't sell the tea in their warehouses for a profit if they had to compete with the lower price of the East India tea. They knew if colonists paid the existing tax, higher taxes would follow."

"Everyone pays taxes, but they destroyed more than three hundred chests of tea. That's worth more than nine thousand pounds." Wilbur leaned back in his chair and sneezed. "Members of parliament are talking of closing the port in Boston until they pay for the tea."

Had he heard right? "Boston is one of the busiest ports in the colonies. How would you close it?"

"We'll send more troops." Wilbur sipped his wine. "No one can beat the British Army."

None of the colonists would like more troops in Boston, especially the Sons of Liberty. Bullying the citizens would only spark more protests. Banner opened his mouth to reason with his brother but realized their viewpoints were worlds apart.

Wilbur dabbed at his runny nose with a lace-trimmed handkerchief. "How long will you stay in London?"

He was grateful his brother changed the subject. His livelihood depended on a peaceful relationship between England and the colonies. "I hope to sail in about a week." He emptied his glass, placed it on the tray left on the sideboard, and resumed his seat. "If my passengers are ready."

Wilbur finished the last residue of wine in his glass and laughed. "Everyone is talking about Lord

Whittington arranging a marriage between his daughter and Lord Dudlee's son. Isn't Eliot a friend of yours?"

Unlike Banner, the honorable Eliot Richmond was the only son and heir to his father's fortune. He had attended the best schools in England and had been given the enviable position of reselling the items shipped from his father's warehouses in London to the merchants and farmers of Connecticut. He had an elegant home in Riverside and left the daily tasks of running the business to his clerk, Glen Stemple. But his pampered life had a price. A baron and a merchant were considered low on the aristocratic order, and marriage to the daughter of an earl would advance the family's standing among the ton of Great Britain.

"After I purchased the *Gabriella*, I needed cargo to ship, and Lord Dudlee needed to transport finished products to the colonies. Eliot traveled with me to begin his work in Riverside overseeing the selling of cargo and purchasing of raw goods to send back to London. We were similar in age and interests and became friends." He leaned forward and met Wilbur's gaze. "What do you know of Lord Whittington's daughter?"

A slight smile creased Wilbur's face as he studied him through narrow gray eyes. "Won't you be spending two months with her on your ship? That should be more than enough time to make her acquaintance."

"I'm the *Gabriella's* captain. I won't have time for tea and exchanging pleasantries with a seasick lass. I only want to ascertain if she's a woman of common sense."

"Does any woman have common sense?" Wilbur laughed and scratched under his wig. "That's why we make the important decisions in life and leave flower arranging and birthing babies to the ladies."

Banner wasn't ready to be dismissed. "Do you know anything about her?"

"The betrothal has been gossiped about since Lady Meg Culbertson arrived last month. She is staying with her aunt, the Viscountess of Rudnack, and her father is staying at his own residence. His fondness for drink and the ladies makes him an unsuitable chaperone for his own daughter."

"What about her mother?"

"The countess died in an accident two years ago when Lady Meg was enjoying her first season. The young lady retired to the country to mourn. When she arrived in London, Lord Whittington and Lord Dudlee immediately announced her engagement to the honorable Eliot Richmond. Lady Rudnack has been introducing her to her friends so she can enjoy the frivolities of parties and social events before matrimony and exile across the sea."

Exile? "We have parties and social events in the colonies."

"I doubt they will measure up to what London has to offer. Lady Rudnack is well connected, and they attend events nearly every night."

"Lord Dudlee is attending the ball tonight and said he would arrange an introduction to Lady Meg's family." Lord Dudlee had been unable to obtain an invitation for Banner, but Wilbur had solved that problem. Rank had its privileges. He stood. "I better dress."

"Do you have evening clothes?"

Clothes identified the gentry and separated them from the working class. "Nothing fancy, but they won't shame the family."

Wilbur ignored his defense. "My valet will provide you with something suitable."

Banner tried not to take offense. His brother believed it was his right to supervise his younger sibling's life. "I appreciate your help."

"What happens if she doesn't meet with your expectations or suit your friend?"

He studied his brother's stoic expression. "Do you know of a fault she possesses?"

"I don't want to sway you one way or the other, but my wife was shocked that Lady Meg's younger sister has been elevated to the status of a companion and attends events with her."

He tried to recall the information given him. "I was unaware she had a sister."

"A natural child, but Lord Whittington has several. He sent his eldest by-blow to school and now employs Owen O'Leary as his steward. He shadows Lord Whittington at most events and keeps his cup full."

He had seen plenty of drunkards along the docks and guarded his own consumption. "He encourages his drinking?"

"And more. They frequent the gaming rooms and bawdry houses in town. With all his scandalous behavior, it's no surprise he would marry his daughter off to a merchant's son."

"Eliot will inherit a title," he defended his friend.

"Baron? Lady Meg is the daughter of an earl and granddaughter of a marquis. She could certainly do better. It is Eliot who benefits from this match."

"Then why would Lord Whittington make it?"

Wilbur waved his hand in the air. "Lord Dudlee has money, and Lord Whittington has debts. The marriage benefits both."

"But why would Lady Meg agree to marry a stranger?"

"She is underage. She had no choice in the matter." Wilbur tented his fingers and raised an eyebrow. "But what of Eliot? Is he for or against the match?"

Banner had delivered the marriage contract to Lord Dudlee the day after arriving in London. He also delivered a letter from Eliot pleading for his father to reconsider.

Lord Dudlee barely glanced at the words from his son and tossed the letter into the fireplace. He added his signature to the betrothal document before sending it off to the bride's family. Eliot's wishes had been ignored.

His brother had shared his knowledge of Lady Meg. He felt obligated to reciprocate. "When the agreement arrived in Riverside last fall, his father sent a letter threatening to disown him if he didn't sign."

"You read the letter?"

Did he think he was no longer a gentleman because he lacked a title? "Never, but Eliot was upset and shared the news, hoping I could offer a solution. The man has no head for business and is totally dependent upon his father for coin. He reluctantly signed the document but begged his father to reconsider in a letter I delivered along with the agreement." Banner met his brother's gaze. "Lord Dudlee did not change his mind."

Wilbur leaned forward, an eagerness in his voice. "Would Eliot defy his father?"

"No." He felt obligated to defend his friend. "Eliot is an honorable man who loves his family. He will not back out of this arranged marriage."

"Duty and honor above all else. That speaks well of

him," Wilbur said. "And doesn't he have younger sisters?"

"Two of marriageable ages whose chances of advantageous matches would be ruined by any scandal."

"I've heard one of the reasons Lord Dudlee is keen for a match is the rumor Eliot has a mistress he wanted to wed." Wilbur didn't wait for an assent. "Is he in love with her?"

Eliot had fallen in love with Cathy Goodheart upon arriving in Riverside three years ago and had planned to marry her, but Lord Dudlee had vowed to disown his son and cut off his allowance if he went through with the ceremony. The daughter of a pastor, Cathy had been ostracized by her family when she began to show her pregnancy. Eliot had taken her in, and their child, Anna, was a year old. Without him, they would have to live as outcasts in an unforgiving society.

Banner couldn't lie to his brother. "Extremely."

"That's unfortunate. Any children?"

"A little girl." A smile tugged at the corners of his mouth as he thought of Anna. "She's the most adorable child."

Wilbur leaned back in his chair and grinned. "I almost wish I could travel to Riverside and watch this drama unfold."

Banner had forgotten how many of the wealthy took pleasure in the misery of others. "I'm more interested in tonight's meeting."

Chapter Three

Meg examined her gown in the full-length mirror. She preferred strong colors, and the blue silk was one of her favorites. Her corset stays supported the soft material in the bodice, which had elbow length sleeves trimmed in layers of lace. The matching skirt was trimmed in ruching of a darker blue that contrasted against the white petticoat embroidered with delicate forget-me-not flowers. The gathered material was draped over wide panniers, and the exaggerated hips created the illusion of a small waist. Her breasts were pressed flat beneath the stiffened stomacher to prevent any movement and blossomed in full mounds above the square-cut neckline.

Meg jumped up and down to test the security of her breasts.

Lilibet clapped as she entered the room. "Is that a new dance?"

"Can you see any sign of my nipples?"

"No, but can I borrow some of your bosom?" She looked at her own gown and modest display of flesh above the green fabric that matched her eyes and accentuated her red hair, which was arranged high on her head with ringlets falling in a cascade down her back.

"You don't need to display your decolletage with your natural beauty." She added a jeweled comb to Lilibet's hair. "That completes your ensemble."

"Are you sure I should attend?"

While Micah was Meg's staunchest supporter in their youthful misdeeds, Lilibet had been her conscience, voicing a warning she too often ignored.

"If Owen can trail Father at every social event we attend, why can't you be my companion? Enjoy yourself, Lili. Who knows when we will return to England?"

Melancholy threatened to ruin the evening. Every new party reminded her she would soon leave London, her friends, and family. She had written to Micah but had heard nothing in reply. She couldn't go without saying good-bye to her brother.

"I must finish your 'air," the maid said.

Meg took a seat in front of the dressing table and watched as the maid struggled to style her shoulder-length hair. What was left of her tresses was piled on top of a pad to create height, but it formed a floppy topknot instead of cascading curls.

"Why not try a wig or 'airpiece?" The maid lifted a clump of fake hair from the stock Aunt Felicity had lent.

She had worn enough of the unnatural hairpieces, and the inner workings of rebellion threatened. She was not ashamed of her natural figure, face, or hair. Meg tore the bindings free and pulled the pad and pins from her hair. She wove her fingers through her freed locks and ignored the maid's shrieks of horror.

"Add a few combs to lift the sides up and back and let nature take care of the rest."

The maid regained her composure and followed her instructions. The simple style framed the strong features of her face. If she resembled a thorn among all the roses, what did it matter? She was off the marriage market.

Parliament had resumed with men talking about politics while their wives and daughters enjoyed the social season of dinners, parties, and military reviews. Events like festivals and races would continue through the spring and summer with the final goal of advantageous weddings.

Aunt Felicity entered the room in a gown that sparkled with tiny pearls sewn on gold silk. Her hairstylist had taken hours to achieve the "tower" with her natural hair pulled up over a pad into a mountain of real and fake curls. The hair was greased, powdered, and decorated with feathers and pearls.

Meg rose and circled around her aunt. "You look beautiful."

"I haven't had so much fun in years." Felicity had been a widow for five years, and her husband had been generous in his will with a townhouse of her own and a comfortable allowance that allowed her to enjoy parties and socializing. "The season was going to be boring until you girls showed up."

Aunt Felicity wanted her to have fun before sailing to the colonies, but Meg was growing weary of the lavish wardrobes, proper manners, and strict etiquette for social events with each host trying to outdo the previous one. Many of her friends had married, and the young ladies vying for attention from the eligible bachelors seemed vain and silly. She was ready for marriage, but was Eliot the husband for her? She would soon find out.

"I'm sorry I couldn't do anythin' with her 'air," the maid said.

"I like it this way." Meg fluffed the curls around her shoulders.

Felicity walked around her, examining her appearance, and gasped. "But this gown exposes your back. I can see some scars."

The scabs were gone and the scars few, but one deep cut had left a pink wound on her shoulder and back. It would take time to fade. "Father will be attending tonight's party. I'm sure he'll be proud to see his handiwork."

"If you don't want to marry this man, I can arrange an elopement or passage to France," Felicity whispered.

"I appreciate the offer, Aunt Felicity, but Father hired several men to watch me and guarantee I do not escape before the ship sails."

"But Eliot has no title." She had made it clear since the announcement that Meg was marrying beneath herself.

"I don't care about a title. I care about the man. I've used the past weeks to find out everything I can about him and have heard nothing but good about Eliot. He could make a fine husband."

Everyone who knew her future bridegroom praised his intelligence, appearance, and gentle nature. By all accounts she was lucky to be his wife. She planned to keep an open mind and develop as much affection as possible toward him.

"Your mother always weighed all her options before a decision. The only choice she made based on pure emotion was marrying Lord Whittington."

"And we know how that turned out," Meg said with sarcasm in her voice.

Felicity sighed as she led the way down the stairs. "Men are on their best behavior before a proposal. She was young and impressionable. He swept her off her feet, and she agreed to marry him before anyone could convince her of his faults. Heaven knows I tried, but she was in love." She placed a hand over her heart. "She believed she could persuade him to give up his sordid indulgences and bad habits. Reform the rake. But she was wrong."

"How soon did Mother know she had made a mistake?"

"After you were born, Lord Whittington revealed his true nature when he ranted about how she had failed him because you were a girl. He barely waited for her flow to cease to breed your brother. He thanked her for doing her duty and returned to his sordid lifestyle."

Lilibet was the result. If Aunt Felicity knew the circumstances of her birth, she never spoke of it. It was not polite conversation.

"Has a letter arrived from Micah?" Ignoring her pleas wasn't like her brother. "Time is running out."

"I'm sure he'll come soon," Felicity said. "He's probably waiting to take his exams."

"I hope you're right." Meg put her arm around her aunt's waist and hugged her.

Felicity grabbed the railing and stood rigid. "Careful. My hair!"

Meg released her and examined the towering mass for any out-of-place tendrils. "No harm done, but you'll have to stand straight as an arrow all night."

"Vanity makes us all fools."

"Then I'm glad I'm not beautiful."

"Hah!" Felicity laughed. "Child, you may not be one of these whimpering pale blondes who nods and smiles at any silly remark, but you are far from plain. And in that gown, you are your mother's daughter."

After her mother's death, the servants had packed Katherine's belongings in her travel trunk, which had remained in London. Upon Meg's arrival, Aunt Felicity had hired a modiste to alter her mother's gowns, update those she had brought, and sew anything she would need for a wardrobe in the colonies.

"I couldn't think or feel after she died," Meg said. "I still miss her."

"But you, my dear, spent hours together and have wonderful memories of your mother."

Meg examined the delicate lace at her elbow. "I'm glad you saved her belongings. I hope I honor her by wearing her gowns."

"Katherine would be proud of you."

Meg shook her head in disagreement. Her mother had wanted her to marry for love and be loved in return. "For marrying a man I don't know? A stranger I've never met?"

"For doing your duty with dignity and grace." Felicity accepted a cloak offered by a servant and led the way to the carriage. "I'm sure you'll grow fond of Eliot once you become acquainted."

Many of the women she had met in London believed a good marriage didn't depend on romantic love. It was based on two people of equal upbringing joining forces to create new life and perform as social leaders in the community. Aunt Felicity hadn't been in love with her husband, but she had liked and admired him. They had produced an heir and lived peacefully together for more than twenty years before his death.

The footman helped the women into the carriage.

Meg arranged her wide gown to make room on the narrow seat. "We're going to have fun tonight and dance until our feet hurt."

"My feet hurt already." Lilibet squeezed next to Meg. "Why are the toes so tight on ladies' slippers?"

"It's to make your feet appear small and dainty," Felicity said.

Lilibet looked at her feet. "Squeezing them into a tiny space only makes them swell."

"Women must suffer for beauty." Felicity cocked her head to one side to keep her high hairstyle from hitting the roof.

"I don't feel any prettier when my feet hurt," Lilibet said.

Meg appreciated Lilibet's honest outlook on life and took her hand. "I'm glad you decided to join me on this adventure."

"My mother threatened to marry me to the butcher if I didn't leave home. I hope I'm not too much of a burden."

"I couldn't make this trip without your company," Meg said with complete honesty. "You always speak the truth and know how to make me laugh."

The coach lurched forward as the team of horses pulled the closed carriage down the cobblestone drive.

"I'm going to miss you girls." Felicity sniffled and searched her reticule. "Have you heard what day you sail?"

"Father informed me the ship would leave for Riverside late March. He said June and July are hurricane season and didn't want to delay the trip or wedding. It makes me wary of my future husband. Why the rush? Why can't I wait until I turn twenty-one in July? Then if he was intolerable, I would have a choice in the matter and not be forced to marry him."

"Have you said this to your father?" Felicity's worry lines deepened in her forehead.

"My words are ignored."

Felicity pressed her lips together. "He's after your trust fund."

This was news to her. "What trust fund?"

"After you were born, your grandfather realized what a wastrel Lord Whittington was and set up a trust fund for you. It was intended to be your dowry if you married before reaching your majority." Felicity rushed her words. "If you didn't marry by then, any money in the trust would be yours."

She needed to understand the statements uttered by her aunt. "Then if I wait, I will receive all of it?"

"Exactly."

"And if I marry before July 17, the money goes to my husband?"

"It goes to Lord Whittington who decides how much to bestow on your bridegroom."

"That explains the rush to the altar," Lilibet said. "He'll use the money to pay off his debts."

Meg agreed with Lilibet and turned to her aunt. "Do you know how much is in it?"

Felicity waved a finger in the air. "The trust is controlled by Lord Whittington's solicitor."

Meg frowned as she looked at Lilibet. "I wonder what the price was for my happiness and freedom?"

Chapter Four

Banner stood among the guests crowded in the entrance hall of one of London's elegant townhouses. Wilbur and his wife greeted others and introduced him to people he didn't know and who would forget his name as quickly as he forgot theirs. He had attended concerts, dances, and other events at the homes of wealthy men in the colonies, but they paled to the opulence of parties in London homes and country manors. Men spent money they didn't sweat or toil for while women competed for the widest skirts, the tallest hair styles, and most expensive jewelry gracing barely concealed bosoms.

Young virgins were paraded before eligible bachelors who could pick and choose the mother of their heir. Marriages were arranged by fathers to join two powerful families with daughters auctioned off for the best match to compensate them for rearing what society considered a worthless female.

Tonight, the only woman he was interested in was Eliot's future bride.

Although Wilbur had offered Banner a wig or powder, he had opted to wear his black hair in its natural state with the length tied in the back with a contrasting silk ribbon. His shirt contained no bows, ruffles, or lace with a simple cravat tied at his neck. A waistcoat of white silk with silver embroidery indicated a gentleman's wealth. The same silver embroidery trimmed the wide cuffs and opening of his dark-blue coat, which matched his trousers.

"Captain, Captain Youngblood," Lord Dudlee hailed across the hallway leading to the ballroom.

Banner nodded a farewell to Wilbur and his wife and joined Eliot's father. Lord Dudlee wore a powdered wig with three rows of curls. A lavender coat was paired with a lighter shade waistcoat and darker trousers. His sleeves and cravat were trimmed in lavender lace. Intricate gold rings decorated his fingers, and he presented a leg clad in white stockings as he bowed. The ornate silver buckle on his polished shoe sparkled in the candlelight.

Lady Dudlee wore a gown of the same colors. Her hair was piled at least a foot on top of her head with precious gems sewn into a knotted silk net encasing the mound. Her necklace was a heavy gold design with matching gems worth a king's ransom. They were trying hard to impress a peerage that disdained them for their low rank and ties to trade.

The couple exchanged pleasantries. Banner needed to talk business before meeting Eliot's betrothed. "I received the inventory of your merchandise for the colonies, and my men should have the cargo loaded by the end of the week."

"I hope there won't be any trouble with the tea."

Banner didn't want to alarm him with Wilbur's prediction of more soldiers. "I don't foresee any."

"I'd like to talk to you about what products will be available from the colonies for the next shipment," Lord Dudlee said.

"I could come by tomorrow," Banner suggested.

"Not before noon. I plan to enjoy myself this evening." Lord Dudlee laughed in a high shrill that made

Banner wince. Others turned at the sound, and he waved in acknowledgment.

Before they could be interrupted, Banner pressed his concern. "Do you have a reply for your son's letter?"

Lord Dudlee's smile froze on his face. "Yes. I'm congratulating him on his upcoming nuptials. I expect Eliot and Lady Meg to visit in a year." He repeated his high shrill of laughter. "And bring along my grandson."

Banner was startled by his confidence of an heir being produced so quickly. People weren't animals. How could two strangers be thrown together and expected to breed? Was it too late to change the fate in store for Eliot? He knew several couples in loveless marriages. They were formal, polite, and lacked joy but by all outward appearances were successful. Too bad Eliot had a transparent nature. His feelings were as easily read as a book. If Lady Meg sought love in a marriage, she would be greatly disappointed.

Lord Dudlee rubbed his hands together. "Do you think Eliot will have everything in order when you arrive in Riverside?"

"I hope so." Did Lord Dudlee know about Cathy and Anna living with him?

"I don't want anything to ruin this marriage." Lord Dudlee's tone turned threatening.

He deftly changed the subject. "What can you tell me about your son's betrothed?"

"Lovely girl. Not like any of those lowborn title chasers from the colonies."

The description insulted the young women who worked hard for a better life in the colonies. It certainly didn't describe Eliot's mistress.

"We're so pleased he's marrying Lady Meg." Lady

Dudlee looked around the crowd. "Our daughters are enjoying the season, and I expect advantageous matches for them soon. Lady Rudnack knows all the important people in society and has been introducing us to her friends. I am so fortunate to make her acquaintance. I invited her and Lady Meg for tea tomorrow."

He could call on the Dudlees at tea time for a chance meeting with Lady Meg. The more he knew about the young woman, the better he could help his friend.

Lord Dudlee pointed toward the hall. "I see Lady Meg's father, Lord Whittington. Would you like an introduction?"

Lady Dudlee made a face at the mention of his name. "I'm going to find my daughters and leave you men to talk." She hastened toward the ballroom.

Banner followed Lord Dudlee toward an older man whose face had seen the ravages of time. His eyes had dark circles beneath them, and his jowls sagged. He burped a bubble of dark wine onto his cravat. Age wasn't his only ailment.

"This is Lord John Culbertson, the Earl of Whittington Hall," Lord Dudlee introduced. "This is Captain Banner Youngblood."

Lord Whittington's bored expression was a telltale sign he had been born to a title. Nothing would impress him. He wore a burgundy suit with stained and worn cuffs, which confirmed his brother's speculation that the bride's father was a gentleman in need of coin.

The earl stared at Banner through puffy lids. "Youngblood? Do I know your family?"

"He's the younger brother of Lord Wilbur Youngblood, the Earl of Stonebrooke," Lord Dudlee said.

Lord Whittington looked around. "Is the earl present?"

"Yes," Banner said, "but I am here about your daughter."

"My daughter?" Lord Whittington attempted to focus on his face. "What is your interest in her?"

"Captain Youngblood will be transporting Lady Meg to Riverside on his ship," Lord Dudlee said. "I told you I had made arrangements for the voyage."

"You're a sea captain?" He didn't bother to hide the insulting tone.

Banner nodded. "A humble but honest profession for a second son."

"Then you'll want to deal with my steward. He handles all my business transactions." He waved to a thin man waiting nearby. "This is Owen O'Leary."

The steward wore a canary-yellow jacket trimmed in black velvet. His pasty skin had a tinge of pink, and with his thin protruding lips and tuft of strawberry-blond hair above his sloping brow, the man reminded him of a baby bird. He bore little resemblance to his rotund father, and Banner was glad Wilbur had filled him in on the family's natural offspring. Had Owen earned the esteemed position of steward, or had his father granted him that privilege?

"Captain Youngblood will be taking Margaret to her betrothed," Lord Whittington said.

Owen's thin eyebrows arched in his wrinkled forehead. "I was expecting an older man. At least one weathered and worn with experience at sea."

Banner had proven his skill. "I was in the Royal Navy before purchasing my ship and have safely transported shipments to the colonies for years."

"He's good friends with my son," Lord Dudlee said. "He's a man you can trust."

Owen touched a lace-trimmed handkerchief to his lips. "I'll have to take your word for it."

Banner ignored the steward and turned his attention to Lord Whittington. "I will do everything in my power to deliver your daughter safely to Riverside."

"I hope you have room for Lady Meg's companion, Miss Lilibet. She insists upon taking the girl with her." Owen raised his chin. "And of course, I will be accompanying them."

"You're going?" Lord Whittington looked confused by the announcement.

"You ordered me, Lord Whittington, and I am always happy to obey." Owen bowed and replaced the earl's empty glass with a full one from a tray held by a nearby servant. "I will offer my protection to the ladies and will witness the nuptials and return with verification."

"We must have verification." Lord Whittington lifted the glass to his lips and drank it empty.

Why was proof of the marriage so important? "You doubt the nuptials will occur?" Banner asked.

"No." The earl's chins shook as he denied any problem. "She has given her word, and my daughter does not defy me."

Yet Lord Whittington was worried enough to send Owen along to ensure the marriage. Would it take much convincing for the lady to call off the wedding? "I would like an introduction to Lady Meg. A voyage such as this is a hardship on a woman. I want her to be prepared."

"We wouldn't want anything to happen to her." Owen stared. "Lady Meg is a precious commodi—"

"Commodity?" Banner asked in disbelief.

"Companion." A slight smile broke the grim line of his lips.

Did he think himself clever with his substitution?

Lord Whittington led the way to the ballroom. "I'll make the introductions, and you can make arrangements with her aunt to call upon the ladies and explain any hardships."

Banner followed last as they made their way along the edge of the ballroom. The center was filled by dancers performing a contra dance. The young ladies were stiff in their movements, executing their practiced steps to the exact beat of the music except for one. A woman in a blue gown added an elaborate arm movement as she turned and flashed a smile that would have disarmed an entire troop of soldiers. He paused as her gaze met his. Lightning had once struck the mainmast of his ship. The jolt was the same. She apologized to her partner for missing a step and laughed as she continued the dance. Who was she?

He had to hurry to rejoin the men who were bowing to a woman whose wealth was displayed by her jewels and expensively embroidered gown. Her hair was teased high and crowned with dyed feathers.

"Lady Rudnack, may I introduce Captain Youngblood?" the earl asked. "He'll be taking Margaret and Owen to the colonies."

"Owen?" Lady Rudnack stared at Lord Whittington. "Why does that creature have to go?"

First, Lord Whittington's shocked reaction and now Lady Rudnack. Owen's addition to the passenger list was a surprise to them. Banner stayed behind the group where he could watch their expressions and listen to the conversation.

Owen bowed. "I am offering my protection to the ladies."

"Protection? My sister had to ban you from the courtyard because you threw stones at the children. Micah has a scar from where you struck him."

"We were children."

"You were fifteen and ten years older than Meg." She turned to Lord Dudlee and the earl. "I know the papers have been signed, but Katherine would have opposed this contract. She wanted her daughter to marry for love."

"Love will come," Lord Dudlee said. "It's a good match. They are well suited for each other."

Lady Rudnack relaxed. "I hope you are right." She glared at the earl. "It is better they don't expect love. Disappointment can shatter a heart."

Lord Whittington dabbed at the sweat on his forehead. The gray pallor of his skin contrasted against the white powder on the elaborate wig he wore. "I have friends waiting in the game room. Where is Margaret Katherine?"

"Catherine?" Banner blurted out. She shared the same name as Eliot's mistress?

Lord Whittington turned his attention to him. "She is named for her mother, Katherine, and my mother, Margaret."

"Katherine called her Meg, and it suits her." Lady Rudnack turned toward the dance floor and raised a graceful hand. "Her partner is bringing her back now."

Banner turned and recognized the woman in blue he had been admiring earlier. This was Eliot's betrothed?

Her brows were darker than her hair and framed

eyes that pierced a man's soul. She didn't bat her eyelashes or cast her gaze downward. He was mesmerized, unable to look away. What did she see?

"Lady Meg, this is Captain Banner Youngblood. His ship will take you to the colonies," Lord Dudlee informed her.

"Don't forget Lilibet." She stared at her father. "I won't go without her."

"Owen will be accompanying you as well," Lord Whittington said.

Her hazel eyes widened, and a soft gasp escaped her pursed lips. Either she hadn't learned the art of subtlety or didn't care to hide her emotions.

"Why?" A hint of anger laced the single word.

"To make sure you marry Eliot as you promised." Lord Whittington lowered his voice. "Owen reminded me about your trickery and schemes. You will not win this battle, Margaret Katherine."

Banner had excellent hearing. What father threatened his daughter?

A slight tremor of her lips betrayed the young woman's distress, and her eyes darkened before she turned to Banner, a smile wide on her face. "My next dance is open. Would you like to partner with me?"

Banner bowed. "I would be honored."

She placed her hand on his sleeve and turned her back on the others.

Lord Dudlee gasped. "Who beat you?"

Banner's muscles tightened as he looked down on her bare shoulders and back exposed by the low cut of the gown. Thin ribbons of pink contrasted against pale flesh. She turned to face her father and raised a delicately arched brow.

Lord Whittington's face reddened, but he offered no explanation.

"Silent, Father?" She turned to Lord Dudlee. "Defiance has a price. Has your son ever defied you?"

"Never. And I would not beat him into submission."

But he would threaten his livelihood and disown him, Banner thought. The young woman's defiance could be Eliot's salvation.

Lady Meg scanned the dance floor. "I think we can join that group. They appear to be short a couple."

He nodded toward her back. He'd seen the same scars on the backs of sailors and was marked on his own. He fought down a memory of receiving the lash. No woman should have to endure the pain. "Are you sure you're up to the task?"

"I love country dances. Besides, those are old wounds."

"Some wounds never heal."

"My father and I have been at war all my life. He was disappointed I was a daughter, and I was disappointed he was my father."

Most victims of a lashing would hide their scars, but Lady Meg ignored the stares and whispers. Obviously, only one person could have beaten her. He leaned in close. "Tell me the truth, Lady Meg. Did the lash force you to agree to this marriage with Eliot Richmond?"

She studied him. "You are a direct man."

"Has no one else asked you this question?"

A smile played on her full lips. "They are too polite to ask."

"Then you consider me rude."

Her smile widened as she took her position. "I consider you honest. I admire that in a man. But I am a woman. I belong to my father. I'm his property. I disagreed with my father's decision initially, but he convinced me the match was in my best interest."

The music moved him closer. "He beat you into submission?" he whispered, his lips near her ear.

"My cowardice forced me to agree to his demands. I barely survived eight lashings before I signed." They parted a few steps and returned to face one another. "Now I can't wait to leave England."

"I cannot be a party to forcing you to marry Eliot against your will."

She shrugged and sighed. "I have to marry someone." She placed her hand on top of his as they formed a star with the other couple. "How well do you know Eliot?"

Her touch was light, but he felt the heat even through their gloves. Her nearness overpowered his senses. "We've been good friends for several years."

"Is Eliot a man who demands obedience?"

She respected bluntness. "Like your father?"

She met his gaze as the music ended. "I need to know if he can be cruel."

"He is an honorable man and would be appalled by the treatment necessary for your father to arrange this betrothal. If you called off the wedding, the fault would not be his. Then Lord Dudlee wouldn't have a reason to disown Eliot."

"Is that his fear?"

"He is a man dependent on his father's coin."

Her brows came together, and she pursed her lips. "If I don't marry Eliot, his father would simply find another bride of nobility for him." She blew out a breath and took his arm as they headed toward her aunt. "Eliot

41

sounds like a just man. I can accept that in a husband."
    She was a practical woman. Eliot was a lucky man.

Chapter Five

Meg stared at a naked statue of Mercury. What other man would be nude except for wings on a helmet and another pair attached to his ankles? Lady Dudlee had decorated her home with what she thought were samples of classical art, but the statues, pottery, and paintings were overwhelming, and Meg was standing in the foyer. What awaited her in the parlor?

She ignored Lilibet's giggles. She might be able to laugh too except her future husband would inherit this house and every gaudy fixture in it.

A maid escorted them to the parlor. "Lady Dudlee will join you shortly."

The parlor exceeded her worst imaginings with dark oak furniture carved in ornate designs and covered in flowery fabric. The walls were cluttered with stern-faced portraits, bloody battle scenes, and nearly naked couples cavorting in the outdoors.

Lilibet pointed at an amorous couple embracing on a grassy meadow. Sheer garments left nothing to the imagination. Her mouth dropped open. "They're naked."

"It's classical art," Meg said. "Lady Dudlee is trying to impress her guests."

"Is she running a brothel?"

Meg stared at her younger sister. "What do you know about places like that?"

Her skin reddened to a shade matching her head of

curls. "One of the stable hands said there was a portrait of a naked woman at the Forsaken Maiden."

"Why would he tell you that?"

"I think he wanted me to get naked." Her blush deepened. "I didn't."

"Now I understand why your mother wanted you to leave Whittington Manor. Father's workers are intent upon making you a forsaken maiden."

Lilibet's eyes widened until the whites showed all around. "Mother said I would have a better chance of finding a good husband in the colonies."

Lilibet would have no trouble finding a husband. She was beautiful, honest to a fault, and an excellent cook. Meg would have to make sure the man who proposed was worthy of her younger sister. She sighed about her own dilemma. "At least you'll be able to choose the man you marry."

"How?" She shrugged. "I don't know what makes a good husband."

What advice could she give that wouldn't make her sound like a hypocrite? "Someone who listens to your ideas and concerns and wants what is best for you." Meg recalled her own dreams of a husband. "He loves you and would risk all to be with you."

"You're a romantic," Lilibet said. "I'm more practical. I want a man who enjoys my cooking. He won't stray with his belly full."

Their laughter brightened the gothic setting. Was there any wonder why she loved Lilibet so much?

Lady Dudlee entered the room in a lavish gown of rose and pink. Her hair was styled in a tower with fewer adornments than at the ball, but with trinkets that dazzled with wealth. "Please be seated." She motioned to a settee covered in red silk with ornate carvings on the arms, feet, and above the high back. She took a seat opposite on a blue-and-white settee made with dark and light wooden pieces joined in an elaborate pattern. Carved wooden leaves covered the back frame.

Lady Dudlee stared at Lilibet. "I was unaware she would be attending. I was hoping to become better acquainted with my future daughter-in-law."

Meg barely controlled her anger. Others saw Lilibet as the illegitimate daughter of a cook, but she was her half sister and dearest friend. "My aunt was ill, and I could not visit alone. Lilibet is my companion, and I think of her as family." She met her gaze, daring her to speak ill of Lilibet again.

Lady Dudlee's hand went to her bosom. "Lady Rudnack is ill?"

"Nothing serious." Felicity's main fault was her vanity. She had overslept and didn't have time to have her hair styled in anything impressive. "She offers her apologies and invites you to tea in the near future."

"I would be honored."

Meg wouldn't miss the lords and ladies fawning over each other as they sought to impress the highest gentry. Her mother had been the victim of vicious gossip and pity for the faults her father flaunted in public. Katherine had fought the shame by finding happiness in spite of her circumstances. She would strive to do the same.

A maid brought in a silver tray and placed it on the table.

Lady Dudlee lifted the delicate teapot and poured the hot brew into small painted cups. "Did you enjoy last night's ball?"

"I found it entertaining and enlightening," Meg said. "Captain Youngblood was a wealth of information about my intended."

Lady Dudlee dropped a lump of sugar from the tongs held in her hand. "You should have asked me about Eliot. I'm his mother." She grabbed another lump from the bowl. "How many?"

"One lump." Was she worried about what the captain had shared? "There are some secrets a man doesn't confide to his mother."

"What did the captain say?" Lady Dudlee's hand trembled as she handed her the saucer and cup.

Meg stirred her tea with an ornate silver spoon. "He said Eliot was an honorable man. How would you describe his character?"

She delivered a lump of sugar into Lilibet's cup and appeared to relax. "He's dutiful and responsible. Eliot has always done what we ask of him."

"Unlike someone we know," Lilibet whispered in her ear as she accepted her cup of tea.

Meg chose a biscuit from the plate Lady Dudlee offered. "You praise Eliot as if he were a saint. I hope he has some flaws, or he will find me lacking as a wife." A short burst of laughter accompanied her remark. She needed Lady Dudlee to confide in her and reveal any family secrets.

"We could never find you inferior in any way." She offered the plate to Lilibet and frowned when she took two biscuits. She turned her attention to Meg. "You are everything we could wish for in a daughter-in-law. I have admired your aunt for some time and met your mother two years ago."

Meg tried to recall meeting Lady Dudlee, but the

memories of that year were marred by her mother's death. "Were we introduced?"

"Briefly at a party before you were claimed by a young man."

"And now I am claimed by your son." Why had he chosen her? And why the urgency? "I'm flattered by the honor of becoming your son's wife, but was there a reason Eliot could not return to England, even for the ceremony?"

Lady Dudlee looked up from stirring her tea. "Eliot did not think it was a good time to leave Riverside with the unrest in the colonies, especially in the shipping industry. He's a responsible young man and felt it was important to remain and oversee the Richmond business. We're so proud of his accomplishments."

"Is it dangerous in Riverside?" Lilibet asked, a tremor in her voice.

"No, no." Lady Dudlee waved her hand to dismiss the idea. "You'll be perfectly safe. Riverside is a quiet town on a busy harbor. Our family investments keep Eliot busy."

"Too busy to find a wife?" Lilibet voiced Meg's thoughts.

Lady Dudlee frowned at Lilibet before turning to Meg with a smile on her lips. "A wife should be an asset to her husband."

"There are no eligible women in the colonies?" Meg hoped her question sounded innocent.

"No one worthy," Lady Dudlee said. "Too many women would take advantage of a man like Eliot."

Did another woman worry them? "How?"

She twittered nervously. "There are some women who are only after a man for his title and wealth."

And some families who were after higher social connections. Meg leaned toward her and glanced about. "Is there someone I should be concerned about?"

"Oh no." Her teacup rattled in the saucer, and she put it on the tray.

Lady Dudlee was hiding something. "You mentioned social standing. I didn't think the people in the colonies emphasized titles. Too many are second- and third-born sons."

"But Eliot is a firstborn son, and someday he'll return to England to take his position in society. A devious woman in the colonies might believe marriage would give her benefits above her birth. What woman wouldn't prefer to live in London rather than a small town in Connecticut?"

She was talking about the threat of a woman in Riverside. "We can't have that." Meg gave her a knowing nod.

She seemed pleased by Meg's words. "Eliot is eager to wed."

Most men dragged their feet to the altar. What was wrong with him? "Do you have a portrait of your son? I would like to recognize him when I arrive."

Lady Dudlee rose from the settee. "It's in Isaac's study. Let me see if he's done with his business. He was meeting with Captain Youngblood about the cargo."

Meg put her cup down and waited until Lady Dudlee left. "I need to discover why his mother considers a devious woman in the colonies a threat to Eliot."

"He could have a mistress."

"Why would that worry them? Most men of Eliot's age have a mistress."

"What if he decides to keep her after the marriage?"

Lilibet asked.

"Then I will only have to do my duty and no more, but I don't like being treated like a child and kept in the dark. I can not only accept a mistress but behave appropriately." Could she? Her mother had settled for a marriage of duty. Although Katherine never complained, her life had been lonely with few ladies comfortable about visiting the manor. She had filled her days with household tasks and raising her children. But Meg had witnessed her mother's melancholy. Katherine had believed in romance and been denied the fairy-tale ending. Could Meg settle for less than true love?

Lady Dudlee returned. "Come. The men have concluded their business."

They followed their hostess to the study in the back of the house. Lord Dudlee rose from his chair behind a mahogany desk with ornate carvings on the legs and sides. Captain Youngblood stood near a bookcase and acknowledged them as they entered.

Meg nodded in return. The captain worked for Lord Dudlee and Eliot. He would be aligned with their interests. Could she turn him into her ally? If he was an honorable man, he wouldn't betray his friend. She would have to learn more about him and Eliot.

Lady Dudlee stared at a painting behind the desk. "The portrait was painted after Eliot finished his education."

Meg studied the man she had been promised to. "Is it a good likeness?"

"I think so," Lord Dudlee said with pride in his voice.

Meg turned to the captain. "You've seen him most recently. What is your opinion?"

"He's older but hasn't changed much."

Lady Dudlee tore her gaze from the portrait. "What do you think of our son, Lady Meg?"

She chose her words carefully. "He's handsome and agreeable looking." But his portrait made him appear quiet and reserved unlike the man standing close by. Banner Youngblood vibrated life from his deep rumbling baritone to his piercing gray eyes. Her imagination ran to thoughts of adventurous pirates kidnapping ladies and stealing passionate kisses. She shivered in response to her wicked thoughts. She needed a husband. Her body was primed to discover the secrets withheld from virgins. She tore her gaze from the captain to the portrait. Would Eliot fulfill her desires?

Lilibet shrugged and stared at the portrait. "He has nice eyes. A nice brown color. Like a cow's."

Nothing like Lilibet to throw ice water on the growing heat in her veins. Eliot's eyes were big and brown, and Meg wondered if he was slow and docile like a bovine.

"He has his mother's eyes," Lord Dudlee said with fondness.

She glanced at Lady Dudlee and then her husband who were staring transfixed at the portrait. "You love your son a great deal."

"Yes, we do. We would do anything to ensure his happiness."

They spoke the truth, and she voiced her thoughts. "Then why is he in Riverside?"

His parents exchanged worried glances. "He'll return soon enough once you are married."

What about the unrest she spoke of? "If Eliot returns to London, who will oversee your business interest?"

"I have a good man working there," Lord Dudlee said. "His name is Glen Stemple. I'm sure you'll like him. He's been supportive of this marriage."

Why would a stranger be interested in her marriage to Eliot? She committed his name to memory. "I look forward to meeting all of Eliot's friends."

Lord Dudlee removed a small box from his desk. "I would like you to wear this as a sign of your betrothal." He revealed a ring with a ruby center surrounded by diamonds.

Lilibet gasped. "That's huge."

"I had it made for this occasion." Lord Dudlee held the ring in his fingers. "May I?"

Meg wanted to wipe the sweat off her hands but extended her left one, and her future father-in-law pushed the ring on her finger. The red stone was beautiful but reminded her of the blood she had shed before signing the agreement. She took a deep breath to steady her fast-beating heart. "Now that I'm officially your future daughter-in-law, I would like a word with you in private."

His eyes widened, and he looked at the others, who hesitated to move.

Lilibet headed for the door. "I'll wait outside."

The captain met her gaze and offered Lady Dudlee his arm to lead her out.

Lord Dudlee closed the door. "What is this about, Lady Meg?"

"I hope I haven't offended you by asking for this meeting, but I feel it's necessary."

He relaxed and took his seat after she sat.

She was terrible at subtleties. "I would like to see the betrothal agreement. I know Owen O'Leary delivered it soon after I signed it, but I did not have a chance to read it."

"It's probably too difficult for you to understand."

She felt the slap even though he hadn't delivered one physically. She was a stupid, useless woman except for one thing. He valued her ability to produce an heir and nothing more.

She bowed her head and fought to control her anger. "All of this is so overwhelming. I was hoping you would help me navigate through it." *Act stupid and men will tell you whatever you want to know to show off their superior intellect.* It was a lesson she had learned but placed on the shelf as useless until now.

"I might be able to explain the terms." He hesitated.

"I would have asked my father, but he isn't a patient man." She let her words sink in. He had to sympathize with her plight. "If you could simplify it for me, I would be grateful."

"Of course." He removed the document from the drawer in his desk. He paused before handing it to her. "I had expected Lady Rudnack to explain everything to you."

"My aunt was not privy to the document." If Lady Dudlee was impressed by the viscountess, then Lord Dudlee would defer to her as well. "She was the one who suggested I read it before traveling to Riverside."

"I understand." Whether he did or not, he handed her the document.

Meg carefully read through the agreement, searching for any hidden promises. It was a simple pledge to marry but no mention of money. "It's a formal and fair agreement, but I see nothing in it about my father's debts."

Lord Dudlee's eyebrows rose to his wig. "That is not a subject for a young woman to discuss."

"But I will soon be your son's wife, and my mother taught me how to keep accounts and run a household. It has been some time since I reviewed my father's ledgers, but I believe his debts are the reason for this arranged marriage. It does not embarrass me to talk about them, and I would expect you to be honest with me. Did my father request any funds or loans from you?"

"Eugenie has no head for numbers, so I am shocked when a woman displays knowledge of debts and credits." Lord Dudlee leaned back and laughed in a high shrill that echoed in the small room. "You have no need to worry. Your father did not ask for any funds from me at this time."

That didn't make sense. Wasn't the marriage about her father's debts? "What do you mean?"

He leaned forward. "I had heard of the financial setbacks of your father and offered a loan, but Mr. O'Leary said Lord Whittington was too proud to accept. I made it clear that if your father needs funds in the future, I will offer my resources." He patted her hand. "I don't want you to worry about him. I am more than willing to offer family assistance if circumstances become dire."

She wasn't worried about her father, but Micah could be left with nothing to inherit. Marrying Eliot would allow her to help her brother and Lilibet when their father's debts caused his fragile world to crumble.

"My brother Micah will be graduating from Cambridge next year. I hope you will assist him in finding a position if he requires help."

"Of course. Once you marry Eliot, we will be

family."

Everything depended upon the marriage. "Owen O'Leary insists upon traveling with us to bring back proof of the wedding. Was that your idea?"

He shook his head, and lines creased his forehead in deep furrows. "No. He asked me to arrange passage for three when the agreement was first drawn up."

The first mention of him accompanying them was last night at the ball, but it had been his plan all along. Once on the boat, she could not escape, and she knew no one in the colonies. Meg spread the parchment on the desk. She ran her finger down the length of the agreement. "No dowry is mentioned."

Lord Dudlee waved his hand in the air. "Because of your father's financial tribulations, I waived any dowry."

But her grandfather had set up a trust. If no dowry was required for the marriage, why the rush to marry before her birthday? Was her father planning to keep all the money for himself?

Grief had blinded her to the threat of Lord Dudlee's visits to Whittington Manor. "How long has my father been negotiating this agreement?"

"Since last year. It takes six to eight weeks to travel between Riverside and London. Correspondence is slow, but now that everything is signed, I will entrust the document to Captain Youngblood who will personally deliver it to Eliot."

Signed, sealed, and delivered like her. She returned the betrothal agreement and rose. "Thank you for answering my questions."

He locked the document in his desk. "I know this has been difficult for you, but all of us want you and Eliot to be happy."

"Is that true? Do you want Eliot to be happy?"

He came around the desk. "Of course. We love him."

"I promise his happiness will be my goal." Now if she could only figure out how to do that without sacrificing her own.

Lord Dudlee hugged her. "Welcome to the family, my dear."

She wasn't sure how to react. She had learned to avoid men who liked to pinch and grope, but his embrace was gentle and brief. It didn't cause her stomach to sour and wish to be somewhere else. She patted him quickly on the back as he pulled away. "I'm honored."

Chapter Six

Banner waited in the parlor, trying not to look toward the study and reveal his concern over the conversation between Lady Meg and Lord Dudlee. What was the man telling the woman? It could be harmless, but something gnawed at his stomach. He had watched Lady Meg study the portrait of Eliot. What did she think of her future husband? What if she fell in love with him only to have her heart broken? Should he warn her? Or would that be a betrayal of his friendship?

Eliot had planned to send Cathy and Anna out of his life, but had he kept his promise? He had paid five pounds when Anna was born, the penalty levied on the couple for fornication and a child out of wedlock. Cathy's father, a respected church leader, hadn't forgiven her for living with Eliot in sin. If he had sent them away, where had they gone?

The door opened, and Lilibet jumped up from the chair where she had been sitting in silence. Lady Dudlee had refused to speak to the girl, her prejudice evident. How would she treat her granddaughter if they ever met?

Lady Meg accepted her cloak from Lilibet. "Thank you for your hospitality."

"Tell Lady Rudnack I hope she recovers from her illness soon," Lady Dudlee said as the butler opened the door.

Lady Meg looked confused before smiling. "I'm

sure she's feeling better already."

Banner followed them outside. The sun was shining, but the air was crisp. He looked for a carriage. "Where is your ride?"

"We walked," Lilibet said.

"It was too nice a day to waste inside a carriage," Lady Meg said. "Aunt Felicity's house isn't far."

"May I escort you home? I wanted to discuss the voyage with you."

"It would be a pleasure." Lady Meg walked beside him with Lilibet near the buildings that lined the brick footway. They took the short distance at a leisurely stroll. "What should we know before sailing across the ocean to Connecticut?"

"I feel obligated to warn you about the hardships at sea. It is a long voyage, and you'll be the only women aboard."

"Will we have to row?" Lady Meg asked.

Was she serious? "There are no oars on board a sailing ship."

Lady Meg appeared puzzled. "Aren't there oars on the longboats?"

"Yes, but we won't be traveling in the…"

She placed her hand on his arm and laughed. "Please forgive me for teasing you, Captain. I forget not everyone enjoys sarcasm and wit."

He wasn't the sort of man women teased. Some flirted, others propositioned, but no one taunted in a playful manner. He stammered for a proper answer. "The wind does most of the work."

"I've been warned that men don't appreciate my sense of humor, so if I offend you, please let me know." Lady Meg tightened the bow on her bonnet. "I know how to curb my tongue."

Lilibet coughed into her gloved hand.

One sister was being more honest than the other. "I enjoy a good ribbing, but I hope you don't expect fun and games. Life is hard at sea, and every man must attend to his tasks, but there are many unique creatures and sights to see on the voyage."

"I've never been on a sailing ship before, but I look forward to the trip with anticipation and fear."

"Fear?" The lady did not lack courage.

Lady Meg turned her head, her bonnet framing her smiling face. "It wouldn't be an adventure if there wasn't an element of danger."

"I will do my best to keep you safe in spite of your perilous wishes." He looked at Lilibet. "Both of you."

"What are the hardships you want to warn us about?" Lady Meg asked.

"More like discomforts. A merchant ship utilizes every available space. You can pack as many trunks as you require, but those will be stored in the hold. Pack one to be placed in your cabin. The weather will be cold on the ocean this time of the year. You'll want to pack warm clothing. The passageways are narrow, so avoid padding for your skirts."

"I think I'll stay in my room," Lilibet said.

"You'll want fresh air," Banner said. "Wear a sturdy pair of shoes or boots and heavy stockings since it will be windy and water washes on deck. You will need cloaks or wool coats to keep warm. There are no fires in the cabins."

"No fires?" Lilibet asked. "Why not?"

"The ship is made of wood. Only the cook has a fire, and it is in a special building on deck. Lit candle lanterns or oil lamps shouldn't be left unattended. You mentioned longboats, but you wouldn't want to be stranded in one in the middle of the ocean."

Lilibet's face had gone pale. "Now I know I won't leave my room."

"How big is our cabin?" Lady Meg asked.

"Small. The only furniture now is a bunk. Lord Dudlee has authorized me to purchase additional furnishings such as a rug, table, and—"

"And what?"

There was no way to put it delicately. "Commode. The men tend to use a bucket or the side of the ship."

Lady Meg turned to Lilibet. "We should go shopping."

"I can purchase the items," Banner said.

"No," Lady Meg said. "If we are living in the space for two months, I think we should go with you. What day are you free?"

Shopping? With two women? He'd heard horror stories from other men and had never accompanied a lady to the shops. "I know exactly what you require."

"We know what we like," Lady Meg said. "When are you available?"

She was headstrong. How bad could a quick trip to the shops be? "Tuesday would be best, but I'd like to get an early start."

"We'll be ready at eleven."

He would have liked an earlier hour but didn't argue. He could scout out the merchandise that would fit in the small space and steer them toward those purchases.

Lady Meg stopped at the gate leading to her aunt's door. "Thank you, Captain. Would you like to come in? I might need to make a list of what we should pack."

"Her mother made lists," Lilibet said. "She had a whole book of them."

"She kept them?"

Lady Meg tilted her chin and raised a finely arched eyebrow. "Don't you keep a ledger of your ship's expenses?"

"I maintain a manifest that tracks cargo, passengers, and crew. The law requires it."

"My mother kept lists of repairs, inventory, and servants," she said. "It's the same thing."

He wanted to argue that a ship's manifest was more important than a household account, but her eyes had darkened beneath delicately raised eyebrows, and he changed the subject. "It's nice you've carried on the tradition."

"I admired my mother. We were enjoying my first season when she died." Her voice shook, and she choked back tears. "The servants packed her belongings into a trunk, and when I arrived in London my aunt asked if I wanted her dresses altered to fit me. This was one of her favorites." She pulled back her cloak to reveal the pale-green silk with yellow daisies embroidered on the gown.

He had taken in the details when he saw her in Lord Dudlee's office. She looked like spring and smelled of lilac when the breeze blew in his direction.

"It's difficult to lose a parent." His voice betrayed his own grief. "I can tell you were close to your mother."

"I loved her and miss her every day. Are your parents alive?"

"No." He conveyed the basic facts. "My mother died three years ago, and my father has been gone two years. My brother Wilbur inherited the title."

"But you've made your own way through life." A

hint of pride praised him from her lips.

"I never liked the idea of taking an allowance from my brother. He puts it in a trust for my children if I ever marry."

"A trust," Lady Meg repeated. "Lord Dudlee allowed me to read the betrothal agreement."

"Is that why you wanted a private meeting?"

"Yes, and there were some peculiarities." Lady Meg touched his arm. "My grandfather set up a trust for me, and I thought it was going toward my dowry, but Lord Dudlee said there was no dowry agreed upon in the betrothal. I know my father is in debt, but you would think he could spare a small amount. It puts me at a disadvantage to bring nothing to the marriage."

She brought more to the marriage than most women. If Eliot didn't appreciate his good fortune, he would have to hit him over the head. "The absence of a dowry makes Eliot more dependent on his father's allowance."

"Doesn't he have any income of his own?" Lady Meg's voice betrayed her worry.

He wanted to reassure her. "No, but Lord Dudlee provides a generous allowance."

They had remained at the gate while talking, but as soon as they neared the door, it opened, and the butler took their wraps and hats. "You have a guest in the parlor, Lady Meg."

A gangly young man with brown curls was seated in a high-back chair reading a small leather-bound book. He placed it on the round table beside him and rose. A grin filled a face that bore a slight resemblance to Lady Meg's softer features. "It's about time you showed up."

Lady Meg tackled him in a hug that sent him falling back into the chair and nearly upending it.

He looked at Lilibet. "No hug?"

She threw her arms around his neck and perched her hip on the arm of the chair. "You took your good time arriving. Meg was ready to take a coach to Cambridge."

Lady Meg turned to Banner. "This is my brother, Micah, if you haven't guessed."

He'd determined the relationship from the family resemblance and their affectionate behavior. "Pleasure to meet you, Lord Micah."

"Oh please, we're both the children of earls and at home. You can call me Meg, and we always call him Micah." She pinched her brother's cheek.

"I received your letter," Micah said, pinching her back. "What's this about you marrying someone in the colonies?" He looked at Banner. "Is that him?"

"No," Meg said as she pushed off the young man to rise. "This is Captain Banner Youngblood. I'm marrying his friend, Eliot Richmond."

Micah rose. "Captain? Why aren't you in uniform?"

"I'm a merchant sea captain."

Meg grabbed Micah's arm. "I was so afraid you wouldn't arrive before we sailed."

"I finished my exams early, packed my bags, and showed up at Father's place last night. I couldn't let you go without a proper good-bye," Micah said. "Why didn't you give more warning?"

She frowned and examined his face. "I wrote you several letters."

Micah removed a missive from his coat. "I only received this one."

Meg examined the note. "I mailed this from Aunt Felicity's house. What happened to the letters I sent from Whittington Manor?"

"Who could have taken them?" Lilibet gave Meg a suspicious look.

Micah took the letter back and returned it to his pocket. "What's going on, Meg?"

"How did Father react when you showed up on his doorstep? Was he displeased?"

"No, but Owen seemed surprised. For some reason he expected me to go home to the manor. It would have taken several more days to reach London. I might have missed you."

Meg hugged him again. "I wouldn't have left without saying good-bye."

Banner watched the exchange. He loved his brother, but their age difference had made it impossible to share more than school breaks and holidays. He envied the easy banter and comradery these siblings shared.

"Aunt Felicity said Owen is going with you," Micah said. "What's that scarecrow up to?"

"You mean what's Father up to." Meg crossed her arms and pouted.

"He wasn't himself, Meg." His voice was filled with concern. "Has he been ill?"

"Mostly drunk." She turned to Banner. "I'm sorry to drag you into our family troubles."

He shrugged. "As captain, I deal with conflicts among my crew and wrangling with merchants on a regular basis. I'm happy to listen and lend any help I can."

Micah extended his hand. "I'm honored to meet the brave man who is sailing across an ocean with my sisters."

Boldness ran in the family. Banner shook his hand and kept his reply lighthearted. "Should I be worried?"

"Ignore my baby brother," Meg said. "He's been at Cambridge and spends all his time with his nose in a book."

"We always went on our adventures together," Micah said. "What if I didn't go back to school next term and ran off to sea with you?"

She took his hands. "As much as I would love that, you only have one year left in school. You can't throw your future away. Besides, we'll be back soon with my husband."

Husband. Banner had nearly forgotten the reason for the voyage. Micah and Lilibet would become part of Eliot's family not his.

Lady Rudnack entered the room in a turquoise gown with matching feathers in a moderate hairstyle. "You're back. How was your visit to Lord and Lady Dudlee?"

"Very profitable." Meg displayed her ring.

Micah grabbed her hand and examined the bauble. "What's this?"

"My future in-laws gave it to me to seal the betrothal. Although he's been cheated. Lord Dudlee told me there was no dowry."

Lady Rudnack looked up from examining the ring. "But your grandfather set up a trust to provide a dowry, and he was a cautious man when it came to investments. Some funds have to be in it."

"Didn't Lord Dudlee waive the dowry?" Banner asked.

"That's an impertinent question, Captain," Lady Rudnack said as she carefully reclined in a plush chair.

Meg waved her hand. "I see no reason to keep secrets from the captain. He's Eliot's friend and knows the Richmond family better than we do." She pulled him toward the settee, and they sat side by side. "Lord Dudlee admitted he was willing to loan Father money, but Owen insisted he wait until after the wedding. With proof of the marriage, Owen can send Father's debt collectors to Lord Dudlee's door. It's shameful."

"Does Lord Dudlee know the extent of your father's debts?" Lady Rudnack asked. "Even a rich merchant has a bottom to his purse."

"I doubt Father knows how much he owes," Meg said. "He leaves all his financial decisions in Owen's slick hands."

"I have some numbers." Micah retrieved the book he had been reading and flipped through several pages. "I found Mother's journal in her trunk."

"You were in my room?"

"I'm your brother. You know I love to explore trunks, boxes, and secret compartments."

"What else did you take?" Meg's tone was suspicious.

"Only the book. I needed something to pass the time and began reading. Do you know she recorded every subject and mark I received in school?"

She shook her head. "That's what you were reading?"

He turned several pages. "This page might interest you." He handed the book to Meg.

Banner leaned over her shoulder as she scanned the list written in neat handwriting. He tried not to let his eyes wander to the low-cut gown revealing the soft mounds of Meg's breasts that rose with each breath.

He looked up to find Micah staring. Let the young pup judge him. He was a man. He could appreciate a woman's figure, especially one on display next to him.

How was a man to gain control if he didn't face temptation?

Meg ran her finger down the page. "It looks like a list of repairs. Garden wall rebuilt. Bannister railing repaired. Marble around parlor fireplace installed. And new stable roof. What's so unusual about that?"

Micah sat beside her, squeezing them tighter together on the settee. He pointed at the book. "I was at the townhouse, and although I didn't look for anything specific, I don't think any of these repairs have been completed. The groomsmen were complaining about all the leaks in the stable roof, and the inside of the townhouse looked run-down."

Meg flipped through the pages. "Mother marked costs next to the repairs."

"Why would she do that if they weren't completed?" Banner asked. "Who was in charge of paying for the repairs?"

Meg and Micah spoke the same name. "Owen."

"Could Father run out of money?" Micah sounded worried.

"He always had money to make repairs before Mother died. She made sure the houses were maintained and the servants paid. If Owen is so bad at managing the properties, shouldn't he be dismissed?"

"Father won't fire him because we say so," Micah said.

"Do you want to inherit his debts?" Her voice was full of concern and fury. "What happens if you have to sell the townhouse or country estate? What about your title?"

"Do you think it's that dire?" Micah asked. "Where did the money go?"

Meg lifted the book. "I believe Mother was asking the same thing."

Meg and Micah were young and reckless. They were jumping to conclusions, and someone needed to rein them in.

Lady Rudnack was showing Lilibet a stack of invitations, ignoring the discourse.

Banner needed to provide a voice of reason. "A list doesn't prove anything. You need to examine the ledgers to prove whether the money was distributed properly or pocketed. You don't want to accuse an innocent man of a crime. Newgate Prison is already full of too many victims instead of criminals."

"Owen guards the financial ledgers with his life," Meg said. "He's not going to allow us to look at them without a fight."

"He won't be around for four months," Banner reminded her.

Meg's eyes grew big, and she looked like she wanted to kiss him. "He's going on the voyage." She jumped from the settee and grabbed her brother's arm to pull him to his feet. "You could look at them while he's gone."

He stammered a reply. "I return to school in a month. Do you think that will be enough time?"

"It's your inheritance at stake." Her voice sounded like a challenge. "Do you want to inherit nothing?"

To his credit Micah squared his young shoulders and stood taller. "No, but what do I look for?" He looked toward Banner who had stood when Meg rose.

He gave orders, not brotherly advice, but took on the role. "You can begin by copying every scheduled repair and the amounts. Then determine if the repairs were made."

"Lilibet can make the list." Meg handed her the book. "Your handwriting is the neatest."

Lady Rudnack looked at them, a curious expression on her face. "What are you children up to now?" She turned to Banner. "They were always getting into mischief when they were younger. I thought they had outgrown it."

Lilibet sat at a small desk and began writing down the information in the book. Micah joined her and pointed to another page to copy.

"When you return to Father's townhouse, you can confirm whether the job was completed or not, but don't let anyone notice you," Meg warned.

"I know how to be discreet," Micah defended. "Unlike you."

Meg stuck out her tongue at him.

Lilibet looked up from writing the list. "But what will this prove other than the work wasn't done?"

Meg bit her bottom lip as if in thought. She turned to Banner. "What can we do?"

"You should talk to your father's solicitor and see if money was paid out for the repairs," Banner said. "If it wasn't used to pay hired workers, where did it go?"

Micah looked at his aunt. "Do you know who is Father's solicitor?"

"Peter Clifton," Lady Rudnack said. "He handles all your father's financial business. Katherine would visit him when she was in London."

"Where is Mr. Clifton's office?" Micah asked.

Lady Rudnack went pale, and the stack of papers fell from her shaking hands and scattered on the floor. "On Cornhill. It's where all the financial institutions are located."

"Are you ill?" Meg knelt in front of her aunt and gathered her correspondence. "What's wrong?"

Banner poured a glass of wine and offered it.

Lady Rudnack downed the drink in one gulp.

He took her empty glass. "Do you want another?"

She shook her head. "It must have been a coincidence."

Micah patted her hand. "What was?"

She studied the concerned faces around her. "Your mother was crossing Cornhill Street when a team of horses bolted, and she was knocked to the ground by the wagon."

"You don't think her death was an accident?" Banner asked.

She looked shocked by his question. "Who would want to hurt Katherine?" Lady Rudnack pointed at the empty glass he held. "Pour me another."

She drank the second glass more slowly. "The coachman brought her home. He said the team and wagon came out of nowhere. We stayed by your mother's side until she passed, but she never regained consciousness."

"I remember crying. I couldn't stop." Meg's voice shook.

"If she was on Cornhill Street, she may have been calling on Mr. Clifton." Micah took the list Lilibet had copied.

"We need to call on Mr. Clifton as soon as possible," Meg said.

Lady Rudnack finished her drink. "If you want to find out about your dowry, he would know."

Meg and Lilibet fussed over Lady Rudnack, and the

men bid their good-byes and headed for the door.

"Walk with me." Micah waved the list at him and then folded it before sliding it into an inner pocket. "What do you make of this?"

"Men don't always listen to women," he said. "We consider them silly, frivolous creatures, so I will repeat what your sister kindly said. You must fight for your inheritance. I have met Owen O'Leary, and I would not trust him with a shilling, but your father is too drunk to question him."

"You shouldn't talk about my father like that."

"The man took a whip to your sister."

"What?" Micah stopped walking. "He would never harm her."

"When you see her next, examine her back. The scars are still fresh. Then grow the same courage she has shown. While Owen is gone, you will have the opportunity to find out the truth. Use it wisely. And don't tip your hand to your father until you can show him proof and sway his opinion to your side."

"What do you think is afoot?"

"I think you will be a penniless lad if you don't take charge of your future."

Chapter Seven

Because of the weekend, Meg had to wait until Monday to visit Peter Clifton, but it gave her time to formulate a plan and rehearse her questions. Her mother had gone to Cornhill Street for a reason.

Micah joined her and Lilibet in the private parlor adjacent to her bedroom.

He waved the list as he paced across the room. "None of the work has been done. And other repairs are needed. The place is falling apart."

"Did anyone notice you examining the house?" Lilibet asked.

"Father has reduced staff, and they were attending church services or sleeping yesterday when I searched," he said. "It didn't take long to assess the damages inside and out."

Meg placed a copy of the list of repairs she had made inside her reticule. "I hope Mr. Clifton will be able to help us."

"Wait," Micah said. "Turn around."

Meg glanced over her shoulder. "Do I have something on my back?"

He tugged on the back of her gown and gasped. "Father did this?"

She hadn't kept her punishment a secret, but his reaction caused her pain. He loved their father in spite of his faults and her apprehensions. "Who told you?"

"Your captain. Why didn't *you* tell me he whipped you?"

"I did in my first letter." The truth dawned on her. "That's why you never received it. They read it and knew you would come home immediately if you learned the truth. The one you received was about the marriage and that I was at Aunt Felicity's home in London."

"And you mailed it from London," Lilibet added. "No one intercepted it."

"This is intolerable." He clenched his fists. "I will not allow you to be beaten into submission."

"It's too late." She kept her voice calm. "The agreement is signed."

"I'm nearly twenty," he said. "I should have a word with Father."

"Don't jeopardize your inheritance by confronting him. Who knows what he'll do in his current drunken state? Mother warned us to be clever and choose our fights wisely. We need to gather information, and then you can talk to Father while Owen is gone."

"Are you afraid of Owen?"

"You bear a scar of his viciousness when you were four years old." She brushed back his thick hair to reveal the scar on his forehead. "I've thought long and hard on Mother's death. Do you think Owen had any role in it?"

"Owen is too much of a coward," Micah said. "He grovels before Father and does his every bidding."

For everyone to see. Owen had a flair for dramatics. "What if he acts the fool to deceive others? In the past two years while I mourned Mother, his influence over Father's affairs has grown. I should have been more vigilant. Only recently have I noticed how Owen guides Father's words and actions. You need to gain his trust and be a positive influence on him while the *trusted* steward is gone." Meg leaned into him. "You have to take responsibility for your future."

"Captain Youngblood said the same thing to me."

She straightened. "He did?" Did her voice squeak?

He studied her. "You two think alike."

Lilibet giggled. "She likes him."

Micah smiled at Lilibet and nodded toward Meg. "She didn't seem to mind when I crowded them on the settee."

"Stop it," Meg said. "The captain is Eliot's loyal friend and is hiding something. If I'm to discover the truth about the man I'm to wed, he is my best source."

Micah leaned forward. "What secret do you suspect?"

Meg took a deep breath to calm her racing heart. The mere mention of Banner had sent her pulse racing. What was wrong with her? "Lady Dudlee hinted about a woman in Riverside."

"But you said most men have mistresses," Lilibet said. "Why shouldn't Eliot have one?"

"I don't begrudge him a mistress, but it would be difficult to develop any tender feelings if he spends his nights with another woman."

"I know you, dear sister. You would not be happy sharing your husband with anyone."

Was Micah right? She thought she was sophisticated enough to tolerate a dalliance by her husband, but what if he loved his mistress? What if a part of her dream for true love died like her mother's?

Meg considered his words as they went downstairs. She wrapped a scarlet cloak around her shoulders and pulled up the hood. Lilibet wore a plain brown cloak and wide-brimmed bonnet over a lace-trimmed cap.

Micah helped them board the closed carriage and sat opposite the women. "You look positively dreary, Lilibet."

She pulled her beige bonnet forward. "It's part of the plan."

"What plan?" Micah looked hurt as he looked from Lilibet to Meg. "Why wasn't I told?"

"I only thought of the scheme last night," Meg said. "Besides, the fewer number of people who know, the greater the chances our deception will be successful."

He waited. "Are you going to tell me? Who are we deceiving?"

Lilibet pointed outside. "It's to fool the guards."

His eyebrows rose. "What guards?"

Lilibet's hands trembled. "We have guards watching us all the time."

"Father is afraid I might elope." Meg looked out the window. "Good, they're behind us."

Micah poked his head out the opening. "You want them to follow us to Mr. Clifton's office?"

"No, we're stopping at the bakery first." Meg finished explaining her plan before the carriage stopped in front of the shop where the smell of fresh bread, cinnamon, and fruit filled the air.

Meg chose a table near the front window, and they sipped tea and ate their sweetbreads while watching the crowd pass. "Do you see them?"

"Lurking by that carriage across the street," Lilibet whispered. "Do you think your plan will work?"

A surge of energy flooded her body. Was it normal for a woman to love intrigue and deception? She had always thrived on it. "We'll find out soon enough."

Micah licked his fingers. "I'm ready."

Meg stared at her brother and shook her head. "Are you sure you don't want another sweet roll? You've only eaten three."

A grin widened his handsome face. "Evading henchmen gives me an appetite."

Meg stood and put on her cloak. "Let's make sure they see us." She walked to the carriage and waited for Micah to help her inside. "I need to stop at Lord Dudlee's home!" she reminded the driver, who knew the phrase as code for their plan.

As soon as they were in the carriage, Meg switched cloaks with Lilibet and tied the wide-brimmed bonnet on her head. "Make sure your red hair doesn't show."

Lilibet tucked her auburn curls under the cap and covered it with the hood. "How will they see me inside?"

"After we escape, lean out the window and wave at someone on the street so they see my cloak, but don't let them see your face."

"Escape?" Micah looked at his companions. "Did you share that part with me?"

"The driver knows what to do," Meg said.

The coach made a sharp turn, and the team broke into a canter to put distance between the two carriages. Once they were out of sight, their vehicle stopped near an alley leading to Cornhill Street. Micah and Meg jumped to the cobblestones and hid in the shadows of a stairway.

The carriage sped away with only Lilibet inside.

"They're following our carriage." Meg took Micah's arm, and they hurried down the alley. She read Peter Clifton's address written on the top of her list.

"There it is." Micah pointed to a wooden sign listing

businesses on the second floor above a counting house. They made their way up the stairs and asked to see the solicitor.

The elderly Mr. Clifton greeted them as they took seats in his office. He wore a simple wig with a single row of curls. His shoulders were stooped as he walked around his desk and took a seat. "I was surprised when I received word you wanted to visit."

Aunt Felicity had sent the notice from the home of one of her friends she was visiting to avoid Owen's spies. She might have complained about their antics but was more than willing to aid in them.

"I'm sorry about the short notice," Meg apologized. "If you haven't heard, I'm leaving for the colonies shortly, and my brother has arrived from Cambridge. We needed to take care of business immediately."

He studied her brother. "You've grown since I last saw you, Lord Micah. Your mother brought you and your sister on one of her visits. It was four, no, five years ago."

Meg had played backgammon with Micah while Mother discussed business with Mr. Clifton. She should have paid more attention to the meeting. "Did my mother meet with you two years ago?"

"Two?" He shook his head. "No. It was four years ago when I last saw her. I was shocked to hear about her death."

If her mother had never met with Mr. Clifton, he might not be able to help. But Owen had visited. She needed to focus on their business.

His voice interrupted her thoughts. "How are you enjoying school?" He was speaking to Micah.

"My marks are good, and I've made friends, but I

would like to become better acquainted with my future estate and holdings."

His eyes widened above his cherub cheeks. "Is your father ill?"

Micah glanced at Meg. "My father overindulges but seems to be cheating death for now."

Mr. Clifton nodded as he focused on Meg. "Mr. O'Leary was here a few weeks ago and informed me he was traveling with you to the colonies to witness your nuptials."

"That's one of the reasons for this visit." She nudged Micah to say the words they had rehearsed at the bakery.

"Mr. O'Leary will be gone for four months. I realized that if anything should happen to him, my father's properties would be in chaos. I thought as heir, I should take on the responsibility of understanding the finances of the country estate and the townhouse."

"I can understand your concern, but that was the reason Lord Whittington had his assets frozen until Mr. O'Leary returns."

"Personally?" Meg interrupted. "You spoke to Father?"

He stared. Had she sounded hysterical? She gave him a smile and waited for his response.

"No." He turned to Micah. "Your father hasn't visited my office since he broke his leg."

Broke his leg? "That was three years ago." Meg looked at Micah, who shrugged and turned his attention to the solicitor.

"I don't understand why that hinders his visits," her brother said.

"Mr. O'Leary told me it still bothers him to climb stairs, and he hates to travel to London." Mr. Clifton looked worried. "The correspondence has his signature authorizing any transactions."

Meg held out her hand. "May I see one of them?"

He looked at Micah.

Meg gritted her teeth. She wasn't surprised Mr. Clifton preferred to do business with a man, but she hated to be reminded of her position when she was perfectly capable of discussing financial matters.

"My sister asked to see it," Micah said. "She would like to verify that it is Father's signature."

Mr. Clifton retrieved a folder. "This is the letter canceling any payments until Mr. O'Leary's return."

He handed it to Micah who handed it to Meg.

"It's shaky but Father's signature," she confirmed.

"The only amount withdrawn was to pay the servants and regular bills next quarter," Mr. Clifton said. "A similar amount will be released in June."

"It's the bare minimum." Meg returned the paper to Mr. Clifton. "Can our father unfreeze his assets if necessary?"

"Of course. If he can travel in person."

"He's currently in London," Meg said, "and fully recovered from his injuries."

"I will talk to my father and bring him to the office," Micah said.

"Next week." She didn't want Owen to know they were investigating their father's expenses. "We have too many appointments this week since I'll be sailing on Friday."

Mr. Clifton studied them. "Is there something I should know?"

"You've worked for my family for many years," Micah said. "When I inherit, I hope I can count on your firm to continue that relationship."

Meg was startled her brother could deliver a warning with a compliment. He'd learn more than scholarly lessons at Cambridge.

Mr. Clifton's bushy eyebrows rose to touch his wig. He nodded in silent understanding. "I take pride in the trust of those I serve. What are your concerns?"

Micah looked to Meg.

They would need the solicitor's help. "Tell him about the neglect."

Mr. Clifton looked startled. "Neglect?"

"I believe funds were allocated for repairs at the townhouse, but they were never made," Micah said. "But the money had to go somewhere."

"I fear Father may have gambled away the funds. I have the dates." Meg handed him the paper with repairs and amounts. "I thought you could check your records and see if those funds were withdrawn."

He rose but hesitated. "I should ask Mr. O'Leary."

She nudged Micah. He needed to make the request.

"Mr. O'Leary is not the heir of Whittington Manor, and if your loyalty lies with him, I need to know that now," Micah said. "You asked if my father is ill. If he continues on his current path of drink and poor health, I may inherit sooner than later. When that happens, Mr. O'Leary will no longer be employed by me."

Meg was surprised by the ferocity of the tone in Micah's voice. When had her little brother grown into a man?

He stood and met the gaze of the older man. "Will I need to find a different solicitor?"

Mr. Clifton wiped the sweat from his upper lip. "My loyalty lies with the family." He studied the paper Meg had given him. "Let me find those dates." He retrieved a ledger and searched through the entries. "This is interesting."

Micah had resumed his seat but moved forward in his chair. "What?"

Meg laid her hand on Micah's arm to keep him from showing his excitement. Mr. Clifton was already suspicious.

"What did you find out?" he asked more calmly.

"The money withdrawn on those dates matches the amounts listed, but it was invested instead of withdrawn for expenses."

"Invested?" they both echoed.

"Please explain," Micah said.

Mr. Clifton returned to his seat and displayed the open ledger on the desk in front of them. "During the past three years, Lord Whittington has sent instructions to invest funds." He paused. "Through Mr. O'Leary."

Meg sighed. "Then the money is lost."

He shook his head and pointed to a figure. "No, the funds have been doing well. If they had been losing money, I would have notified Lord Whittington for permission to move them to safer investments."

Micah frowned as he tried to read the upside-down numbers. "How much does the money total?"

He hesitated. "More than six hundred pounds, Lord Micah."

"What?" Micah leaned toward her. "Why is Father sitting on six hundred pounds when the house is crumbling around him?"

"It's not only the house," she whispered back. "Collectors come around quarterly, and Owen only pays a small amount to keep them happy until the next payment."

"But why invest the money?" Micah asked. "What is he planning?"

"What's going on?" Mr. Clifton asked.

"That's what you're going to find out," she whispered to Micah. She rose and raised her voice for Mr. Clifton to hear clearly. "We thank you for investing the money so wisely. My brother and I are glad such a competent man is handling Father's money."

"Thank you, Lady Meg, Lord Micah."

She paused to make it sound like an unimportant afterthought. "One more thing, Mr. Clifton. I am betrothed to Eliot Richmond, the son of Lord Dudlee. He told me no dowry was paid, but my aunt, Lady Rudnack, said my grandfather had a trust arranged for me for that purpose. She said you might know the details."

He looked to Micah.

"It's my sister's dowry," he said. "Answer her."

Having a man around who could command respect was nice, but why weren't women treated with the same regard when unescorted? She hid her frustration with a warm smile.

"When your grandfather died, I took over the management of the trust. It becomes yours when you turn twenty-one unless you marry," Mr. Clifton said. "I mentioned the trust to Mr. O'Leary because I knew your birthday was in July but I wasn't sure of the year."

"When was this?"

"Last year before the March quarter ended. He was surprised to learn about the trust and eager to learn the details. I reviewed the terms with him and tallied the amount you would receive on your twenty-first birthday if you remained a spinster."

She was more interested in the motive for her upcoming wedding. "But if I marry, who collects the money?"

"It goes to your father. He's to give it to your husband as a dowry, but I need proof of the marriage first. That may be the reason no dowry was mentioned in the betrothal agreement."

"Did Mr. O'Leary say he would provide the proof?"

"He said that was the purpose of his journey to the colonies." Mr. Clifton closed the ledger and straightened papers on his desk. "Once he returns with proof, I will release the funds."

"And if I marry after my twenty-first birthday, the funds are completely mine?"

"Yes, although I don't think a woman alone should handle such a large amount of money." He looked at Micah. "When do you reach your majority?"

"May of 1775."

"Ten months after I reach mine," Meg said.

"Your father could handle the money until then."

He would be the last person to trust with her funds. "How much is in the trust?"

He hesitated.

She didn't hide her anger. "Did you tell Mr. O'Leary the amount?"

He took a deep breath. "Nearly ten thousand pounds. Your grandfather made some wise investments for you, and they've grown over the past twenty years. You're a lucky young lady."

Meg gripped the back of the chair, stunned by the amount. Micah had to take her arm to lead her out the door.

"We're almost outside," he said. They exited the

building and crossed the street. He waved his hat in front of her face. "Are you all right?"

She collapsed on a bench. "I know the value of my happiness. Ten thousand pounds. At least it wasn't sold cheaply."

"It's a fortune and should be yours. Can't you ask Eliot to postpone the wedding until July? It's only a couple of months."

"Which is the reason for the rush. If I marry before my birthday, Father will receive it." She stomped her foot. "And I can guarantee he won't give Eliot any for a dowry."

"Are you sure Father knows? Owen lied to Mr. Clifton about Father's ability to climb stairs. What if Owen didn't tell him about the trust?"

She didn't like giving her father the benefit of the doubt, but the only person she distrusted more than him was his steward. "It would explain why Owen is personally escorting me to Riverside and no mention of a dowry is in the agreement. Why settle for six hundred pounds when he can have ten thousand?"

Meg grabbed Micah by his jacket lapels. "I've been a fool in underestimating Owen. You have four months to sober Father and examine the ledgers. Find out if Owen is taking advantage of him and make him see the truth."

"Then what?"

"Use the six hundred pounds to pay off Father's debts and fix the townhouse and estate. Owen can't take possession of buildings." She squeezed his arm. "You did me proud upstairs the way you handled Mr. Clifton. You'll make a fine earl when you inherit."

"What about your inheritance? When Owen returns

with proof of your marriage, he'll collect the ten thousand pounds from your trust," Micah said. "What are you going to do?"

"I'm going to try to not marry Eliot Richmond."

"How are you going to accomplish that?"

"I haven't the slightest idea, but I have two months to think of something."

Chapter Eight

Banner arrived promptly at eleven on Tuesday, expecting to wait on the ladies, but Meg, Lilibet, and Micah were waiting in Lady Rudnack's spacious foyer. He welcomed another man on the shopping spree. Women were a mystery. He had limited interactions with the female gender and had never formed a strong bond beyond a casual acquaintance. Not that he didn't wish for a relationship that went beyond short-term passion.

He looked forward to seeing Meg and longed to spend time with her, but how far could their friendship advance before it threatened her future happiness with Eliot? He couldn't betray his good friend by seducing the woman he was going to marry. He should focus on Lilibet. She was pretty and sweet, but his heart didn't pound with excitement when he looked at her. A short-haired blonde with hazel eyes was the one who haunted his dreams.

Micah helped place a cloak around Lilibet's shoulders, and Banner took the opportunity to help Meg with hers.

She turned her face, and her lips brushed his fingertips. "Do you have a list of what we need?"

His hand shook. "Yes, I do."

Lilibet laughed. "You two are so much alike it's scary."

"I admire organization," Meg said.

He shared his list. He'd already located the shops where the necessary items could be found. "I think we can find everything today."

Meg opened her reticule. "Who will pay for our purchases?"

"Don't worry." Banner studied the arch of her brows and the graceful line of her nose. "Lord Dudlee gave me a letter of credit to cover all the expenses."

Meg twisted the large ring on her finger. "He seems to be generous."

"He is with those in his favor." Which was why Eliot was marrying the woman before him.

"I'm afraid only a few items will fit. The room is wider at one end, but the bunks take up nearly three feet along the inner wall." He turned over his list and showed her a diagram. "You'll have to choose your pieces carefully."

She studied his drawing. "Will everything on your list fit?"

"If it's the right size."

The coachman opened the door to the carriage. Banner helped Meg and Lilibet inside and waited for Micah to enter and choose a seat. He gave the driver directions and sat in the remaining unoccupied seat next to Meg. The coach lurched forward, and the hooves of the horses echoed on the cobblestone street.

"We went to see Mr. Clifton yesterday," Meg said.

"Do you trust him?" Micah nodded toward Banner.

"We talked about seeing Father's solicitor in front of him. It would be rude not to update him on our visit."

Micah frowned. "But he isn't family."

"And he can give us an unbiased opinion." Meg turned to face Banner and openly studied his face. "Are you a man of integrity, Captain?"

The question was straightforward and deserved an equally honest answer. "I consider myself a man of moral character."

"Oh, I hope not." She turned to Micah and laughed. The sound was musical and played on his heartstrings. "How will we ever corrupt him?"

He stared at the three, who burst into laughter. He should have been angry but realized they were testing him before taking him into their confidence. They were like playful children, unlike his serious brother who doled out dreary advice. But their youthful exuberance could lead to trouble. What were they plotting?

"What about loyalty?" Meg asked. "If we told you something in confidence, would you feel compelled to tell your friend Eliot?"

"I might if it impacted him." Banner guided them to the original topic. "How did your meeting go with your father's solicitor?"

Micah raised his hands into the air. "Did you know our father was an invalid?"

"What? He was a little drunk when I met him but seemed mobile."

Meg bounced against his side, her hand touching his knee when the carriage hit a rut. Thick wool separated their skin, but the slight pressure had his body reacting in a way that surprised him. How could an innocent touch spawn such an arousing reaction? It had never happened before. She appeared to be unaffected. He concentrated on her words and fought to gain control.

"He broke his leg three years ago, and according to Owen, he couldn't maneuver the steps leading to Mr. Clifton's office," Meg said. "This blatant lie required his *faithful* steward to deliver any correspondence."

Banner reviewed her words. "Has he been stealing from your father?"

"No." She sank into the leather seat. "But he hasn't made repairs to the estate or townhouse. He asked Mr. Clifton to invest the money instead."

"And he lost it?"

"No," Micah nearly shouted. "He's accumulated six hundred pounds in the past few years."

That was a large sum of money to gain. "Then what is the problem?"

"Why would Father invest the money instead of making repairs or paying off his debts?" Meg asked. "The money remains untouched."

Banner recalled the wear on Lord Whittington's coat. "Who has access to the funds?"

"Father," Micah said. "It's his signature on the letters sent to Mr. Clifton."

"And Owen," Meg added. "In Father's current state, he'll sign anything Owen puts in front of him. Sometimes it is difficult to discern if Father controls his steward or if he's the puppet."

Banner had wondered the same thing. "Mr. O'Leary didn't appear to usurp your father's power, but the man's behavior is suspicious."

"He is always groveling, but he may have more influence than I thought," Meg said. "Father never could have arranged this marriage alone. I wonder how Owen benefits."

"He could be after the money," Micah said.

"But this marriage arrangement alerted us to his scheme, whatever that may be."

"Mr. O'Leary can't remove any funds while on this

voyage," Banner said. "Whatever he is doing, it will have to wait. Is there anything else I can help with?"

"Do you know how to sober a drunkard?" Micah asked. "Don't sailors drink ale or rum'?"

Did he think his sisters would have to worry about the crew getting drunk and ravishing them? "Many enjoy too much alcohol when on shore, but I portion out the rum during a voyage. Meg and Lilibet will be safe on the voyage. I guarantee it."

"I'm asking for Father," Micah said. "How do I sober him?"

That was a relief. "Hide all the liquor and substitute coffee or tea. And keep him busy so he doesn't crave a drink."

"If I can sober him, Father can ask Mr. Clifton for the money that's been invested to make repairs and pay his debts," Micah said.

"If he's been duped," Meg said. "What if Father has other plans for that money? He loves to gamble."

Micah frowned at his sister. "I think you misjudge Father."

"When he earns my respect, I will give it," she said. "If he'll listen to anyone, it will be you."

"Then I'll try to convince him to use the money for the estate as you suggested." Micah leaned back and crossed his arms. "When Owen returns, he will be surprised to find the funds unavailable."

The carriage stopped in front of a carpet shop. Rugs of all sizes and decorative patterns hung from the ceiling or were stacked on tables. They debated between a floral pattern and one of geometric design.

"They'll pick the flowers," Micah said in a low voice. "They're girls."

"I heard that," Meg said. "And because you won't be going along, we'll take the rug with the roses."

Banner checked the dimensions to make sure the rug would fit and gave instructions to deliver it to his ship. They moved to the furniture store a few shops down the road, and their carriage followed. A plainer one trailed close behind with two rough-looking men staring out the windows.

"Do you know you're being followed?"

"My father is worried I might elope."

"Would you?" Did he sound excited? He couldn't show his face in Riverside if he eloped with Eliot's bride. Or could he? Eliot would be relieved but disowned.

"No, although it might be fun to try." An impish smile played on her lips. "But I think I've discovered the reason he's in such a hurry to see me wed. Mr. Clifton said my grandfather established a trust for me, but I can only receive it if I wait until after my twenty-first birthday on July 17. Father receives the funds if I marry before then." Her tone turned judgmental. "More money in his pockets to waste."

Banner removed his watch from his waistcoat. "It's growing late. We need to make some decisions."

"This is lovely." Lilibet pointed at an armoire.

"There is no room for it. You'll store your clothing in the two chests permitted in your room, and there are pegs on the walls for daily items of clothing." He pointed at the squares and rectangles in his drawing. "You have room for a commode, a washstand, and a small table. If you place cushions on your trunks, they can serve in the place of a settee. My carpenter can add shelves for items like books and small containers. Don't pack anything breakable."

Meg examined his drawing. "Do you shop for all your passengers?"

"No, usually a woman travels with her husband, and he sees to her needs. You'll spend most of your time in your cabin, so I'd like you to be comfortable and safe. I've added a sturdy lock to your door and window."

"We have a window?" Meg asked. "Where is our cabin located?"

"You'll have one of the officers' quarters," Banner said. "It's in the stern, and the window will provide a nice breeze when the weather warms."

"Where will those officers sleep?" Lilibet asked.

"Some of them will share the cabin with Mr. O'Leary. He's on the other side of the ship. I didn't think you'd want him next door."

Meg shivered. "You were right."

"My quarters are in between. You are invited to dine with my officers and me whenever you choose. I can have the cook serve your meals in your cabin if you wish to dine alone."

"I don't think I would like being cooped up," Meg said. "I hope your officers and crew won't mind the company of two women."

"There will be certain times you cannot be on deck, but when the men are done with their personal tasks, you can enjoy the fresh air."

Meg looked around the store. "Then we should finish shopping."

"We'll look at washstands while you look at tables," Lilibet suggested, pulling Micah away.

Meg headed for a row of tables and writing desks with different chair styles. "These are nice."

He opened a drawer built into the table. "This can

be used for dining and writing upon. The drawer locks."

"I trust your opinion. Buy it."

She had said the words spontaneously, but they meant more to him than she realized. Trust took time to win, yet she deferred to his judgment. If only he could warn her about Eliot.

Lilibet and Micah chose a washstand that could store the bowl and pitcher underneath. The final purchase was a commode.

They visited another shop to purchase towels, blankets, and pillows.

"Now all we have to do is pack," Lilibet said.

"Don't forget to bring along items to pass the time. I know ladies favor needlework, but it can be difficult if the seas are rough."

"We can sneak some books from Father's library." Meg's voice was filled with excitement even though she had reduced it to a whisper.

"He won't let you borrow them?" Banner asked.

"I don't want to ask him for any favors." Meg crossed her arms. "Besides, all his books are gathering dust. I don't think he's read one in years."

"I'm borrowing what will be mine in the future." Micah raised and lowered his eyebrows several times. "Which ones do you want me to pilfer?"

"Anything about sailing," Meg said. "And see if you can find *Robinson Crusoe*, and Lilibet likes *Gulliver's Travels*."

"I thought I was named after Lilliput," she said with a giggle. "But I would like to read it again."

"I'll see what I can find," Micah said.

"And try to find a book on pirates," Meg added.

"I have a copy of *A General History of the*

Robberies and Murders of the Most Notorious Pyrates by Captain Charles Johnson if you're interested in buccaneers," Banner said.

"I'd love to read it." Meg's smile lit up her face with excitement. "Is it an honest account of piracy?"

"It makes them a bit glamourous, and some parts may be too violent. I may have to censor it for your reading."

"Please don't," Meg begged. "We want our trip to be an exciting adventure."

"You crave danger. I want to reach land as soon as possible," Lilibet said. "No pirates, shipwrecks, or storms."

"Don't worry," Banner said. "Most voyages are uneventful."

"Did you ever want to be a pirate, Banner?"

Meg had used his given name. Was she aware their relationship had shifted from stranger and captain to friend? "I think there's a bit of piracy in every sailor, but I didn't know women dreamt of danger on the seven seas."

"We have plenty of drudgery and boredom in everyday life," Meg said. "We dream of everything from sentimental love to thrilling adventures to escape from our mundane reality. Do you think Eliot will approve of my unnatural tendencies?"

"I think Eliot will have no complaints." Eliot had better be a good husband. She deserved nothing less.

Chapter Nine

Meg stared out the window of her carriage as they passed the familiar sights of London. The day of their departure had arrived. Lilibet sat next to her, sniffling into her handkerchief. Micah sat opposite.

He reached into his coat pocket and handed her a leather-bound journal. "I want you to write about your journey."

She ran her hand over the cover and flipped through the pristine pages. "It will be like I'm sharing the adventure with you."

He handed Lilibet a similar journal. "This is for all the recipes you collect."

She clutched it to her chest. "I've heard they eat all sorts of different foods in the colonies. Do you think they'll share the ingredients in their dishes with me?"

"Of course." Micah's smile was warm as he patted her hand. "You could charm the most secretive cooks out of their coveted dishes."

"I can't believe the day has finally arrived." Meg wouldn't see her brother for a long time. She felt like crying but forced a smile instead. "Isn't it exciting? I'm sure I'll fill this journal with all sorts of wondrous things." She tucked his gift into a cloth bag, and Lilibet shoved her book into a similar bag she carried.

"Are you ready to travel across the ocean?" Micah asked Lilibet.

She shivered and shook her head. "I never traveled before coming to London, and that trip was scary. This voyage is terrifying."

Meg took her hand. "Would you rather stay home?"

"Mother said this is my chance for a better life, but why can't I be a cook in England?"

"You can be a cook anywhere," Meg said. "But in the colonies no one will know about your birth. You'll be like everyone else."

"Miss Lilibet Dugan." Her smile quickly disappeared. "It's a bit frightening. What if they don't like me or find out the truth and hate me for being a liar?"

"Everyone loves you, Lili," Meg said. "And they'll love your cooking. You are going to have a wonderful time in Riverside."

Lilibet looked worried. "What about you?"

"I'll find my happiness." Did they hear the tremor of fear in her voice? She leaned out the window of the carriage as they neared the Pool of London, south of London Bridge. "What's that?"

Micah was seated on the same side and looked to where she pointed. "Those are the masts of the ships."

"There are so many of them."

"London is a busy port. Everyone complains about all the ships, but no one wants to make any changes." He pointed in the distance. "The imported cargo has to be delivered to the quays on the north bank for inspection and assessed by the custom officials. Then the captains try to find an open wharf, mooring post, or other ship to tie up to in order to unload. The unfortunate ones ferry cargo in smaller boats to the shore and warehouses."

Meg stared at her brother. "How do you know this?"

"I spent some time watching the ships come and go

with my mates when we had time off from our studies. I honestly envy you and Lilibet for your opportunity to sail on a ship."

Their carriage pulled onto a side road and stopped at a warehouse with the Richmond name painted on a sign above the wide doors. Up and down the Thames, the different wharfs were crowded with wagons and carts. Workers loaded or unloaded barrels and crates of various sizes.

Lilibet clutched her handkerchief over her nose. "What's that smell?"

"Life." Meg inhaled the scents of fish, spices, and humanity.

Lilibet pointed to a woman leaning against a barrel. "It looks like she's seen plenty of life."

Her gown was faded and the skirt torn at the hem. Her breasts rose above laces that haphazardly held the bodice together.

"A little too much," Meg said.

Lilibet stared at the ships crowded on the Thames River. "How safe is a ship voyage?"

Meg patted her knee. "Captain Youngblood has practically guaranteed a safe crossing."

"For you." She sank into her seat. "I'm ballast."

"Ballast? See, you already know a nautical term."

"Only because I have to quiz you. Why do you want to know about sailing? You aren't planning to become a member of the crew, are you?"

Micah laughed. "She wants to be first mate."

Meg tried to pinch him, but he evaded her hand. "I'm only trying to learn as much as I can about sailing to converse with Captain Youngblood and his crew. I think he's keeping a secret about Eliot, and I have every intention of discovering it before the voyage ends."

"He'll blabber everything he knows if you wear a low-cut gown," Micah said. "You don't need to know how to tie a bowline."

Meg arranged the fichu draped around her shoulders and covering her bodice for a modest look. She pulled her cloak about her. "We should have left you at the townhouse with Aunt Felicity."

"And drown in her tears? Why are women so emotional? It's not like you'll be gone forever. Eliot is a nobleman. He has to return to claim his title and lands."

"Lord Dudlee is far from the grave," Meg said. "But, hopefully, in a few years I can convince Eliot to return home." Hopefully, sooner.

Lilibet turned to Micah. "What will you do while we're gone?"

"I'll make the most of my time with Father. Today, I'll see you safely to the captain's ship. Once you're on board, what you do will be entirely your decision."

Meg stated the obvious. "I'm planning to marry Eliot."

"Then try not to fall in love with Captain Youngblood," he warned.

She smacked his knee. "You're imagining things."

"I've never seen you glow with the inner light he's ignited, darling sister. You stare at the man as if he's a god on Mount Olympus."

"You're only teasing me so I don't cry when we say good-bye."

"Promise you won't shed a tear, or I'll start sobbing, and it's unseemly for a man to cry."

Lilibet sniffled into her handkerchief. "I don't promise anything."

Meg glanced out the window as the other carriages arrived. "We don't have much time, and we can't talk in front of the others. Promise me you'll look into the ledgers and find out if Father is a coconspirator of Owen's or his pawn."

"I will. Captain Youngblood and I had a long talk about taking on responsibilities."

"When did you talk to him?"

"While you were listening to that woman sing last night, we stepped outside and talked about your future."

"He talked about me?" Even she couldn't deny the excitement in her voice. Was her brother right? Did she have tender feelings for Banner? That could complicate matters.

"You do fancy him," he said as if it were fact.

She snorted and avoided his perusal by tying her bonnet. "I'm only curious about what he might have said."

"You have the man befuddled. If you weren't marrying his friend, he might consider kissing you, but he's an honorable man." Micah grinned and leaned toward her. "It'll be interesting to see which one of you crosses the line of propriety first."

"I don't believe in lines. Besides, I'll need every weapon in my armory to find out the captain's secrets."

The coachman opened the door. Micah exited first and helped her and Lilibet maneuver the small metal steps safely to the ground. They wore plain gowns with modest necklines, heavy cloaks, and wide brim bonnets as Banner had instructed.

A three-masted ship was moored to the posts on the waterfront, the square sails furled against the yards.

Lilibet stared at the towering masts. "It's bigger

close up."

"It won't seem big after a few weeks aboard her," Micah said.

Her father, Lord Dudlee, and Owen exited their carriage and joined them. They crowded into the open space on the dock among barrels, crates, and trunks. Men carried the cargo up the gangplank and stacked it on the deck. Other men lowered it into the hold.

Captain Youngblood stood near the rail, tall and imposing as the commander of his ship. His thick wool coat and trousers were black with only the white of his cravat showing at his neck. He wore knee-high boots instead of shoes and stockings. His tricorn hat shielded his eyes as he surveyed the work.

She tried not to stare, but he cut a stunning picture. Why hadn't the portrait of Eliot stirred her even a fraction of what she felt now? His gaze fell upon her, and her heartbeat thundered within her chest.

He nodded and strode down the gangplank to greet them. "We have a few more items to load, and we'll be ready to set sail." He signaled his men to gather their belongings. "Which trunks do you want in your room?"

Meg pointed to her mother's trunk in which she had packed her daily gowns and personal items. "That one and the other one for Lilibet." The other two contained fancier gowns and items they would need in Riverside. "Those can be stored until we reach Connecticut."

"Any other bags?"

She lifted her cloth bag. "Only this." It contained herbs and medicines for illness and their monthly flows. Aunt Felicity had added a box of dried fruit, and she had stored her journal inside.

Owen pressed his handkerchief against his nose and

mouth as he watched the servants unload his trunk from the second carriage. "I hope the air is fresher on the ocean."

Lord Dudlee turned to Banner and handed him a leather satchel. "Inside are the betrothal agreement, special marriage license, and funds for the wedding. I have a letter for Eliot and another to Glen Stemple for you to deliver."

Banner put the strap over his shoulder and exchanged words with Lord Dudlee she couldn't hear.

Micah leaned in close. "How long before you read the letters?"

She watched the men carry her trunk aboard. "They're not addressed to me."

"When has that stopped you in the past?"

Meg had learned the trick of removing a wax seal from her mother who said it was necessary to read all the correspondence arriving at Whittington Manor because Father shared none of the information with her. "I don't like secrets."

"Last night I may have told the captain about your bad habit of reading other people's mail."

Was he crazy? "Why would you do that?"

"You said we could trust him, and the wine loosened my tongue." He cringed and lowered his voice. "I didn't know you would be tempted."

She smacked his arm. "What else did you tell him?"

"I don't remember everything. We bounced around from one topic to another." He hugged and kissed her. "But it should make your trip more interesting."

Before she could scold him, he offered his arm to Lilibet and escorted her aboard the ship.

Lord Dudlee reached out his hands to Meg. "I'm

glad you're marrying my son. I wish you both all the happiness in the world."

Meg relaxed when he hugged her. She would have to learn to enjoy the touch of a man. "I'll do my best to guarantee your son's happiness."

Her father stood to the side as Lord Dudlee retreated to his carriage. He looked at her with no affection but raised his hands as if to hug her, too. She backed away. He let them drop to his sides. "Have a safe journey."

"It would ruin your plans if the ship sank."

He appeared startled. "You might want to curb your tongue in the presence of your future husband."

"Giving me fatherly advice? I have been assured Eliot does not own a whip."

He looked at the ground. "I regret it was necessary."

"It was only necessary because you put your trust in the wrong people." She glanced at Owen who had safely reached the deck and was strutting about.

Micah left Lilibet aboard and hurried down the gangplank toward them.

"You should ride back with your son, your heir."

"Your mother tried to give me advice. If I had listened…"

She stepped closer. "Listen now." She gave him a quick peck on the cheek, and his eyes widened. She turned to Micah and hugged him tightly. "Plant the seeds, Brother."

He looked past her. "Did you forgive him?"

"No. I can't forgive him for being a terrible father or husband to Mother. He has to live with his choices, and I will live with mine. But I don't have to keep seeking his love or approval. I choose to love those who are worthy, like you." She kissed his cheek. "You'll do great things, Micah."

Captain Youngblood stood near the gangplank and helped her board his ship. She turned and watched as Micah joined their father in his carriage.

"Micah will be fine." Banner's whispered words reassured her. "He's more mature than you think."

"I'm beginning to realize that, but I will always think of him as my little brother."

"My older brother treats me like I am six years old and have broken my mother's favorite vase. He is always warning me to stay out of trouble."

"Do you?"

"We shall find out."

The sparkle in his eyes promised trouble in her future. She gulped.

The hull creaked with the movement of the water flowing out to sea and the strain of the ropes to keep the ship tethered. Meg moved her feet to stay balanced.

"Cargo is secured, Captain," a man announced.

"Cast off," Banner shouted as mooring lines were tossed aboard and the gangplank pulled in.

The crew scattered to do their assigned tasks.

Banner removed his tricorn hat. "Let me show you to your quarters."

"Don't you have to take us down the river?"

He looked toward the bow. "The ship needs to be towed around all the other ships until the river widens. The first mate will handle that."

Her mouth twitched into a smile. "Do you mean you're rowing the boat?"

His eyes widened as he looked past her. "Would you like to man an oar?"

"I believe you are teasing me, Captain."

His deep rumbling laughter made her heart race. Owen was absent from the deck and had missed the exchange, thankfully. Her flirting was harmless but necessary to find out more about Eliot, but she didn't need Owen suspecting more of her behavior.

She took Lilibet's trembling hand and followed Banner aft where a door opened into a narrow passageway.

"My first and second mates are in this cabin."

They glanced through the open door. The bunkbeds were on the inside wall with a trunk at one end. Another trunk served as a seat in front of a table. A chair hung on the wall.

"It's awfully gloomy," Lilibet whispered.

Banner continued down the hall. "This is your cabin."

He stood in the doorway and allowed them to enter. The floral rug she had chosen covered the floor. The commode and washstand were near the door, and the writing desk and two chairs were on the far wall where sunlight streamed through a window.

"It's lovely." Lilibet gasped as she clapped her hands and entered.

It was a sharp contrast to the other room. "You were clever to let us see the mates' cabin first. Thank you for making this one lovely and comfortable."

He pointed to her trunk at the foot of the bunk. The other one was near the window. "You can step up to the upper bunk. There are cubbyholes for storing shoes and personal items." Banner pointed to built-in compartments at the head of the beds.

Lilibet stared. "I have to sleep up there?"

"I'll take the top." Meg gathered a pillow and

stroked a quilt she hadn't purchased. "Did you buy this?"

"Along with soap and other items I thought you might need."

"Thank you." Was she gushing? Her face felt warm.

"One of the crew will empty the bucket from the commode every morning," he said. "But don't place it in the hall like a chamber pot. There's a hook on the wall to keep the contents from spilling." He seemed embarrassed to talk of personal hygiene. "If you need anything, let me or Issy know. He's the bosun. He's in charge of the crew and repairs to the hull, rigging, and sails."

"Issy?"

"That's me." Issy stood in the open doorway. He bobbed his head and removed a knitted cap. He had light-brown hair framing a round face and pug nose. "It's short for Isidore."

"I hope the others don't give you grief for waiting on a couple of women," Meg said.

"Issy is married," Banner said. "That was one of the reasons I chose him."

"I have a wife and two children in Rochester."

"Won't you miss them on such a long voyage?" Lilibet asked.

"I'll be sailing back on the first ship to England. Then I'll spend so much time with her she'll beg me to join the first crew to leave in the fall." He replaced his cap and hurried down the passageway.

Meg leaned against the door and pointed to the door across from them. "Where does that lead?"

"My quarters. Would you like to see them?"

She turned to Lilibet.

"Go ahead. I think I'll unpack a few items."

"We'll keep the doors open," Banner said. "We wouldn't want a scandal for lack of a chaperone."

Banner's quarters were double the size of the officers' cabins. Rugs covered the floor with a bed situated between two windows on the stern wall. Shelves lined the walls where chests, barrels, and crates contained whatever items were too valuable to store in the hold. A large trunk was placed at the foot of the bed with another against the wall. To her right was a table and chairs for six. A washstand with a mirror and a small commode were located on the opposite wall near another door.

Banner removed the letters, documents, and money Lord Dudlee had given him from his satchel. "Do you have anything of value you want locked up?"

She twisted the ring on her finger and removed it. "You should take care of this. I'd hate to lose it before reaching Riverside."

He knelt by his desk and unlocked a metal box built into the floor. He placed the documents and money inside. He took her ring, placed it in a small velvet bag, and added it to the contents. After locking it, he took the two letters from Lord Dudlee and placed them in the desk's top drawer. Was he tempting her? Why had Micah told him about her penchant for reading others' mail?

"Micah gave me a journal to record my adventures aboard your ship." She pointed to a capped container of ink in a box secured to the top of the desk. "May I borrow some?"

"Feel free to borrow anything you need. There's paper in the desk." He opened a drawer.

"You don't lock your desk?"

"The ship's log is public record. Other items are of

no interest to my crew."

Curse Micah for sharing her vices. Banner *was* testing her.

He pointed to a small chest on the floor below the shelves. "You might find something useful in there."

"Treasure?"

Laughter was his response. "Nothing that valuable. It contains clothing and items left by previous travelers. We use it mostly for rags and bandages." He lifted the lid and pulled out a jacket. "This might ward off the cold wind better than that cloak you're wearing."

She examined it. "I like it. Are there matching trousers?"

He gave her a peculiar look. "Why would you need them?"

She placed the coat on the bed. "Winds tend to travel up petticoats." She lowered her voice to a whisper. "And we wear nothing underneath."

He cleared his throat and sat at his desk. "Take a look."

She found the trousers and a cap. She pulled out a large nightshirt. "Yours?"

He looked up from the log he had removed from his desk drawer. A single eyebrow rose along with the corners of his mouth. "No. I don't use one."

She tried to imagine him naked. Even in his clothing, he was handsome with long legs, broad shoulders, and agile hands. She knew he would be magnificent undressed. She needed a husband. Soon.

He made a notation in the log book. "Have you found everything you need?"

She folded the nightshirt and placed it in the chest before closing the lid. As she rose, she pointed to a door.

"Where does that lead?"

Banner rose and opened it. "To another passageway. Quarters for the carpenter, sailmaker, and cook."

Owen's voice rose in indignation from behind the closed door to their left. "What do you mean I have to share a room?"

Meg laughed. "Who is the poor unfortunate soul who has to share with Owen?"

A grin spread across his face. "All three of the aforementioned."

"Four in a room?" She looked across the captain's cabin. "Is it the same size as the one I'm sharing with Lilibet?"

"Aye." A hint of humor flavored his voice.

"How does everyone fit?"

"Owen and the cook have bunks, and the other two men use hammocks." He pointed to the beams overhead. "Hammocks can be suspended about anywhere."

A man with hair that rivaled Lilibet's stepped out. His face was covered in freckles, and he shook his head. He paused in the hall and tipped his cap.

"This is Duffy. He's the cook and doctor when needed."

Duffy stabbed his thumb back at the door. "That one is already turning green, and we've barely left the dock."

Meg chuckled. "It would serve Owen right to be seasick."

Banner raised a dark eyebrow. "All passengers get sick."

Was he warning her? "Good to know."

Banner escorted her across his quarters to the opposite hallway.

She stood outside the door. "I'd like to go on deck

and watch the ship travel down the Thames."

He looked surprised. "If you want."

Meg entered her room and placed the clothing from Banner's trunk on her bunk. "Lili, do you want to watch as we leave England?"

She grabbed her cloak and bonnet and joined them.

Chapter Ten

Banner followed the women as they climbed the companionway leading to the afterdeck. The supporting spindles were ornate and matched the taffrail that surrounded the stern.

Meg's hand rested on the smooth railing. She turned as she reached the deck. "You have a beautiful ship."

He considered the *Gabriella* his pride and joy. "She has some years on her, but she's served me well."

They stood near the helm as the ship moved slowly through the maze of vessels crowding the Thames. Buildings of brick and wood rose on each side. Businessmen in fancy attire mixed with rugged dock workers and beggars in rags. A boy fishing off a pier waved. Meg and Lilibet waved back.

"Mother took Micah and me to Kent years ago to watch the ships heading out to sea." Meg lifted her face to the sun. "I envied the passengers. Now I'm one of them."

"I'm not as adventurous as you," Lilibet said. "I liked staying at home and helping Mother in the kitchen."

"Your mother kicked you out of the kitchen so you couldn't hide behind her skirt." Meg spun around. "Look at all the spectacular sights around us, Lili. Embrace it."

Lilibet stumbled as the ship shifted.

"Better hold on to the railing." Banner pointed to the

rail in front of the helm.

Lilibet looked toward the buildings, turned to the sails, and then stared at the deck. "I think I'll go back to the room and embrace the mattress."

Banner expected Meg to follow Lilibet, but she remained nearby, waving to those on shore. Her face reflected the awe and wonder he had experienced his first time at sea. Everything was fresh through her eyes.

She turned to watch men emerge from the hold in the center of the main deck. "What merchandise are you taking to the colonies?"

"Fabric, clothing, tools, household items, tea, and spices," he said. "Items they can't make themselves in the colonies although they are weaving their own cloth and growing apples for cider."

"Everyone in London was talking about the tea being tossed into the sea," Meg said. "Why would the natives do that?"

"Those were Bostonians dressed as Mohawk natives to avoid prosecution." As a merchant, Banner was familiar with the details, some he didn't share with his brother. "The East India Company has a monopoly on the tea trade, and colonial merchants were losing money. They boarded three American ships, the *Dartmouth*, the *Beaver*, and the *Eleanor* while they waited to unload and pay the duty. Even though there was other cargo, only the chests of tea were thrown overboard."

"But why? I heard it was worth nearly ten thousand pounds. Some people would lie and steal for that amount."

"They weren't thinking about the value," Banner said. "Many colonists did not approve of the destruction of private property, but every time parliament tries to tax the colonists, they protest or refuse to buy the items taxed. Sometimes it works."

"I have learned that resisting authority can result in harsh punishment," Meg said.

Like a lashing. He stepped closer so others couldn't hear his words. "You're right. My brother said the king will send more troops to Boston. That will only inflame those aching for a fight."

"But the British Army is the best in the world. Why would they aggravate them?"

He shrugged. "Some have nothing to lose. Others have a great deal to gain."

Meg shook her head as she walked across the deck. "Women aren't encouraged to have an interest in politics. I didn't consider how it would affect me, but I think I was wrong to ignore the news."

"Some events we can't control."

The longboat towing them released its line. The ebbing tide along with the backing and filling of the sails would carry the ship out to open sea.

Meg stopped and pointed upward as the crew climbed the rope ladders. "What are they doing?"

"They're climbing the ratlines to unfurl the sails," Banner said. "The men position themselves in the footropes and over the yards to loosen the gaskets and release the canvas."

Meg shielded her eyes as she looked up at the men perched above her. "Aren't they afraid to be so high?"

He chuckled as he recalled his own experience wobbling above the deck and ocean. "They wouldn't be seamen if they were."

"Do you climb up there?" A note of worry laced her words.

"When it's necessary." He pointed at the ropes. "Don't touch any of the lines. You might get tangled and end up hoisted upward in the rigging. I wouldn't want to see you hurt."

"I finished reading a book on sailing, but all it did was confuse me." She waved her hand from one side of the ship to the other. "I admit I'm woefully ignorant of how everything works."

"No one learns how to sail from reading a book, but I'll answer any questions you have."

"I know the three masts are called the foremast in the bow, the mainmast, and the mizzenmast, and the sails are named for each mast," she said.

Banner pointed from top to bottom. "The sails on the mainmast are called the main royal, the main topgallant, the main upper topsail, the main lower topsail, and the main course."

The men dropped to the deck and formed groups for pulling the lines.

"What are they doing now?" Meg asked.

"Each square sail has a head, which is attached to the yard. Each side is called a leech, and the bottom is the foot. On the bottom corners are clews where the lines are attached. The crew will pull on the lines until the canvas is taut, and then they'll tie the lines around the belaying pins along the rails of the ship."

"How do they know how to work together?"

"They sing chanties and pull on the beat. Every seaman learns to navigate, handle the lines and equipment, unfurl or reef the sails, and steer the vessel. A group is assigned to four-hour watches with specific tasks. Now the crew will pull or ease the braces to set the angle of the yard."

"Why do they have to change the sail angle? Doesn't the ship go straight?"

He knew better than to laugh at her ignorance and chose to educate her even though she wouldn't have any use for the knowledge. "A sailing vessel can't sail directly into the wind or directly from it, or we lose the ability to steer. We set a course about sixty degrees away from the wind to control direction. To reach the colonies, we'll have to change course back and forth so the wind comes from the opposite side."

"Is that called tacking?"

"You did learn something from the book." Banner pointed at the helm. "The sails are set to fill with the wind for speed or go slack to slow the ship for tacking." He pointed to the sail in the stern. "The spanker is used to turn the ship."

"It's like a dance between the sails and the wind," Meg said. "And you're an excellent dancer."

Banner prayed he wasn't blushing and stepped toward the helm. "This is my first mate, Arthur Griffin."

Griffin turned the rudder, and wind filled the sails. The ship jolted forward.

"That's wonderful!" Meg lowered her bonnet and looked back, the wind blowing her hair from her face. "I may not see England again for a long time. Do you call London your home or Riverside?"

"I told my brother Riverside was my home now, but it took years for me to claim the colonies as mine. Don't worry. You'll return to England one day with your husband."

"I hope it's not too long. I miss my family and friends already."

He had seen her kiss Lord Whittington on the dock.

"What about your father?"

Her face relaxed, the pain falling away. "I don't hate him. I feel sorry for him. My mother was a wonderful woman, but he never appreciated her. He missed out on the happiness she could have given him. For that, I pity his choices."

She would have been a good daughter if he had given her the chance. "Some people never find happiness even when it's right in front of them."

"You have to fight for it," she said. "It's been two years since my mother's death, and I still have a void in my heart. I don't know if the ache will ever go away."

She openly shared her feelings. He felt obligated to do the same. "When my mother died, I lost the most important person in my life."

"What was she like?" Her voice had a soft tenderness to its tone.

"Beautiful, kind, and funny. When I was away, I couldn't wait until I would see her again and share my adventures with her. She wanted to know everything about the places I went and the people I met. She made me feel special even though I was a second son. While she was alive, she was home."

"What about your father?"

"He didn't know how to show affection or relate to children. He never learned. By the time I was a grown man, I was away at sea. I didn't find out how much he cared until after his death."

"How?"

Banner confided his personal life to only a few close friends, but he had seen the pain Meg's father had caused her. "I always thought my father was a cold man who enjoyed finding fault in my actions, but after his death, his solicitor explained that he had transferred funds into the trust my mother left me when she died. The money allowed me to leave the Royal Navy and buy a ship of my own. He helped me without being obvious."

"He left you your pride," she said. "But why did you leave? Didn't you like the Royal Navy?"

He looked toward the helm before meeting her gaze. "I learned to sail and discovered a love of the sea, but my captain was a cruel man."

"He was an idiot," Griffin said as he steered the course of the ship.

Meg turned to face him. "You served with Banner in the Royal Navy?"

"Second mate."

She stepped toward Griffin. "What happened with the captain?"

He remained quiet, looking to Banner to explain.

Only Banner's closest friends knew the story, but Meg of all people would understand. "I was twenty-five. I had received my commission when I was nineteen and had worked my way up to first mate. We had returned from a voyage to Jamaica with a full cargo and were docked in London. I always sent word to my mother when I arrived in town. It was evening when my father sent a messenger back. Gabriella Banner Youngblood was dying, and the doctor didn't think she would make it through the night. The captain had left to meet his mistress and had placed me in command for the night watch." He turned to the helm. "Griffin agreed to stand it for me, and I left, which was against orders."

Meg looked confused. "Did something happen to the ship? Was the cargo stolen?"

"No, but the captain didn't like my decision to

abandon my post." He let the bitterness show in his voice. "He accused me of neglect of duty."

Her face lost color. "Were you punished?" Her voice shook.

"I could choose to be publicly court martialed and shame my family or receive twenty lashes by the captain's hand in his private quarters and keep it out of the ship's log." He looked at Griffin. "For each of us."

"At least it wasn't a cat o' nine tails," Griffin said. "They don't use those against commissioned officers."

"But twenty." Meg went pale. She had to be thinking of the eight she endured. "That's awful." Anger marred her features. "But what was the harm? The ship was in port."

"The captain demanded absolute obedience. No exceptions. I knew the consequences and went anyway."

She nodded. "For your mother."

"I stayed with her through the night, placed cool cloths on her forehead, and read a few psalms to comfort her. She passed shortly before dawn." He fought back any display of emotions.

She touched his arm. "You made the right decision."

He looked at her hand on his sleeve. "I don't regret it, but I thought it unfair to punish Griffin."

"By agreeing to take your watch, I was just as guilty," Griffin said.

"My father came to take me to my mother's funeral and saw what the captain had done and why. I never saw him so angry. In my delirium, I thought his anger was directed at me for disobeying an order."

He cleared his throat as words failed him. "He said he was proud of me. I'd been seeking his approval all my life, and an act of defiance had won it. A few days later the solicitor presented me with the money my mother had left me."

"And your father," she interrupted.

"He encouraged me to resign my commission. I heeded his advice and purchased the majority of this ship. Lord Dudlee and another merchant paid for the cargo, and I began my career as a merchant sea captain. The first man to sign aboard was Griffin."

"And I don't regret it," Griffin said. "Captain Youngblood can catch a wind on a calm sea and battle six-foot waves in a storm. The *Gabriella* is the best ship on the ocean with him at her helm."

"And you named your ship the *Gabriella* to honor your mother."

Meg's smile was stunning. She had a face already haunting his dreams. If only he had met her sooner.

"She was a grand lady," Banner said. "I wish she could have seen what I've accomplished with her help."

"I'm sure she was always proud of you." She blushed and turned toward the railing. She raised her hand to her brow. "What is that in the distance?"

They had reached the North Sea. "Across is the shoreline of the Netherlands and Belgium. To the south is France. We'll sail along England's coast until we reach the ocean."

"I've never seen the Atlantic. Is it frightening?"

He doubted anything would scare Meg. "Some passengers are overwhelmed by the vast openness of endless water, but the beauty takes your breath away with colorful skies above and every imaginable sea creature below."

Issy approached them. "Dinner is served, Captain."

Banner offered his arm to escort her to her room.

She knocked, and Lilibet answered.

Meg entered. "Are you ready for dinner?"

She looked pale and gripped the bedpost. "Almost."

Meg hung her cloak and bonnet on the brass hook attached to the wall while he waited in the doorway. She removed two turquoise decorated combs from her hair and looked around. "Is there a mirror?"

Lilibet pointed above the washstand where a square mirror had been attached to the wall.

Meg smoothed her hair, replaced her combs, and looked at her sister. "Ready?"

Banner followed them across the hall. The overhead lanterns were lit, and Duffy had set the table with a linen tablecloth, porcelain plates, and silverware. "You've outdone yourself, Duffy."

"Men don't value frivolities, but ladies do."

"I've never seen a nicer table setting," Meg said.

Duffy's chest puffed out and threatened to pop his waistcoat buttons.

Lilibet stumbled sideways when the ship shifted. "Why does the ship keep leaning?"

Meg helped her sit down. "You need to learn to lean with it."

Banner seated Meg to his right.

Owen entered and rubbed his hands together. "Why is the ship so cold?"

Banner remained seated. "It's March."

"Then light a fire."

"Mr. O'Leary, we don't have fireplaces on a ship," Banner said. "The only person allowed to build a fire is the cook in the galley where he has sand, bricks, and buckets of water to prevent stray embers from spreading. I suggest you dress for the cold."

Owen buttoned his coat and looked around. "Why do you have this room to yourself and I must share a tiny space with three other men?"

The man was testing his patience. "I'm the captain. If you don't like sharing the officers' quarters, you can join the crew in the foredeck. I'm sure we can find a hammock for you."

He waited for Owen to argue, but his sour guest took his seat, unfolded his napkin, and studied the pattern on his plate instead.

Duffy lifted the lids from the platters on the sideboard, and the spicy scents filled the air. He had prepared chicken with bread stuffing, pickled beets, and apple cobbler.

"This looks delicious," Lilibet said. "I didn't realize you were such an accomplished chef. I collect recipes. I hope you'll share yours."

"I'm a sea cook, not a chef, and don't get used to fine meals like this one," Duffy said. "By the end of the journey, the chickens and eggs will be gone, and we'll be eating fish, smoked pork, and what's in the bottom of the barrels."

"Enjoy," Banner said as he raised his fork.

Owen took a few small bites. "This is passable for peasants."

Meg frowned. "When did you become a condescending gentleman?"

"A gentleman is more than his birth." Owen stroked the fabric of his coat. "He is recognized by his dress, behavior, and wealth."

"Then you fall short except for your fine clothes. They are better than any I've seen Father wear in recent years. Did you order a suit for him and take it upon yourself to claim it?"

"You impudent chit." He slammed down his fork and stood. "You are under my guardianship and will not question anything I say or do."

Banner stood. "She is under my protection while aboard my ship. Then she will be under the protection of the honorable Eliot Richmond. I warn you to give her the respect she deserves."

"Because she's the daughter of an earl and born a lady," Owen said with a sneer. "You forget your place, Captain. Except for lack of a marriage license, I would be a lord."

Owen's suspicious handling of Lord Whittington's funds, airs of superiority, and threats to Meg aggravated Banner's patience. "I was born the son of an earl, but here, I am the captain, and anyone who does not obey me aboard my ship is severely punished. I rarely flog a man, but I might make an exception in your case."

His face turned red. "I am a passenger, not a member of your crew."

"Which is why you are receiving a warning this time. Lord Dudlee entrusted me with delivering Lady Meg safely to Connecticut. I intend to fulfill my obligation."

Owen sat and stabbed at his chicken. He tore the tender flesh from the bone. "Then our goal is the same. Once she is wed, I will return to England."

"And what are your plans when you return?" Meg's tone was suspicious.

"Does it matter?" He smiled in a way that was threatening. "You'll be satisfying your husband's need to produce an heir. The one thing a woman is good for."

"Women did not create the system of

primogeniture," Meg said. "Only rich and powerful men benefit from it."

"Which is why the rest of us must do what is necessary to grab the morsels dropped on the ground from their grand tables of opulence."

Meg's face had gone pale as she stared at Owen, who focused on his food.

The tension between them was palpable. "Let us enjoy dinner and the many sights on the voyage ahead." Banner hoped a change in subject might lighten the mood. "The orcas are beautiful creatures with white markings on their black skin."

"But they are called killer whales for a reason," Issy said. "I saw one toss a seal into the air and gobble it down in one bite."

"But other creatures are harmless." Banner shook his head to warn Issy to steer clear of killing as a topic in front of the ladies. "There are dolphins who can dance on the water."

"They act as if they can talk to you," Issy added.

Suddenly, Owen groaned and pushed away his empty plate. He stared at the lantern hanging from the ceiling. "I'm not feeling well."

Duffy grabbed his arm and ushered him out of the room. He returned moments later, shaking his head. "I'm glad he knows where the slop bucket is, but he wasted a good meal."

Chapter Eleven

During the first week, Meg and Lilibet remained in their cabin away from the cold winds and busy crew members except for dinner with the officers and an afternoon walk about the deck. She began her journal for Micah but was discouraged by the lack of information to share.

"We saw a whale," Meg repeated to Lilibet. "One whale. Our great adventure has turned into a colossal disappointment."

"The officers could share stories after dinner. I liked the one about a parrot that talked."

"I hope Owen doesn't join us." Meg closed her journal and placed it in the table drawer. "His dour mood dampens every meal. I never realized what a complaining bore he was until now."

"If the sea is rough, I doubt he will be able to keep a meal down," Lilibet said. "He gets more seasick than me."

The swoosh of waves against the hull bore witness to the rough waters. "I wrote about how he ran from the room and hurled his meal into a slop bucket." Meg laughed. "Micah should enjoy that."

Lilibet wrapped a quilt around her as she sat on her trunk. "I wonder how he is doing with Lord Whittington."

Meg listened for footsteps above them and sat next

to her. "I always blamed Father for everything, but I think Micah is right. Owen kept him drunk so he could control the funds for the estate and townhouse."

"But to what end? No one would hire him without references."

"You've seen the way he dresses and heard how he talks. Owen has loftier ambitions than as a steward." Meg recognized Owen's threat. "He could steal the money he authorizes for investments along with my trust fund and live like the gentleman he brags to be."

"But the money doesn't belong to him," Lilibet stated the obvious.

"If my brother doesn't sober Father and convince him Owen is a thief, Owen can take it before anyone is the wiser."

Lilibet shook her head. "But you've warned Micah."

"And he'll be away at school when Owen returns." Meg stood and paced across the cabin. "I've been foolish. He took advantage of my mourning to gain complete control over Father's business dealings. Even Mr. Clifton trusted him. If I marry Eliot, I will be stranded in Connecticut and helpless to stop him." She recalled the last time she spoke to Owen. "I shouldn't have baited him into an argument. You need to intercede the next time I belittle him."

"He would think it odd if you didn't insult him."

A knock on the door interrupted their giggles.

"Dinner is served," Issy announced.

Owen begged off dining with them to everyone's delight.

Meg had been patient about extracting information about Eliot. Banner was guarded when talking about him or praised him effusively. She hoped the other officers would be more forthright or let something slip during casual conversations. She suggested a game of backgammon after supper and asked Banner to be her partner. Others played checkers and chess.

Meg had heeded her brother's advice and wore a gown with a square-cut neckline without any fichu to aid in her quest for answers. She sat opposite Banner with the backgammon board between them. Although she noted his interest in her decolletage, he was careful not to stare openly. She began with a casual inquiry. "What is Riverside like?"

"It's a small village with about two thousand citizens," Banner said.

Two thousand? "Everyone must know each other. How big is Boston?"

"It has about fifteen thousand people. Philadelphia is the largest town with about twenty-three thousand residents."

London was crowded with more than seven hundred thousand citizens. She rolled the dice. "Are there shops in the village?"

"The main streets have shops and homes, and many of the people in the surrounding farms bring their produce to market to sell. Plenty of foods are native to the land like potatoes, tomatoes, corn, peppers, and beans. If you want fish, you throw a line into the river, and you have a meal. Horses, cows, goats, and sheep have been brought over along with grains and other plants. No one starves in Riverside."

Lilibet was playing checkers with Issy. "You make it sound like a paradise."

"Riverside is beautiful but in a simple way," Banner said. "There are no grand cathedrals or palaces, but we have churches and townhalls for dances and entertainment. I think you'll enjoy the activities available."

Meg took advantage of the opening. "Does Eliot entertain often?"

The other officers looked to Banner. They weren't going to tell her anything without his permission.

"I have been to his home to dine many times," Banner said. "He has an excellent cook."

"But what about parties? Doesn't he enjoy company?"

Banner hesitated before answering. "He has never hosted a large gathering, but you could change that."

A mistress living under his roof would have prevented him from entertaining in his home. She needed to catch Banner off guard. "Do you attend many parties?"

"A few. I don't feel as comfortable with the gentry as you do."

"Young ladies are taught to behave a certain way at social events, but I was only at ease in London because I had no pressure to impress anyone."

"You appeared to enjoy the party where we met."

"Any event can be boring without the right partner to pass the time." She smiled at Banner before realizing it was an intimate revelation. "Is Eliot amusing?"

He nodded. "He possesses a sense of humor and a charming personality."

Banner was sidestepping her barrage of questions. She went to the heart of her concern. "Do you think Eliot is capable of love?"

"I'm sure of it." His outburst was met by a cough from Griffin.

She pressed her advantage. "Is he in love with someone now?"

"He has yet to meet you." He had recovered with a compliment. The men at the table visibly relaxed. "I believe you will impress everyone in Riverside and make many friends."

"You can be anything you want in the colonies," Griffin said. "Men don't have to be born to privilege. They can claim fortune and respect with hard work and honesty. There is a saying that all brothers are created equal in the colonies."

"All brothers?" She nodded as she understood. "Not everything goes to the firstborn. All brothers inherit." No mention of the sisters inheriting anything.

"There is plenty of land and wealth to go around," Banner said.

"Do you have a house in Riverside, Captain?"

He laughed. "I have a rented room above a tailor's shop, but I purchased land upriver of town for a home."

The captain was building a house. Did he plan to marry? Panic caused her heart to beat more rapidly. "Are you planning to quit the sea?"

Banner moved his pieces. "Not immediately, but I want to invest some of my profits into something permanent. You never know when a shipment could be lost at sea."

"Are we in danger?" Lilibet's voice was near a screech.

"Of course not. Everyone wants a home," Meg said in a tone to reassure Lilibet. "I used to draw my dream house when I was younger. But then Micah pointed out that I would have to live in my husband's home."

Banner rose and removed a roll of paper from a

cubbyhole where maps were stored. He spread it out over the backgammon board. "I've designed my own house. By the time we arrive in Connecticut, the land should be cleared to begin work. Would you like to share your ideas?"

Meg studied the drawing. Details like windows, doors, and dimensions were clearly marked. "You have a talent for design."

He pointed at the features. "This is the entrance and parlor. I have a study over here with the dining room and kitchen in the back."

Meg recognized a shortcoming. "If I were to build a home, I would want a larger kitchen."

He looked puzzled. "For servants?"

"No, I love to cook. Lilibet's mother taught us, and Lili recorded the recipes."

"My mother was illiterate, and it was easier to write down her directions than try to remember every detail. We would experiment with different ingredients." Lilibet laughed. "We made disastrous messes."

Meg laughed with her. "But we had fun eating the mistakes."

"Well, since I don't cook, I won't need a large kitchen."

"Your wife will, and this will be crowded." Meg pointed to a wall. "And where is the pantry or cellar?"

He studied his drawing. "I could enlarge the kitchen toward the back."

"You should add a couple of bedrooms above it," Meg added.

He frowned. "Two should be enough."

"Aren't you going to have any children?"

He leaned back and glanced at the other men. "How

many do you suggest?"

"Families tend to be large in the colonies. My mother had ten." Duffy had won his game of chess and was storing the pieces. "Eight boys. It's all the fresh air, clean water, and food. You better plan on adding more rooms above the larger kitchen."

Banner looked from Duffy to Meg. He rolled up his plans. "I'll take your suggestions under consideration."

Meg and Lilibet said their good-byes and prepared for bed.

Lilibet stored her gown in her trunk. "The captain didn't like your suggestions for his house."

"I only gave him my honest opinion. I saw an improvement and suggested it. I don't think that was a reason to become angry."

"He's probably redrawing his plans with your suggestions," Lilibet said. "He listens to your ideas."

"But he doesn't answer my questions." Meg paced along the length of the bunks. "What do you think they're hiding?"

Lilibet climbed into her bed and pulled the covers up. "About what?"

"About Eliot. You saw how they looked to Banner every time I asked about him. Has he turned into a monster?"

"You saw his portrait." She yawned. "He looked nice enough."

"You said he looked like a cow."

Lilibet giggled. "I said he had eyes like a cow. Do you think he's gotten fat? Duffy said people eat well in the colonies."

"Fat? I was thinking he had gone bald."

"Fat and bald," Lilibet repeated. "That would be

bad."

"Thank you for giving me that *lovely* image of my betrothed. What am I going to do if he's ugly or dull?"

"It would give you a reason to refuse him." Lilibet yawned and closed her eyes. "The portrait misrepresented him."

Meg climbed into her bunk and looked over the side. "I could overlook some flaws if he was willing to wait until after my birthday to wed."

"Do you think Owen would allow that?"

Meg knew the answer.

"He's made it clear he plans to return to England as soon as possible but after you wed," Lilibet warned.

"So he can steal my trust fund." Meg either had to postpone the wedding or prevent it. Neither choice seemed feasible with Owen intent on seeing her married.

Chapter Twelve

By the fourth week into the voyage, the April sky provided plenty of sunshine and had warmed the air for Meg and Lilibet to spend more time on deck. Banner had the carpenter build a canopy at the stern to protect their fair skin from the sun. A bench seat allowed them to enjoy reading, but today, Meg was tying knots. She had been fascinated by all the different knots the sailors used, and he had cut a few short lengths of thinner strands for practice.

"Try a mooring hitch," Banner suggested. "It's easy to tie and releases instantly."

"Why would I want the knot to come undone?"

"It's as important to know how to untie the rope as it is to tie one. The slipped half hitch is another knot that can be easily released."

Meg laughed as she followed his instructions and then untied her work. "Why are there so many different knots?"

"Each one has a purpose. Some are to secure a bundle, to anchor another rope, or connect two objects."

"What happens when you can't untie the rope?"

He pulled a knife from a sheath on his belt. "You cut it."

"My mother carries a knife all the time." Lilibet removed a small sheathed blade from her skirt pocket. "She gave me this one before my trip to London. She said it can cut trouble short."

Banner turned to Meg. "Do you have one?"

She withdrew a similar small knife from her skirt pocket.

Banner held his large blade next to hers. "Most men carry knives like this. Do you see the problem?"

"I need a bigger knife?"

He turned his head to hide his grin. "A knife is useful, but don't depend on it to protect you. Yours won't do much damage, but you can cut or stab and give yourself a chance to run away."

"Or travel in groups," Meg said. "Mother said there was safety in numbers. We never traveled around the estate alone. Father had some unsavory friends."

"Men are supposed to protect women," Banner said. "I don't understand those who prey upon them."

"That's what makes you an honorable man." She secured a knot and showed it to him.

Even with the canopy, Meg's hair had bleached to a lighter shade of blonde and had grown long enough to secure it in a ribbon or braid along her scalp. Her face was red.

"You're getting sunburned."

She scooted along the bench into the shade. "I try to stay under the canvas, but the sun keeps moving."

He laughed so loudly the crew turned to stare. He was spending too much time in her company but was drawn to her, listening for her footsteps or voice. Her presence made the voyage speed along, and yet he wished it would never end. They would arrive in Riverside to meet Eliot in a few weeks.

She had consistently asked questions about him. He had answered those relating to the man, but had avoided any reference to a woman in his life. Meg either knew about Cathy or suspected he had a mistress, but she was careful not to ask directly. Not yet.

His friend was a fool if he thought he could keep Cathy a secret. A bigger fool to think Meg would tolerate another woman. He would set his friend straight on what it was to be a good husband. But what did he know? He had never imagined taking a wife until... He couldn't entertain that possibility. Meg was promised to Eliot, and he wouldn't betray his friend. Meg considered him honorable, but he'd never felt more dishonorable.

Meg raised the rope for his inspection of another knot. "I'm doing something wrong."

He pointed out her error. "Go over not under."

Meg made the correction and pulled the length of rope tight. She handed it to Banner. "How does this look?"

"Not bad for a beginner. Should I assign you to a watch?" He was learning to tease her the way she teased him.

"Don't give her any encouragement," Lilibet said. "She loves to shock people by breaking rules."

"Your brother warned me of your irreverence for the norms of society."

She looked worried. Briefly. Her misdeeds were infrequent and harmless by her brother's account.

"You can make Owen part of your crew if you need another hand," Meg said. "Knowing he was at sea in misery would be reward enough for me."

He looked around at the crew working the lines and sheets. "The sea isn't for everyone. Poor Mr. O'Leary still spends most of his time in his cabin."

"For which we are eternally grateful." Meg stored

her knot samples in the seat of the bench and retrieved a book.

"What story are you going to read today?" Did Meg realize he spent every minute with her when she was on deck? Banner couldn't concentrate on his duties when she was near. Issy kept the crew busy at their tasks, but those not on watch found time to be near the young women. How could he judge them when he was guilty of the same distraction? He looked through his spyglass to pretend he was doing something seaworthy.

"I'm going to read the one about pirates you let me borrow." She showed him the table of contents. "I didn't realize there were so many colorful characters."

Meg had rare taste. "I didn't think women enjoyed pirate stories."

"Not only do I enjoy them, but I've dug for buried treasure."

Was she serious? "Did you find any?"

"One summer Micah, Lilibet, and I buried some of Mother's jewelry and drew a map. When Mother realized what we had done, she ordered us to return her valuables. Only the map wasn't very good, and we had a horrible time finding the right location. We dug dozens of holes before we found the chest."

"The gardener made us fill in all the holes," Lilibet said. "My hands were covered with blisters."

"Playing buccaneers was the most fun we had all summer." Meg flashed a smile at him as dazzling as the sun. "Do you have trouble with pirates in the Atlantic?"

He looked around at the expanse of ocean. "Not for fifty years."

She sighed as she looked out at the horizon. "Then we won't encounter any on our voyage?"

He laughed at her naiveness. "You sound disappointed."

"If you read my journal, you would understand. Nothing exciting has happened. Poor Micah will be bored reading what little I've written."

"I like a voyage to be boring." Or did he? Meg had brought an excitement to his blood he had felt on his early voyages but was now missing.

Meg flipped through the pages of the book. "Do you recommend a pirate I should read about?"

He had a favorite. "There was Black Sam Bellamy."

She searched for the chapter with his name. "Tell us what you know about him."

He leaned against the rail as he recalled the passage he had nearly memorized and stories he had heard from others. "He was an Englishman who captured at least fifty ships and was considered one of the most successful pirates during their seventy-five-year reign."

"Tell us more," Meg urged.

"Bellamy captured the *Whydah Gally* in February 1717 in the Bahamas from Captain Lawrence Prince. She was a slaving ship, and he set the African slaves free and hired them as crew with equal shares."

Griffin was at the helm. "That was unheard of, but the men loved him for it."

Meg looked around the deck. "What made the *Whydah Gally* special?"

"She's similar to the *Gabriella* in size," Banner said. "The *Whydah* was a three-masted galley ship a hundred and ten feet long and three hundred tons. She was rumored to have five tons of gold and silver on her when she sank."

"Five tons?" Lilibet repeated. "How much is that?"

"It was a king's ransom," Griffin said. "Enough to make the entire crew rich men."

"When did she sink?" Meg asked.

"It was during a spring storm in April of 1717."

Meg's eyes were as bright as emeralds. "Was any of the gold found?"

"No." He shook his head. "The surviving crew said the gold, silver, and jewels were stored in sacks and placed in between the ship's decks. Scavengers found bodies and some worthless items but nothing of value."

"Did the English blow the ship up?" Lilibet asked.

"Nothing like that. A nor'easter caused her to crash off Cape Cod. A hundred and forty-four men perished. Only two survived."

Lilibet turned to Meg. "What's a nor'easter?"

She shrugged and looked to Banner.

"A nor'easter is a big storm with gale-force winds and towering waves," Banner said. "The mainmast broke, and the ship capsized."

"A ship can do that?" Lilibet's voice rose in fear as she grabbed Meg's arm.

"When she's carrying cannons like the *Whydah*," Griffin said. "The guns tore her apart."

"It was an unusual storm that hit the area," Banner said. "The *Whydah* wasn't the only casualty. Another of Bellamy's ships, the *Cathy Anne*, also wrecked near Pochet Island. Seven men survived it."

"They were lucky," Meg said.

"Not really. All nine survivors were locked up in Barnstable Gaol, and in October, six of them were tried in Boston for piracy and robbery, convicted, and hanged. The two ship carpenters were acquitted because they were conscripted by Bellamy to become pirates or die.

The last member was sold into slavery. He lost his freedom."

She closed her book. "That's so sad. I don't know if I want to read about him now."

Banner tapped the cover. "Read it. But remember a good story embellishes the truth. A hero must have a flaw to overcome, and a villain must nearly succeed before facing judgment. Absolute truth can sometimes be boring."

"Do you think I should embellish the writings in my journal?"

She wouldn't have any trouble stretching the truth. "Will Micah enjoy it more?"

A broad smile turned her face into a vision of loveliness and mischief.

"Captain!" Griffin pointed toward the bow as winds whipped the sails. An urgency in his voice made Banner search the skies with his spyglass. Dark clouds gathered in the distance.

Meg stood and raised her hand to her eyes. "What is it?"

Banner pointed at the turbulent sky on the horizon. "Storm ahead."

Lilibet clutched Meg's arm. "Is it a nor'easter?"

Banner didn't answer. It could be a mild rainstorm, but the air had turned colder, and he feared something fiercer. He helped the ladies toward the stairs. "Go below and secure any loose items." He smiled to reassure them, but Meg looked toward the horizon with a fear she rarely showed.

The swirling clouds rolled toward them, and raindrops began to fall. "Reef the sails," Banner shouted to the crew.

Men scrambled up the rigging and folded the sails against the yards, tying them in place. The winds increased, and waves crashed onto the deck. Meg stood near the rail on the lower deck.

"I told you to go below."

"Give me something to do," she shouted over the wind.

He turned to Griffin. "Once the lines are secure, pick four men to stay on deck. The rest are to stay below. I'll be back to take the helm once I've changed."

He grabbed Meg's arm and led her to his cabin. "You like tying knots. Thread rope through the holes in the shelves to keep the kegs and containers in place and secure everything in my cabin, including the shutters." He gazed into her eyes. "Can you do that?"

"Yes." She nodded.

He exchanged his coat for a longer wool coat and pulled a knitted cap over his hair. He grabbed a pair of gloves. "I won't be back until we've cleared the storm. Do not step foot on the deck. You better warn Owen to stay in his room."

She had a stubborn look on her face. "Do I have to?"

He knew her threat was harmless. She judged people by how they treated others and had good reason to dislike Owen. But she had been surrounded by love from her mother, Micah, and Lilibet, and he couldn't imagine her being cruel. She had even treated her father kindly at the dock, a man who had used a whip against her.

He waved his finger at her and frowned. "You're a better person than Owen."

She shrugged. "He could stand near the railing, and a big wave could wash him overboard. It's not like I'd push him."

137

"I know you're teasing, and I appreciate your humor, but someone might take you seriously and harm him."

"Owen is such a sourpuss the sharks would probably spit him back on the deck."

He shook his head as if to disapprove but found her too entertaining to silence her. He didn't dare tell her how dangerous this storm could be, but she must have recognized something in his face.

"Banner." She placed her hand on his chest. "Be careful."

"Once you're done in here, stay with Lilibet so Issy can find you."

"Do you think we'll have to abandon ship?"

"Storms are common." They might not have time if the ship capsized. He wanted to kiss her. If they didn't survive, he would regret never showing the depth of his feelings. Her hand still rested on his chest. He covered it with his own.

"Do you have to go? Can't someone else do it?"

"I'm the captain."

She nodded. "You're responsible for the ship and crew."

"And passengers. I'll be able to do my job knowing you're safe down here. Promise me you'll stay below."

"It's that bad?" Her voice trembled.

"Do you want me to lie to you?"

"Never."

"It's all right for you to lie and scheme, but I have to be honest?"

She smiled in a way that teased and tormented him. "One of us should have some morals." She closed her eyes. Did she expect him to kiss her?

"Are you going to marry Eliot?"

Her eyes fluttered open. "Not if I drown."

The thought of losing her whether in a storm or to another man was impossible to imagine. Her life had become the center of his universe. His arms pulled her tight against his chest. She looked up, waiting, her heart beating against his. His lips brushed against her mouth, capturing the softness. He had meant the kiss to be quick. He was in a hurry but lingered as her arms went around his neck, and she molded her body against his. Her kisses were tender and a bit inexperienced. He allowed her to play a light dance on his lips before he became serious and plundered her mouth, demanding a response. Her primal groan echoed his own. But she didn't belong to him. He set her apart from him.

He pointed his finger. "No hysterics."

She stood rigid. "Never."

"Try to keep Owen from screaming. It frightens the crew."

She smiled at his joke. "I'll put a stocking in his mouth if he starts."

He took a step to leave, turned, and kissed her again. "If we make it to Riverside, this didn't happen."

"Who's the liar now?"

He had no excuse and forced himself to leave.

Banner relieved Griffin at the helm. Nearly all of the square sails had been secured to the yards or lowered and stored with the staysails. The crew had gone to their quarters, praying or cursing, depending on their faith. Only a few men remained on deck to help with the jibs and spanker. The rain struck his face like stones, and beads of water remained on his coat.

"Drop the sea anchor, and I'll use the spanker to

keep the wind aft," Banner shouted as the increasing winds fought against the remaining canvas. Waves rose in crescents that broke over the bow and sides and crashed on the deck before flowing back through the rails.

Meg would be fearless. What was he going to do about her? He couldn't keep her as a mistress while she was married to Eliot. No, he would go insane even if Eliot didn't exert his marital rights. He couldn't think about their future course. There might not be one if he didn't concentrate all his efforts at battling the storm. He needed to keep the ship upright.

Chapter Thirteen

After Meg finished securing the captain's cabin, she found Lilibet in bed under the covers. "Are you awake?"

She poked her head above the blanket. "We're going to drown."

Meg sat on the bunk and stroked tangled curls back from her tear-streaked face. "We're not going to drown. Banner won't let his ship sink."

"His precious ship. What about us?"

Should she tell her about Banner's kiss? No. Lilibet had enough worries. What would she do once she reached Riverside? Would Banner tell Eliot he loved her? Did he love her? A kiss meant desire, but did it confirm deeper feelings? He hadn't declared any.

A sea captain as young and handsome as Banner probably had any number of women vying for his favors. Did the kiss mean anything to him? Her world had changed with a touch of his lips. She couldn't imagine kissing anyone else.

But Owen was determined to see the wedding occur, whether the money was for her father or for him. And once on land, he would have the authority to force her to wed Eliot. She could lose Banner forever.

The storm reflected the violence of her emotions as the ship rose and fell with every wave. Boards creaked with the assault, and the window rattled on the stern wall.

Lilibet covered her ears. "Stop it!"

Rain pelted the windowpane in rapid fire. Meg closed the wooden shutters that covered the glass and latched it tight like she had done in Banner's cabin. The ship tilted, and something crashed on deck.

Lilibet screamed. Meg needed to keep her calm and sang a hymn even though the wind battled to drown her voice out. She removed her gown and crawled into bed with Lilibet to coax her into a troubled sleep. She heard the bell toll the changing of the watch before she fell asleep.

Meg woke suddenly, sensing a change in the weather. She left Lilibet's side and dressed in a simple gown. Issy was in the passageway.

"Is the storm over?"

He nodded. "It's abating, Lady Meg, but it was a bad one. Captain Youngblood battled through more than one watch to keep the ship ahead of the worst of the storm."

She looked toward his cabin. "Where is the captain?"

"Mr. Griffin went to take the helm. The captain will be coming below soon."

Banner had to be cold, soaked, and exhausted. She had been taught to give orders and take charge in a crisis. "The captain will need towels and blankets. Where can I find them?"

"In the large trunk at the end of his bed."

"Can you ask Duffy to make him coffee and something to eat?"

He nodded and headed down the passageway toward the deck.

Meg slipped inside Banner's cabin. She opened a shutter and folded it back against the wall. The raging storm had turned day into night, but now the setting sun displayed a brilliant canvas of magenta and cyan among parting clouds. She placed a lantern in the center of the desk and grabbed a tinder box from a drawer. She rubbed the steel striker against the bumpy flint to create sparks, careful to keep them within the box and light the small pieces of rag and hemp. Once a flame appeared, she lit the wick of the candle inside the glass lantern and latched the opening. She put the lid on the tinder box to extinguish the flame.

Banner's bunk had a blanket and thick quilt. She folded them down. She searched the chest at the end of his bed and found a couple of worn blankets and two towels. She placed them on the table and removed a chair from the hooks that had secured it during the storm.

The door flew open, and Banner stumbled into the room with a limp cap in his hand. He looked like a drowned rat, his clothes dripping with water. Sea salt caked his dark hair and the stubble of beard on his face.

His eyes were glazed. "What are you doing in here?"

"I'm going to save your life." She turned the chair so the back rested against the table. "Sit."

He took an unsteady step toward her. "I'm tired not dead."

He collapsed on the chair, and she threw a towel over his head and rubbed the salt and water from his hair.

"Duffy is making something to eat."

"I'm too tired to dine."

"You will be dead if you don't warm up and eat something before going to bed."

He stared at her with soft gray eyes, the fight extinguished but defiance smoldering in the way he cocked an eyebrow. "This isn't my first sea voyage."

"I don't want it to be your last." She pried the soggy

cap from his grasp, wrung it out over the slop bucket, and tossed it on the floor. She tugged his gloves free and added them to the cap. "How many storms like this have you been through?"

His body shivered in a violent spasm. "None. We almost capsized."

Was he telling the truth? "I don't think I want to hear that." Her voice trembled.

"We didn't, but she took some damage. The crew will be busy with repairs."

"Your bravery deserves my gratitude." She unbuttoned the wool coat, heavy with water, and peeled it away from his shoulders before dropping it on the floor.

He tried to help undo the buttons on his waistcoat, but his hands shook, and she brushed them away.

"Let me do this." Meg unfastened the small buttons.

The vest was added to the pile of wet clothing. The cravat around his shirt collar was knotted, but she worked the sopping fabric free from his neck. "You were right about learning to untie knots. It comes in handy." His wet shirt clung to his skin, and she tugged it over his head, wrung the water from the fabric, and added it to the growing heap.

She stared at his naked chest, wondering how he could be so broad in the shoulders and narrow in the waist. He put Lady Dudlee's statues to shame. She grabbed a blanket and massaged the hard bulging muscles of his bare chest and arms. She pulled him forward to continue the treatment on his back and saw the faded scars from a whip.

She swaddled the blanket around him and tucked it in front.

"Thank you." His words shook, and his body shivered.

"I'm not done." She leaned down to grab his foot. "Give me your boot."

"I don't need my boots removed."

"Water has been splashing down inside them for hours. Your feet are probably rotting away as we speak."

His teeth chattered. "That's disgusting."

She pulled off each boot and a wet stocking. She dumped the water from the boots into the slop bucket, wrung out the stockings, and added them to his wet clothes.

"Now the pants."

He raised a single eyebrow. "I thought you were a lady."

She braced herself for a fight. "I know you prefer sleeping naked, but for modesty's sake, I know something you can wear." She ran to the rag chest and found the large nightshirt, wool socks, and a nightcap. "Perfect."

Banner's head had fallen forward. He was nearly asleep.

She unfastened the trouser buttons below his knees. "Can you stand?"

"Of course." He stood and wobbled. "I'm a bit dizzy." The blanket fell to the floor.

She retrieved it and rubbed it over his shoulders and chest to remove any remaining dampness. The friction returned color to his skin. She gathered the nightshirt and pulled the opening over his head. She slid his arms through the sleeves like dressing a child for bed. "Now hold still." Meg fumbled with the buttons at the top of his drop trousers and let them fall to the floor.

145

He stared at her face. "Did you peek?"

"What do you think?" She dried off the chair and pushed him into it. After wrapping the dry blanket around him, she grabbed a bare wrinkled foot, rubbed it with a towel, and repeated her action with the other foot. She tugged on the wool socks.

Duffy entered with a pot of coffee and a loaf of bread. "Lady Meg, I wasn't expecting to find you in here."

"I was helping the captain get ready for bed. He's exhausted, but he needs to eat something. What do you have?"

"Some bread and cheese and hot coffee."

"You take his wet clothes and see if you can dry them out," Meg said. "I'll feed him and put him to bed."

Duffy hesitated.

She pointed to the pile. "They'll dry quicker by your firebox."

"Yes, Lady Meg." He gathered the wet bundle along with the boots and made a hasty retreat.

Meg held the cup of hot coffee to his lips. "Sip, don't gulp."

"Are you always a mother hen?"

"Only with those who need it." She offered him a slice of bread topped with cheese.

Once he had eaten and finished a cup of coffee, she pulled him to his feet and helped him across the room to his bed. He fell onto the mattress, dragging her down with him. The ropes creaked beneath their weight. She wiggled out from under his body.

"Where are you going?" His voice was hoarse and dreamy.

"You need to sleep." She pulled the covers up and

added the dry blanket over them. "Are you warm enough?"

He patted the empty spot beside him. "I'd be warmer with you in here with me."

She laughed and added the nightcap to cover his damp hair. "Aren't you the flirtatious rake?"

He yawned. "Who are you, my lovely?"

"You're muddled." She leaned forward and kissed his cold lips. His arm went around her as he returned her passion but fell limp to his side as sleep overtook him.

"I could ravish you, and you wouldn't remember a thing. Poor baby." *Poor me.*

Chapter Fourteen

Banner yawned and stretched as sunlight streamed into his room through the open slits in the shutters. It was morning. The storm had lasted for hours, ending as the sun set. Had he slept all night? He looked around and recognized his surroundings but couldn't remember how he had reached his bed.

His last memory was gripping the helm as rain pummeled the boards, and the wind howled at his back as he raced to escape nature's fury. Every muscle in his body ached from the strain of keeping the ship upright as it plowed through the waves, straining to reach calmer seas.

He groaned as he tossed the covers aside and threw his legs over the side of the bed. His feet were encased in thick wool socks. He stood, and a cocoon of fabric fell about his body. A sleeve edged with lace dangled over his hand. What was he wearing? He headed for the door. "Issy!"

The door flew open, and Issy stood in the opening. "What is it, Captain?"

He raised his arms outward and spun around. "What am I wearing?"

"It appears to be a nightshirt, Captain."

"And why do I have it on?"

He looked confused. "Because you were sleeping?"

Meg appeared in the doorway. "You're finally

awake." She turned to Issy. "Have Duffy bring him some food."

"Yes, Lady Meg."

Had Meg taken over command of his ship while he had slept? "I'm not hungry."

"You must be starving. You only had a slice of bread topped with cheese before I put you to bed."

"What?" The words must be in error. He looked around his cabin, trying to recall the events following the storm. "You put me to bed?"

She opened the shutters on the windows, and the room was flooded with light. "You were exhausted." She pointed to the trunk where his clothes were neatly folded on top. "Duffy cleaned and dried everything and polished your boots."

He lifted his lace-edged sleeve. "Duffy undressed me?"

She smiled broadly, her hand on a hip. "No, I did."

He stared at her, unable to grasp her words. "You did what?"

"Your hands were numb with cold and shaking so badly you could only fumble with your buttons. Don't worry. I've undressed lots of little boys."

"I'm a man. There's a big difference."

"I'm fully aware of that. Now," Meg said in a sultry whisper.

He looked toward the open door. "Where was Issy during all this?"

"He went to tell Duffy to make you coffee and bring some food."

"He left you alone with me?" Did he sound scared?

"Since you normally sleep naked, I could only find that nightshirt for you to wear."

"I don't need a mother, wife, or…" He hesitated on the word mistress. He'd entertained himself on deck at the helm with thoughts of her naked and in his bed. The heat the image produced had kept him from freezing to death. His thoughts were leaning toward lover, but he quickly squashed those. Eliot was his friend and business partner. He would never have an affair with his wife. Even if there was no love in the marriage. "Why did you undress me?"

"Someone had to take care of you." She walked around him. "You were nearly frozen from the storm and would have caught your death from the cold."

He looked at the nightshirt. "I look like a bloody virgin bridegroom on his wedding night."

Her smile widened, and she gave him a lusty laugh. "I assure you, Captain, I did not deflower you."

He searched his memory. "What did happen?"

She raised a dainty eyebrow. "You don't remember?"

He sat in a chair by the table, hoping his body had not acted without his mind. "Tell me what you did."

She looked confused. "I put you to bed."

He looked toward the rumpled covers. "You? All by yourself?"

"Well, it was a bit difficult. The ship was still tossing, and you were heavy."

"Did I hurt you?"

"Only when you fell on top of me, but the bed cushioned us."

"Us?" Had he taken advantage of her in his confused state?

"You wanted me to stay and keep you warm." Her sultry voice was maddening.

"Did you?" His voice squeaked.

She laughed, but any answer was interrupted by Duffy as he brought in a tray. He grabbed the coffeepot and cup. He was dreaming and needed to wake up.

"Mr. Griffin said we went slightly off course and may be a few days late reaching Riverside," Duffy said.

"Did he? How long have I been asleep?"

"Two watches, sir," Duffy said.

Meg set a plate and silverware at the table. "Sit down and eat, Banner. I mean Captain. Griffin will give you a full report once you've eaten and dressed." She smiled. "You do look adorable."

"What?"

She laughed as she closed the door.

"She is a bold one, Captain," Duffy said.

Bold, beautiful, and promised to another. He was lucky the voyage was coming to an end.

Banner ate what Duffy had brought him, surprised that he was hungrier than he thought. He dressed and headed for the deck to inspect the damage from the storm. The bowsprit and masts were intact. Two staysails needed replaced, and the men were unfurling sails and checking for any damage to the canvas. Lines would need to be inspected and replaced if necessary. A section of the railing had broken. The carpenter was already working on the repairs.

Griffin was overseeing the work.

"Have you slept?" Banner asked.

"I finished my watch at the helm and closed my eyes, but there was too much to do to sleep long. That was the worst storm we've been through, but the ship weathered it well."

"What about the cargo?"

"Dry in the barrels and containers. The men were a bit shaken but grateful they came out of the storm alive. Did you hear Lady Meg singing hymns?"

He'd heard the haunting melodies but had dismissed them as the mythical siren's song preceding shipwrecks. "I didn't realize what it was at the time."

"She was singing to Lilibet to calm her. Had the same effect on the men. Poseidon won't sink a ship with an angel aboard."

Banner had a different opinion. "She's no angel."

Griffin chuckled as they walked the deck. "Issy said she insisted upon undressing you and putting you to bed."

Banner looked around at the crew. "How many men know what she did?"

"Only myself, Duffy, and Issy. None of them will speak of the matter."

"It could ruin her reputation." Banner tested a line. He needed to keep busy and not think about the woman who occupied his every thought.

"Eliot can't refuse to marry her," Griffin said. "Pity. He's a bit of a milksop."

He felt obligated to defend Eliot. "He's my friend."

"I know, but must loyalty trump love?"

"What do you mean?"

"I've known you a long time, Captain. Once you satisfied your curiosity about women, you were selective and never took more than a brief notice until now. She's a good match for you, and we know where Eliot's heart lies. Tell her you love her before it's too late."

"That would only complicate the situation."

"I've told three women I love them. One refused me. One married another. And one agreed to be my wife. I never regretted declaring my feelings."

Banner had never told any woman he loved her. He was too honest to lie in order to warm his bed. But he wanted Meg for more than satisfying his base desires. "Where is she?"

"Mr. O'Leary is on the lower deck, so she's probably in her room," Griffin said. "She tries to put as much distance between that man and herself as possible aboard a ship."

Banner spotted Owen near the bow. "I don't like the man either, but he represents her father."

"He represents himself and has a lofty opinion of his worth."

Banner headed toward Meg's room but changed his mind. What could he say to her? The voyage was closer to an end than beginning. He could wait and see what Eliot decided. His friend could refuse to marry Meg. Then he could declare his love.

Chapter Fifteen

Meg paced across the small space of her cabin. Since the storm, the captain and his men had been busy with repairs and making up lost time. Banner had been polite but distant, refusing to talk about what had occurred between them. He wasn't going to carry her off and marry her like a princess in a fairy tale. She needed to rescue herself.

"We have one week left before reaching Riverside. I can't wait any longer. I need to read the letters Banner placed in his desk."

Lilibet had been sprawled on her bed but sat and marked her book. "What do you need me to do?"

"The canopy has been repaired. Take your book and sit at the stern. Make sure Banner doesn't go to his cabin."

"How will I stop him?" Her book shook in her hands.

"Engage him in conversation about *Gulliver's Travels*."

Lilibet gathered her bonnet. "I can talk to Issy and Duffy, but your captain terrifies me. He's big, loud, and I jump every time he gives an order."

Meg thrilled at the sound of his booming voice. "Those orders are for his men, not you."

"Must he shout them?" She put on a lightweight jacket. "How long will it take?"

Meg would need to open, read two messages, and reseal them. "At least fifteen minutes."

"Do you think you'll learn anything from the letters? Why risk it?"

"I won't know until I read them. The voyage is almost over, and I don't have a plan for avoiding this marriage. I haven't learned anything more about Eliot from Banner or the crew. Everyone tells me what a fine gentleman he is."

Lilibet giggled. "A fat bald gentleman."

"Exactly," Meg said. "I'm not blind. When they think I'm not looking, they whisper and share worried glances. I have a bad feeling about this whole situation."

"It's the Irish who can sense calamity." Lilibet pointed at herself. "Why would the captain leave the notes in his desk and not locked in his safe with your ring?"

"Micah told him about my letter reading before he realized there would be letters to read. Banner made sure I saw them when we first boarded. That's why I've waited all this time." She shrugged. "Well, I wouldn't want to disappoint him. I'll join you when I'm done."

Lilibet touched her hand. "What if he finds out?"

"What can he do? I'm already facing a life sentence for the crime of being a woman."

"The captain is going to be disappointed in you if he finds out you read the letters."

She valued Banner's respect, but the knowledge gained from reading the information might help her navigate her future. "Men make the laws and expect us to follow them. I'm making my own rules. Who am I going to hurt reading two letters? I don't even know if there will be anything in them of interest, but I need to know what Lord Dudlee wrote to his son and his clerk. The scales of right and wrong are tipped toward the need to know."

"I hope it's worth the gamble." Lilibet glanced in the mirror and tied her bonnet.

"Make sure Issy goes out with you." Meg opened the door. "Tell him I'm going to take a nap until supper."

Meg gathered her knife, mirror, and a lit candle. She peeked through the opening in the door to make sure no one was left in the passageway and crossed to Banner's quarters.

She glanced about, sat at his desk, and placed her tools on the polished surface. She opened the top drawer but didn't see the letters. Did he move them? She searched through loose papers and lifted a ledger. Beneath were the sealed messages and a hair ribbon she had lost. Why had he kept that? Did he even remember the kiss they had shared? She replaced the ledger and papers in the drawer and placed the two notes on the desk.

The seals were intact. Banner hadn't read them. He wouldn't. Snooping would be against his personal code of conduct. She looked at the wax. A hot knife would do the trick.

She heated the metal in the flame of her candle and slid the warm blade beneath the wax seal on the first missive. She carefully lifted the intact seal and placed it on the square mirror. She opened the letter to Eliot, noting the folding pattern, and read it. She committed several phrases to memory before refolding the paper. She dripped fresh wax from her candle onto the opening and replaced the old seal, using her knife to keep it from cracking. Satisfied it revealed no tampering, she heated her knife and used the sharp edge to remove the seal from the correspondence to Glen Stemple and read the contents.

The message was cryptic, and she read through the passages again.

A breeze of salt air came from the window behind her, and she turned. Banner climbed through the open window. He had a frown on his handsome face.

"Do you always come in through the window?" She kept her voice nonchalant.

"It was cloudy, and I saw a light shining from inside."

Her candle. "Where's Lilibet?"

"Duffy is sharing a recipe."

"You knew Lilibet couldn't resist." He had bested her. She waved him forward. "Come here. This is fascinating."

He strode across the short distance. "Your brother warned me about your bad habits, but I don't detect any guilt or remorse in your voice."

She made no apology. "Haven't you read someone's letters before?"

He placed his hand on her shoulder. "Only those addressed to me."

His fingertips burned against her flesh. Was he angry? "But don't you want to know what Lord Dudlee says?"

"No." His warm breath tickled her ear as he bent over her.

She looked up, her lips inches from his mouth. "I didn't realize you were a Puritan."

"I don't believe in religions." Banner's deep baritone rumbled as he straightened. "But I do believe in respecting others' privacy."

"Too bad, because I think Glen Stemple has been sabotaging Eliot's plans." She was fishing for information to confirm her hunch.

"What?" He reached for the letter.

She moved it away. "You're not interested."

He stood stiff at attention. The war between curiosity and his principles was obvious.

She kept the paper turned away from his view. "How long have you known Glen?"

"Since I began working for Lord Dudlee. He's a clerk who handles the business reports for the company."

"Have you read any of those business reports?"

"I have copies of the manifests when we ship products for the Richmond family."

"He's been writing about more than cargo by Lord Dudlee's reply in this message." She placed the letter on the desk and pointed to a paragraph.

He leaned over her shoulder and folded the paper. "I'm not going to read it."

"I admire your moral integrity. But the only way to find out what Father was plotting at Whittington Manor was for my mother to read his mail. As her daughter, I'm not above bending a few rules."

"Your mother encouraged this behavior?" His voice rose in disbelief.

"It was necessary." She carefully folded the letter in its original pattern. "If you'll forgive me for being less than perfect, I'll tell you what's in it that I find so interesting."

"I fear you're a bad influence on me." He pointed to the drawer. "I left the correspondence in my desk to see if your brother was telling the truth, but I'm surprised you waited this long to read them."

"I do have some self-control." She reattached the seal.

"You're good at that."

She wondered what Banner knew and bluffed with the most pressing question. "Why didn't you tell me Eliot has a mistress?"

His brows rose in surprise. "I didn't want to prejudice you against him."

Confirmation. "I'm not shocked." She kept her voice steady. "Most men have a mistress, but it would be nice to know there will be three in this marriage."

"Eliot promised to vacate Cathy from the house before you arrived."

Cathy. She had a name. "She lived with him?" That was unusual.

He coughed. "I shouldn't have told you that."

He had let his guard down, and she took advantage. "What is she like?"

He paced to the front of the desk and placed his hands on the surface. "What do you mean?"

She lifted the letter to Eliot. "Lord Dudlee appears to have a low opinion of her. In his letter he reminds his son to do his duty and marry me upon my arrival and to forget the woman who has bewitched him."

"Bewitched?" Banner's brow wrinkled, and he stared at the resealed letter.

"That was his word, not mine." She blew out her candle. "Lady Dudlee believed that a woman was after Eliot's title and wealth. Is Cathy an ambitious woman?"

He laughed. "Cathy Goodheart? She's a pastor's daughter." He sobered and stared. "You didn't know that."

She felt the corners of her mouth rise. "I do now."

He walked away, turned, and strode back to the desk. "I didn't tell you about Cathy to spare your feelings."

"I have no feelings for Eliot, yet." She placed her knife and mirror in her pocket. "You put me at a disadvantage by not telling me what you knew."

"Nevertheless, I won't tell you anything more." He turned away.

"When you know the truth but keep it from someone, that's a lie," Meg said.

He spun around. "Are you saying the absence of truth is a lie?"

She lifted the other letter. "This one is more interesting. Lord Dudlee thanks Glen Stemple for keeping him informed of MCG's nefarious schemes and promises to reward him. He thanks him for offering the solution to their problem, and hopes he will aid Owen in making sure the marriage proceeds without incident. Is there anyone else with those initials?"

"Only Mary Catherine Goodheart." He grabbed the letter, examined the seal, and dropped it on the desk. "Nefarious schemes? From Cathy? She's the sweetest woman I know."

"We have a mystery, Captain. Why would Glen paint an unflattering picture of Cathy to Lord Dudlee?"

"I don't know. Could you have misread the letter?"

"I read it twice to clarify any meaning." She leaned back in the chair. "How old is Glen?"

"I believe he's a little older than me. What does age have to do with it?"

"Did Eliot deliver his letters directly to you, or did he send them through Glen?"

He sat on the corner of the desk. "All correspondence came through his clerk, and Glen always offered to deliver the letter and manifest to Eliot when I docked."

She pointed at the seal. "What if Glen wasn't above reading other people's mail? Did he know Eliot intended to wed Cathy?"

"The banns were read in church two years ago."

Banns? "Eliot was confident his father would approve?"

"He had no reason to doubt it. He was shocked when his father refused to sanction the marriage and threatened to disown him. Eliot depends entirely on his father's allowance."

"As his clerk, would Glen know that?"

Banner nodded. "He's the one who pays Eliot out of the business profits."

She placed the sealed letters back in his desk and stood. "Two years ago when I entered society, my mother warned me about people who liked to manipulate others with lies. I was to base my decisions on facts, not rumors. I believe Lord and Lady Dudlee want what is best for their son. Do you believe that Cathy Goodheart would make Eliot happy?"

"Yes."

She studied his face. "You didn't hesitate."

"My words are true."

She stood and moved close to him, meeting his gaze. "Then why is Glen painting a vicious picture about her?"

"I think you must be mistaken." He moved away, turned, and paced across the floor. "Glen was the Richmond's clerk long before Eliot arrived in Riverside."

She leaned against the desk. "What are his responsibilities?"

"He receives the Richmond share of the cargo and stores it in their warehouse. He sells the goods and uses the profits to purchase merchandise Lord Dudlee wants shipped to England," Banner said. "He keeps records of orders and transactions for Eliot."

What was left? "Does Eliot do anything?"

"He represents his father," Banner said. "Glen gives Eliot the paperwork, and he reviews it."

She couldn't stop now no matter how he reacted. "Do you ever compare your manifest of what you delivered to the Richmond warehouse to the one Glen gives Eliot?"

"No. That's his business." He crossed his arms and glared. "He's worked for the family for years. He's a *trusted* employee."

So was Owen. Was she prone to unwarranted suspicions, or were her instincts true? Only time would tell. She stepped closer and touched the buttons on his coat. "I think we should discuss the kiss we shared."

He stiffened. "I was wrong to do that. You belong to Eliot."

"Belong?" She took a step back. "Am I a piece of cargo to be delivered to your business partner?"

"I didn't mean it that way." He kept his gaze locked on hers. "I made a promise to take you to Eliot, and I've kept that part of my pledge."

Meg's lofty visions of being swept into his arms with declarations of love crashed to the ground along with her broken heart. "Oh, your honor is intact, Captain. You're not the first man I've kissed, and you won't be the last." It was a lie, but Meg's shattered illusions forced her to lash out like a wounded animal. He would never know how special his kiss had been. "I made a promise to Lord Dudlee to make Eliot happy, and I aim to fulfill *my* pledge."

His jaw tightened, but he said nothing. Banner wouldn't do anything dishonorable such as eloping with her. She would have to save herself from this unwanted marriage.

"Don't worry." Meg's voice quivered as she gathered her candle from his desk. "I wouldn't think of compromising your precious honor. I won't kiss you again. Do you think Eliot will appreciate my kisses?"

"What?"

She spun on her heels, strode to her own room, slammed the door, and grabbed a pillow to muffle her sobs as she burst into tears. Meg was on her own. Too bad she had no idea how she was going to free herself from this dire situation.

Chapter Sixteen

Meg had taken all her meals in her room for the final week of the trip. Because of the storm, they were scheduled to arrive May 21 according to Issy. If she went out on the deck, she made sure Banner was on duty and too busy to spend time with her. She had never been in love with a man before, but she recognized the signs. She thought of him constantly. She wanted to be near him, to hear his voice, to share a smile.

But he had rejected her before she had a chance to learn his feelings or declare her own. Her mother had failed to warn her that love could swell to euphoria and then crash to agonizing agony. The time alone had reduced the wounds from a deep gash to an aching bruise. No one married their first love, did they?

She could look forward to meeting Eliot without the burden of loving another, but the two men were friends. She couldn't escape his company forever. She wouldn't let him know how much he had wounded her tender heart. Her pride and training as a lady meant true feelings were hidden beneath a smile and gracious manners. Aunt Felicity had been right. It was better to marry someone she could respect and had common life goals. Love only made the relationship more difficult.

She had saved one of her mother's dresses to wear when she met Eliot. It was a rich plum with a white underskirt. Her hair was long enough to be pulled back and up with a cascade of curls that gave the appearance of more length. She wanted to look her best. She had no plan on how to escape the nuptials, so she needed to make the marriage work. She didn't add her fichu. Why hide her bosom? She wanted to impress Eliot, didn't she? The sun was shining, so she chose a wide-brim bonnet.

Lilibet answered a knock on the door.

Issy handed Meg a small velvet bag. "The captain said I should return this to you."

She removed the ruby ring he had placed in his safe and slipped it on her finger. She had forgotten about the symbol of her betrothment. Was Banner reminding her she belonged to another?

"Your other trunks have been loaded," Issy said. "Are you done with these?"

Meg nodded, and Issy ordered two men to carry out the packed trunks and followed. Meg looked around the room that had been home the last two months. She would miss the *Gabriella.*

Owen waited in the passageway outside their room. "Go ahead, Lilibet. I'll have a word with Lady Meg."

Lilibet hesitated, but Meg nodded, and she headed for the deck. Owen had no respect for women, but he respected Meg's title. Most of the time. "What do you want, Owen?"

"I didn't have to worry about you escaping while on the ship, but now that we're about to be on dry land, I don't want you to think you can run away."

"Where would I go in this wilderness?" Bitter sarcasm laced her words.

"I will attain my goals," Owen said. "You will marry the man."

She acted surprised at his stark revelation. "When

did my marriage become your objective?"

He looked startled but recovered. "My intentions are the same as Lord Whittington's."

"You have nothing to worry about." Meg smiled with her new resolve fresh in her mind. "Why wouldn't I marry Eliot? Everyone I've spoken to assures me he'll make an excellent husband."

"Good, because if you don't do exactly as I say, I will take Lilibet back with me to England and drop her off at the most notorious brothel in London."

What? Several moments passed before she comprehended what he had threatened. "She's an innocent."

A glimmer sparked in his cold eyes. "And they pay a high price for virgins."

Raped like her mother. But not by one man. Bile and anger rose in her throat. "She'll stay here with me under my protection."

Owen pushed her against the wall, his hand remaining on her shoulder, the pressure building as if he wished to squash her. "I will not have my plans ruined by a mere girl. You marry Eliot, or I take Lilibet back to England with me. I have a letter from your father authorizing me to act as guardian for both of you in his absence." He released her. "But if you marry Eliot, I will leave her care in your husband's hands."

He turned and walked away.

Meg had been too shocked at his brazen behavior to cry out or protest, but now her body shook in terror, and moisture filled her eyes. Owen had never abused her directly, but she had seen him beat and degrade servants. She had no reason to doubt his threats. She took several deep breaths, used her handkerchief to wipe away any tears, and headed for the deck.

Owen was standing next to Lilibet, a slight smile on his thin face as if nothing had happened between them. Her heart still raced from their encounter. He knew her weakness, her love for Lilibet, but he expected her to be frightened by his threats. She would play that role while she plotted how to outmaneuver him. She would never allow him to force Lilibet into the service of a whore for strangers to use her body for their pleasure. Never.

"Thank God we've reached land." He looked around, a sneer on his lips. "Where is your betrothed?"

"I see a carriage." It was empty, and she saw no one who looked like Eliot's painting standing nearby. Her future husband would need a good reason not to welcome them personally.

Lilibet searched the crowd and shrugged. "I don't think he came."

His absence could be a blessing. A public meeting would be awkward, especially with her heart racing and her mind preoccupied after her encounter with Owen. She wanted to be calm and in control when they were introduced.

Owen began the descent down the gangplank, his arms waving to maintain his balance. Meg and Lilibet followed to the dock and looked around. A wagon was loaded with their trunks.

Banner was speaking with the driver and turned. She steeled her heart from reacting to his presence. He was a man like any other now, but few could compete with his ruggedly handsome features and commanding presence. His clothing was finer than what he wore aboard the ship, and his face was freshly shaved. Who was he trying to impress? Certainly not her.

Banner studied her as she approached. "I hope you're feeling better."

"Women have times they need to remain in private." She kept her voice cool. "I'm recovered."

His brow wrinkled at her explanation. Men avoided any talk of a woman's monthly cycle. That it had coincided with her broken heart was convenient.

"Where is Mr. Richmond?" Owen demanded.

"Is it possible Eliot doesn't know we've arrived?" Meg asked in disbelief.

"We signaled our arrival when we entered the harbor." Banner studied her. "I'm sure he has a good reason for not being here. I've finished filing the manifest and arranged for transportation. We should be able to leave shortly."

"I need to find out when the next ship sails to England," Owen said. "Where's the harbormaster?"

Banner pointed out the building.

"I won't be long." He stared at Meg. "Don't run off without me."

"We wouldn't think of leaving you behind." She twisted the ruby ring on her finger. "I'm sure Eliot is looking forward to meeting all of us."

"Come along, Lilibet." Owen grabbed her arm. "You can accompany me."

She looked at Meg with fear in her eyes. Owen was already making good on his threat, but he couldn't harm her here. "Go along. Owen won't allow anything to happen that might ruin the upcoming nuptials."

He nodded and released Lilibet's arm. She glanced back as she walked with Owen.

Meg gave her a reassuring smile and turned to Banner. She picked the safest topic she could think of.

"When do you unload the ship?"

"Once the cargo is inspected and duty paid, my men will move my portion to my warehouse, and Eliot's men will pick up his goods over the next few days. The items we've brought are needed in the colonies and will sell quickly."

"You'll be busy." And gone from her life. She twisted the handkerchief in her hands and stared at his feet. "Then this is good-bye." Her voice cracked even as she fought to control her words.

"After my business with Eliot, I'll return to my ship."

"Then I'll thank you now for a lovely voyage." She extended her hand, and he took it. She felt the pleasant shock his touch sent through her body even if he didn't. She tipped her head back, the brim of her bonnet high enough to look directly at his face. "You made the crossing as pleasant as possible."

He squeezed her hand before releasing it. "Even with the storm?"

"I will remember the nor'easter in a special place in my memories." The sincere message was spoken from her heart, and if he didn't know what she was referring to, he had to be an idiot. Meg headed for the carriage.

Banner offered his hand to assist as she climbed the small metal steps. She gripped his fingers as he lifted her upward and took her seat. He studied her, concern on his face, but she turned and stared at the building Owen and Lilibet had entered and waited nervously until they emerged.

Lilibet and Owen sat opposite her, and Banner took the space beside her. If she protested, it might betray her turbulent feelings.

Owen had a paper in his hand. "The *Manchester* sails May 28. I hope you have everything you need for the wedding."

"In a week?" Meg didn't hide the outrage in her voice. "How am I to be ready for a wedding that soon? What about the three weeks to read the banns?"

"No need to wait with the special license your father obtained. I'm sure you can manage," Owen said. "The ship sails at one. I will have proof of your marriage in my hand before I board."

She lifted her chin. "I don't turn twenty-one until July 17. We can wait until then."

Owen's face flamed. "Lord Dudlee wants you to marry immediately, and I want to return to England as soon as possible, so you'll wed before I sail, or I'll take Lilibet home with me." He placed his arm around Lilibet's shoulder.

"What?" Lilibet stared at her for an explanation.

She reached across the opening and squeezed her hand. "You aren't going anywhere without me."

She had enough experience with authoritarian men to know butting heads would result in her being beaten. Not with a whip this time, but by the numerous rules men had established from the beginning of time to limit a woman's power. She needed to think and find a strategy. Thank goodness Banner was out of her life. She needed to focus on the enemy before her instead of the man beside her.

Owen was in too much of a hurry for her to wed, gain proof, and return to England. "I would think, by how much you disliked the voyage, you would be in no rush to begin another one."

"Lord Whittington depends on me to take care of

him and his properties." Owen examined the lace on his cuff. "I would not like to think he is suffering because of my absence."

Hopefully, Micah had gained their father's confidence and was spoiling any plans Owen had devised when he returned. "I'm sure the servants are providing him with comfort in a bottle."

"That's why he depends so much on me." Owen turned to Lilibet. "Once Meg is wed, you'll be in the way here. I'm sure your mother could use help in the kitchen."

Lilibet scooted away from Owen. "I didn't plan on going home, yet."

"Eliot and I will make plans for Lilibet." Meg dismissed Owen by turning her attention to the town. As they left the warehouses in the dock area, a sawmill came into view with wood workshops for barrels, wheels, and furniture nearby. A blacksmith stood in the open doorway of his shop, hammering a red-hot rod on an anvil. A man loaded sacks of flour into a wagon outside a mill. They passed taverns and small homes in an assortment of styles and sizes.

"Look at that log house, Lili," Meg said. The house was made of hewn logs with mud between the large squared timbers. It was primitive but sturdy. Two small windows faced the street with a solid wooden door between them. A short porch was supported by log posts.

"I thought you were more civilized in the colonies," Owen said.

"I like it," Meg defended.

"There are a few log houses, but most are white weatherboard or brick. We even have glass windows." Banner had been silent during her heated debate with

Owen and acted as if nothing had transpired. He nodded at her and pointed out a small white house with a picket fence. "There's a charming example of the homes in Riverside."

"It's lovely." She fought to keep her voice calm.

The driver turned down a cobblestone street lined with brick footways and wooden buildings that reminded her of small towns in England.

"This is Main Street," Banner said. "Most of the businesses and shops are located along here."

"What's that?" Lilibet pointed to a large open area.

"That's the town square. In the morning farmers bring their crops to sell."

"Are those stocks?" Meg shuddered. Two matching structures of wood with a central hole for a head and two on each side for wrists were on display in the open area. A whipping post stood in the center of the grassy area. "It's out in the open?"

"Public punishment is the way the colonists deal with criminals," Banner said. "But after a trial. That's the courthouse on the other side of the common square. There's a jail in the cellar for those who need to be transported to the state courthouse or back to England."

A few vendors remained on the square and hawked their wares as they passed.

"There's a place you might enjoy." Banner pointed at the millinery shop. Straw bonnets trimmed in ribbons and dried flowers were displayed in one of the windows.

Meg was more interested in the building next to it. "Didn't you say you lived above the tailor shop when in port?"

He nodded. "I rent space with two rooms. It's quieter than sleeping aboard my ship in the harbor. A separate entrance is located along the alley."

A narrow opening between the buildings allowed a glimpse of a steep set of stairs leading to the second floor. They would soon part ways. A melancholy settled over her, but she attempted a smile as he pointed out other sights along their route.

"I smell fresh bread," Lilibet said. "And cinnamon. It reminds me of my mother baking in the kitchen."

Meg turned to Banner. "Do we have time to purchase some pastries?"

"Don't tell Duffy," Lilibet said. "He tried hard to provide meals we would enjoy, and I wouldn't want to hurt his feelings."

"Unless you think Eliot will have cakes and tea ready for us when we arrive," Meg said. Although if he didn't remember to come to the dock to welcome his betrothed, he most likely forgot something as mundane as tea.

Chapter Seventeen

Meg welcomed the delay. She did not look forward to meeting Eliot and never seeing Banner again. But she would need to convince Eliot to keep Lilibet in Riverside and thwart Owen's plans by spending time with him and gaining his confidence.

Banner stopped the carriage and signaled the luggage cart to go ahead. He helped the ladies out, and Owen followed. They made their choices, and Banner paid the baker.

A woman entered the shop. "Captain! Captain Youngblood! I thought that was you I spied through the window. Such a yummy pastry."

Did she mean the roll in his hand or the man? Meg's defenses went up in spite of her resolve to dismiss Banner from her life. Her tanned skin and simple hairstyle made her feel dowdy by comparison to the woman who smiled at the captain as if he were the only person present.

The woman was strikingly beautiful with dark-brown hair artfully arranged high above her forehead with perfectly curled tendrils gracing her shoulders against the palest skin a woman could possess. "Everyone has been talking about your return."

He looked startled. "Why?"

She turned her attention to Lilibet and Meg. "Which one of you is the lucky lady?"

"This is Miss Lilibet Dugan and Lady Meg Culbertson," Banner introduced. "Miss Victoria…what is your last name now?"

"Bucholzer. Awful sounding, but he was wealthy." She touched the necklace that graced her slender neck and ample bosom. "And extremely generous, which is what I like in a husband."

She was a widow? The woman wore a scarlet gown with a black petticoat. The daring neckline displayed heaping mounds above the stiff stomacher.

Owen was staring, and a drool of spit escaped his gaping mouth.

"I'm so sorry for your loss. When did your husband pass away?" Meg asked politely.

She shrugged. "A month ago."

"Aren't you still in mourning?" Lilibet asked the question Meg thought. Most widows wore black for a year or at least a few months.

"I never mourn long. Life is too short to live in the shadows. I prefer the front row." Her laughter was rich, and she rested her hand on Banner's arm. "Since I'm between husbands, I will need an escort. I hope you'll be available."

"If he's not, I certainly am." Owen raised his hat, and a tuft of strawberry-blond hair stood at attention. "Owen O'Leary at your service."

She fluttered her fan before her face and extended her hand, which Owen kissed. Her flirting was scandalously obvious, and she did it with the confidence of someone well-practiced in the art.

Banner looked in Meg's direction with a befuddled expression. "I'm afraid I'll be busy with selling my cargo and the upcoming wedding between Lady Meg and

Eliot."

"Of course." Victoria turned to Meg. "Everyone in the colonies has been talking about Eliot's bride, and you do not disappoint, my dear."

Everyone knew about the marriage and had been gossiping about her? How mortifying. Meg looked around and saw the other patrons of the shop staring and digesting every word.

"On behalf of everyone in Riverside, I welcome and congratulate you on your upcoming nuptials." Victoria gripped Meg's arms and gave each of her cheeks a light brush with her own.

She didn't trust Victoria's praise or superficial congratulations. What did the woman hope to gain by pretending to be her friend? And what was her relationship with Banner?

"The wedding takes place in a week." Owen spat the words out as he stared at Victoria. "I hope we can become better acquainted before I return to England."

"A week?" She recovered from her surprise and nodded toward Owen. "I'll let you know if I need an escort."

"It's time we left," Banner said. "Eliot will be waiting."

"I wish I could join you, but I'm meeting a dear friend." She blew a kiss and departed with a swish of her wide skirt.

Meg stared at the empty space still vibrating with life. Victoria had all the confidence and grace that came with numerous victories. Had Banner been one of them?

"Lovely lady," Owen said. "Did she say she was widowed twice?"

"They were both wealthy and influential men,"

Banner said. "Victoria is popular at social events. She knows everyone and everything of importance in the colonies. She is always the center of attention."

"I hope to see more of her," Owen said as he boarded the carriage without helping the ladies.

Meg stared at her uneaten pastry after taking her seat. She shoved it at Lilibet. "I'm not hungry." She rode in silence as Banner continued pointing out sights on the western part of town. Could the day prove to be any worse?

They turned onto a dirt road where houses were farther apart with larger yards, gardens, and multiple outbuildings.

"There's Eliot's home." Banner pointed to a symmetrical brick building two stories high. The wagon hauling their luggage was stopped near the back, and servants were unloading it. The carriage pulled up to the front door. Newly planted wildflowers filled the wooden boxes beneath the tall sectioned windows. It was an oddly feminine touch for a bachelor.

Owen stepped out of the carriage and waited at the door.

Banner stepped down and offered his hand. Meg was looking at the house and slipped on the step. He caught her about the waist and held her until she gained her footing.

"Thank you. It wouldn't do to meet my intended flat on my face."

He nodded toward her bosom and lowered his voice. "You might want to tuck a pink bud back in that has escaped."

She examined her bodice and found she was exposing a nipple. She covered her breast with her hand

and adjusted the fabric. She was too embarrassed to look at Banner, who turned his attention to Lilibet.

The door opened, and the butler welcomed them inside. She looked around the foyer. A steep oak staircase led upstairs to her right, and a wide hallway extended to the back where another door was opened to allow a breeze to blow through the house.

"Where's Mr. Richmond?" Banner asked the butler.

"In his study, Captain."

Banner looked to their right where a door was closed. "Tell him he has guests."

He nodded. "Yes, Captain."

Meg studied her new home. It was modest compared to the townhouses in London but clean and comfortable with painted floors and tall windows that allowed natural light to brighten the interior.

Fortunately, Eliot did not have his parents' taste in décor. No naked statues greeted them, and the artwork on the walls consisted of landscapes. A needlepoint was framed to her left. The initials *MCG* were stitched in the corner. Cathy Goodheart had left a bit of herself behind.

Eliot Richmond came out of his study and left the door open to reveal a section of a desk with two padded chairs in front of it. A half-empty decanter rested on a small sideboard on the far wall.

Eliot bore a resemblance to the young man in the portrait hanging in his father's study but had aged with lines around his tired eyes and a slump in his shoulders. His hair had thinned, and the beginning of a belly pressed against his waistcoat. Lilibet's joke about him being fat and bald would soon come true. He didn't smile but extended his hand to Banner. "You're back."

"May I introduce Owen O'Leary, Miss Lilibet

Dugan, and your betrothed, Lady Meg Culbertson." Banner's voice had an edge of disapproval to it, the tone he used when one of his crew had made an error.

Eliot's gaze barely acknowledged her. His lack of interest was unnerving. Was he made of ice?

She curtseyed. "Eliot, I'm so happy to make your acquaintance." It sounded silly. The man was betrothed to be her husband. They would be married in a week. Would marriage to Eliot be as bad as she imagined? One man was as good as any other. Or so she had thought before she met Banner. She looked at the captain. He refused to meet her gaze. He was studying their host. Something was wrong.

Eliot's eyes were red. Had the man been drinking? Panic seized her. Drunkards were unpredictable and often cruel like her father. She had hoped a plan would come to mind by now to avoid the union, but she saw no escape.

"Let's go into the parlor," Banner suggested. An arched opening to the left led to a comfortable sitting room. The windows were framed in full-length draperies in fabric that matched the settee and two chairs. The floor had a colorful rug that complemented the fabric. Someone with taste had decorated the room. Pillows and a vase with flowers added a feminine touch. Was Cathy still in residence?

Eliot made no move to say anything or direct their next action.

"I signaled our ship's arrival for today." Banner's voice was harsh. "I expected you to be at the dock."

Eliot looked confused. What was wrong with the man?

"I had to obtain a wagon and carriage." Banner

tapped his long fingers on his knee as he waited.

"I forgot." Eliot looked at his guests. "I'm terribly sorry."

Meg stood, and the others rose. "Lilibet and I would like to freshen up before tea."

"Tea?"

English homes were run on a schedule. Breakfast upon rising, dinner at three p.m. with tea at six p.m. and a light supper of leftovers at nine p.m. "You do have tea, don't you?" She offered a smile.

He looked around as if confused.

She turned to Banner as panic grew in her stomach. "I hope you will join us." Did he recognize it as a ploy to keep him at her side a little longer? "Or is this the last we'll see you?"

"I'm standing up for Eliot, so I'll be available to him if he needs me until the wedding."

"You take care of the bridegroom, and I'll take care of the bride," Owen said.

She recognized the threat in his voice and made sure he didn't suspect she wasn't going to be intimidated. "This bride would like to be shown to her room."

"Of course." Eliot waved to a servant.

"We'll join you shortly for tea." Meg and Lilibet followed the maid upstairs. Owen waited below, watching. He was not going to give them a chance to escape.

Meg needed to know the arrangements. "Where is Mr. Richmond's room?"

The maid pointed ahead of them. "At the head of the stairs."

Meg paused as the maid led them down the hallway. "I don't have an adjoining room?"

"There is one, but Mr. Richmond assigned you a different room until after the wedding." A hint of disapproval was in her voice. The maid showed her to a room down the hallway and in the back. "Will this be acceptable?"

She looked out the window and turned. "Oh dear. I can't tolerate the morning sun. Is there a room available on the front of the house?"

"Yes, across the hall, miss." Again, her voice had a hint of disdain.

Meg needed to intimidate the servant enough to prevent her request from being denied. "Most people call me Lady Meg."

The maid nodded several times and hurried to open the door to the room at the front of the house.

Meg looked around. "This will do."

"I'll have your trunks moved, Lady Meg."

"We'll need water and towels to freshen ourselves."

She curtseyed. "Yes, Lady Meg."

Lilibet shut the door and crossed the room to the windows. "You love the morning sun."

She pointed to the floor. "But the study is directly below."

"I knew you had a reason." Lilibet pushed down on the mattress. "What's wrong with Eliot? He seemed lost, and he barely acknowledged you."

"I might be offended if he was the man I was going to marry."

"He is the man you…" Lilibet sighed. "How can you joke about it?"

"I agree that something is upsetting him. That's why I want this room."

"Do you think you'll be able to hear through the

floorboards?"

Meg lifted the area rug near the four-poster bed. "Look." She pointed to a knothole in the pine flooring. "Watch the door." She knelt on the floor and peered through the hole. Light from the front windows illuminated the desk and items on it below. "It's perfect."

She straightened the rug and tossed her bonnet on the bed.

The maid brought in a pitcher of water, and two men carried their trunks inside. "Would you like me to unpack?"

"No, we'll unpack later. I'll have clothes for you to wash and press."

"Yes, Lady Meg." The maid curtseyed and backed out of the room.

Lilibet poured the water from the pitcher into a washbasin. She soaked a cloth and handed it to Meg. "It was a dusty ride."

She wiped her face and stared into the mirror. "I must have looked a fright next to Victoria."

Lilibet washed her face. "She's old and vain."

"She's beautiful and fawned over Banner like he was a tasty pastry."

"He didn't appear to be interested."

"Thank you for that lie." Meg circled the room, touching objects as her thoughts whirled in her mind.

"If you care for him, why have you been avoiding him?"

"He doesn't return my feelings. I need to cultivate Eliot's instead." She returned to the washstand and stared at her reflection in the mirror. "I look like I've been on a sailing ship for two months. Do you think Eliot was horrified by my peasant appearance?"

"You could do with a long soak in a hot bath."

"Later. I don't have much time to make myself presentable." She dumped her personal bag on the bed and searched through the items.

"What are you looking for?" Lilibet asked.

"I don't know." A sob escaped before she pressed her fingertips against her lips to silence her fears.

"Let me style your hair." Lilibet removed the combs and smoothed out the tangles. "Your hair is so light and silky. And look how long it has grown." She pulled it up, placed the combs, and created curls around her finger. "A few loose strands to frame your face, and you're beautiful."

Lilibet was trying to cheer her up. She wouldn't worry her by complaining. She twisted the ring on her finger. She needed to figure out a plan to stop a wedding in seven days.

Chapter Eighteen

Banner tried to engage Eliot in conversation, but the man couldn't concentrate. He would make a simple response and then lose his train of thought. Owen looked to him for an explanation, but he had none. This was not the man he knew.

He was relieved when Meg and Lilibet entered the parlor. Her hair was combed and curled. A short tendril fell near her temple. Why did he notice every little detail about her? She had spent the week in her cabin for female problems, but he wondered if the excuse had been convenient to avoid him.

He had wanted to apologize for his bad behavior. He had told her kissing her had been a mistake, but only because it had fueled feelings inside him that would only complicate the situation. He had missed her horribly and wanted to take her in his arms and whisper the words that couldn't be spoken.

He had expected Eliot to be overjoyed at meeting his wonderful bride-to-be. Instead, he barely acknowledged her.

Meg smiled at Eliot, ignoring his bad manners. "I'm so happy to finally arrive. Your parents praised your many accomplishments."

He looked startled. "You spoke to my parents?"

"Yes. Your father gave me this ring to seal the betrothal." She extended her hand and displayed the ruby ring.

"It's beautiful."

Banner waited for him to compliment Meg, but none came. Was the man blind? He clenched his fists to keep from punching some sense into his friend.

"We are placed in an awkward situation, but I'm sure we will make the most of it and find happiness in the end." Meg's voice was soothing but determined.

Her enthusiastic declaration surprised him, but he saw a glance between Owen and her that mimicked their odd behavior in the carriage. Had he threatened her now that she was no longer under his protection? He would have to warn Eliot. Better yet, he would have one of his men watch Owen.

A maid brought in a serving tray with a porcelain teapot and delicate matching cups and saucers. Gingerbread cakes were arranged on a plate.

"Do you have any coffee?" Meg asked the maid.

"Yes, Lady Meg."

"The captain prefers coffee." She turned to Eliot. "What do you prefer to drink, Eliot?"

He looked up, a confused expression on his face. "Tea?"

"Why don't we all have tea?" Banner said.

She looked at him, her eyes wide. Was she seeking an explanation for Eliot's strange behavior? He had none. He shrugged.

Meg served the tea, and everyone settled into the conversation about the weather, voyage, and décor. No one broached the subject on everyone's mind until Owen spoke.

"As I have told Lady Meg, I wish to return to England on the *Manchester*. It sails in seven days. I will need proof of the wedding before I leave."

Eliot looked surprised. "I don't know if we can arrange a wedding so soon."

"You don't know your bride as well as I do," Owen said. "Lady Meg can accomplish anything she sets her mind to, and she is eager to wed."

"Owen has more confidence in me than I warrant, but I will try to meet his deadline," Meg said. "We wouldn't want anyone to suffer because of my lack of trying."

She had said the words pleasantly enough, but the look she gave Owen conveyed the hostility she felt for the man. Why was Owen adamant to see her wed? Was he after the family fortune as Meg had suspected? He had dismissed her intrigues as a frantic woman hoping to escape an unwanted marriage, but Owen clearly had ambitions. Ones that required wealth. Was Micah guarding his future inheritance?

Eliot stared at Meg. "I shall leave the planning in your hands."

"I am honored you would allow me to make the decisions," Meg said. "My father never considered my opinions. You are a rare man indeed. I do believe we will get along well, Eliot."

Eliot's eyebrows shot up at the compliment. "Of course," he stammered.

"Is there a church you prefer for the service?"

"The Community Church is the one I attended."

"But Eliot…" Banner glanced at Meg and turned back to Eliot, who had reddened.

"I'll visit those nearby and see what will suit my needs," Meg said.

Banner prayed she would choose one of the other

churches. She couldn't choose the Community Church. Cathy's estranged father, Thomas Goodheart, was the pastor.

"I have a dress, but I'll need to purchase some items in town." She turned to Owen. "Will you be paying for them?"

Owen coughed. "I was under the impression your bridegroom would pay for any expenses."

Everyone looked at Eliot.

"Your father sent money for the wedding." Banner removed a purse from the leather bag he carried. "He also sent you a letter and the documents you'll need."

Eliot stared at the items Banner placed on the table. He opened the purse and withdrew several gold and silver coins.

"I think it would be better if Lady Meg charged her expenses to your account and then you paid them," Owen said. "She might become a target of thieves if she was seen carrying coin."

Was Owen worried she'd run off with the money? He couldn't blame her. Eliot had hardly shown his best character so far. Although he could complete a sentence now.

"I'll write a letter of credit," Eliot said.

"Thank you," Meg said. "I'm exhausted from the trip. I think I'll bathe and rest until supper."

Meg and Lilibet rose, and the men stood.

"I think I'll retire as well." Owen followed them upstairs.

Banner watched as they parted at the top of the stairs. He turned to Eliot. "We need to talk."

Eliot headed for his study. Banner gathered the documents and coin bag where he had left them in the parlor and deposited them on the desk where Eliot sat, slumped in his chair.

Banner remained standing. "What's wrong with you? You forget we're arriving, you hardly say two words to Lady Meg, and then you mention the Community Church."

Eliot gripped his head in his hands. "I wasn't thinking. You don't know what it's been like without them. I can't think about anything but Cathy and Anna. I miss them so much."

"Do you think the Reverend Goodheart wants to perform the ceremony? He expected you to marry his daughter, especially after reading the banns. He's not going to want to marry you to another woman."

"That was two years ago. Even though my father refused to approve the match initially, I thought he would change his mind." Eliot groaned like a man in despair. "But every letter was more adamant about disowning me if I went through with the marriage." He sniffed an embroidered handkerchief and ran his fingers over the initials sewn in the corner. "What could he have against a woman like Cathy? She's the daughter of a man of God. How could he think so ill of her to refuse my one request to make her my wife?"

"What did he write?" Banner pointed to the letter on top of the betrothal agreement and special license for the marriage.

Eliot picked up the letter and examined the seal. He didn't seem to detect any alteration to the wax before breaking it from the paper and unfolding the missive.

"Should I leave?"

"No, stay." Eliot read the letter Meg had already seen. "It's all praises and well-wishes for my upcoming nuptials. He believes Lady Meg is the ideal wife for me and will elevate my station in English society."

Banner agreed as he took a seat and tried to relax. "Her family has important connections."

Eliot let the letter drop to his desktop. "I'm a coward. I love my father and mother too much to go against their wishes. He's given me everything, and I cannot be ungrateful."

"You're a good son."

Eliot searched his face. "But?"

"Obligations such as yours and my brother's make me glad not to be firstborn," Banner said.

"All my life I've been told privilege comes with great responsibility."

Banner sympathized with the promise of wealth and power. "It's difficult to give up the privilege."

"I would have nothing to offer Cathy if I went against my father's wishes." Eliot looked up from staring at the letter discarded on his desktop. "You spent time with her. What do you think of Lady Meg?"

"I believe she would make an ideal wife." *For me.*

"Is she a practical woman?"

Banner was brutally honest. "Yes, but she doesn't like to abide within the constraints of rules."

His eyebrows rose on his forehead, and his eyes widened. "Do you think she would accept sharing my bed with a mistress?"

Absolutely not. "Some women do, but I don't think she is one of them."

"It doesn't matter." Eliot groaned. "Cathy would not. I kept delaying her departure because she said it would be better to cut all ties. She's shamed her family enough by loving me outside the boundaries of marriage, but I intend to provide for her and Anna."

"Lord Dudlee seems to believe Cathy is after your title and wealth. What did you tell him about her?"

He looked shocked by his words. "Nothing but praises. I don't know what he bases his opinion on. He's never met her, and I'm the only one who's written about her."

If Meg was right, Greg Stemple had shared information. Why had he painted Cathy in a negative light to Lord Dudlee? "Do you have the letters he wrote you?"

Eliot shook his head. "I burned them. They were too vicious to keep."

"What did he say?"

"How Cathy had poisoned me with deception and manipulations. He called me a fool for falling for her lies, and she would ruin me. If I didn't heed his advice, I would suffer the consequences with no title and no source of income. I would have to return to England alone and in disgrace."

Meg had read both letters from Lord Dudlee. He had condemned her for snooping, but she had discovered something important. "What about Glen? He writes your father every time you do."

"About shipments. He came to Riverside before me and set up Father's business. He introduced me to Cathy and her family. He would never say anything disparaging about her. He has the highest regard for her."

"Then who else writes your father?"

"I don't know. He has no friends here, and the servants are from this area." He gripped his head in his hands. "What am I going to do? Cathy is gone."

"Well, I'm glad she isn't here. Having your mistress

under the same roof as your future wife would be awkward." He needed to talk to Cathy. "Where is she staying?"

Eliot reddened and stammered before replying. "I had no other place to send her. Her parents would never take her back, and you're building a house."

He jumped to his feet. "You sent her to my lodging? You had four months to relocate her."

"I only moved her out a few days ago." Eliot's voice rose in pitch.

"Where am I to stay?" Banner blurted out.

"You can stay here. No one in town would take her in, but she wrote her aunt in Philadelphia. She may not need your rooms for long."

He could sleep on his ship, but he wanted to keep an eye on Owen. "I'll accept your offer."

"Why is that man in such a hurry to return to England? I was hoping after time Lady Meg would change her mind and call the wedding off."

"Her father has commanded she marry you, and Owen is here to make sure she obeys." Banner thought of the scars on her back. "She has no choice."

Eliot's shoulders sagged. "And I cannot break the agreement."

"Why not? Do you think Lord Dudlee is going to disown his only heir because you marry the woman you love?"

"My father does not threaten without consequences." Eliot shuddered. "It's how he became rich, and his ambitions have grown since inheriting his title."

"He thinks you're making a mistake." The portrait in his office was of a boy. "Don't you want to fight for the woman you love?"

"What do you know of love? No woman has ever captured your heart."

Until Meg, but he had no right to claim her. She was promised to Eliot and appeared determined to go through with the wedding.

Eliot sobbed.

Banner didn't know how to comfort him. "I've never seen you so distraught." He poured him a drink from the sideboard.

"I keep thinking of sweet Cathy. She left without any hysterics. So brave." He wiped his face. "I lost the woman I love. I lost my daughter. Poor Anna couldn't find her doll."

He placed the glass on his desk. "You can buy her another doll."

"She didn't want another doll. She cried for her baby." Eliot groaned. "She's walking and talking now. Simple words, but she's so precious."

He pushed the drink closer. "Get ahold of yourself, Eliot."

He downed the drink. "Have you no heart? What will she do without my protection? While Cathy lived here, she had servants and no one was allowed to treat her unkindly. Now she's alone."

"I'll need some of my belongings. I'll visit Cathy after I check on the progress of unloading my cargo and emphasize the reasons you have to marry Lady Meg."

A board creaked above them.

Banner studied the ceiling. "Which room is Lady Meg in?"

"I don't know. Does it matter?"

Someone was above them. Meg probably had her

ear pressed to the floor and had overheard everything they said. She was incorrigible, but he was learning to accept her shortcomings. Or were they admirable traits?

Chapter Nineteen

Meg felt a hand on her shoulder shaking her awake. She had tossed and turned, struggling to sleep without the gentle rocking the ship had provided. She groaned as she rolled over. "What?"

"You told me to wake you early so you could explore," Lilibet reminded her.

She stretched and stared at her surroundings. "Where are we?"

"In your future home if you don't do something."

She was in Eliot's home. He was in love with Cathy Goodheart but couldn't marry her because someone had turned his father against her. She had a pretty good idea Glen was the guilty culprit, but why would he spread lies about her? She needed to find out more information and rubbed the sleep from her eyes.

She had spent the night dreaming of Banner. Was it adultery to imagine another man performing acts reserved for a husband? Only after she was married. Which was why she needed to find a way out of the wedding. But Owen's threats loomed. Without a ceremony, Lilibet would be in danger.

She kicked off the covers and crossed the room. They had unpacked only a portion of their belongings. Hopefully, they would not be staying. She was no longer on a ship or traveling and needed to dress like a titled lady. She had asked the maid to iron two of her mother's dresses and chose a linen gown of dark brown with a yellow pattern. She remembered to add the pannier side pockets to give her gown width. "Where should we begin exploring?"

Lilibet looked confused. "What are we looking for?"

"Answers."

Lilibet shrugged. "I don't have any questions."

"I do." They ignored Eliot's room and opened the door to the one next to it assigned to his future wife. The room had a honeysuckle scent lingering in the air. Wilted spring flowers remained in a vase. The dressing table was clear of items, but dust outlined where a mirror and several bottles had been placed.

"Eliot told Banner last night that Cathy left only a few days before we arrived. She's living in Banner's rooms above the tailor's shop."

"How do you feel about that?" Lilibet asked.

"He's not going to live with her," she defended. "He's going to stay here. Besides, he's not in love with Cathy Goodheart. Eliot is."

Lilibet frowned. "Shouldn't that bother you?"

"I'm not in love with Eliot." And she doubted she could ever fall in love with him. She preferred a man who took charge, not someone who wilted in the face of adversity. He couldn't even defy his father for the woman he loved.

"But you're going to marry him in six days."

She opened the drawers. "That's why we're searching the house."

"I still don't understand what we're looking for."

"Anything to help our situation."

Lilibet stood frozen in place. "Our situation?"

In the past she would have spared Lilibet any

worrisome details, but she needed to warn her of the danger. "Remember when Owen talked to me on the ship?"

"Yes. I couldn't hear anything he said, but you looked worried when you came out on the deck."

Meg hesitated.

"Don't protect me. I'm not a child." Lilibet met her gaze. "I'm nineteen and old enough to know the truth."

She took her hand. "If I don't go through with the wedding, Owen threatened to take you back to London where he will deposit you at a notorious brothel."

Lilibet paled. "I could jump overboard after the ship sails and swim toward shore."

"You swim like a rock." She pulled her close and hugged her trembling body. "I'm not going to sacrifice you for my happiness. If I can't think of a way out of this marriage, I'll go through with it."

A tear slid down Lilibet's cheek. "Eliot doesn't seem so awful."

"Two months ago I would have agreed."

"Is it the captain?" Lilibet whispered.

"He won't marry me. He thinks it was a mistake to kiss me."

Lilibet pulled away and stared into her eyes. "He kissed you?"

"I may have kissed him." She shrugged. "He said it was a mistake. He'd rather kiss Victoria."

Lilibet's mouth dropped. "Did he say that?"

"No, but you saw them." Meg sniffled to keep the threatening tears at bay.

Lilibet offered her a handkerchief. "Why don't you tell me your plan?"

She wiped her tears. "When I have one."

Lilibet mirrored her fears and desperation. "You'll figure out something. You always do. Didn't you hear anything useful last night?"

"I uncovered a few clues. Eliot mentioned he attended the Community Church. Banner was upset because it's the Reverend Goodheart's church and first on my list to visit."

"Today?"

"It's Sunday, and the reverend will be busy. I'll send a note to meet with him tomorrow."

"What can I do to help?"

"Most of the servants will have the day off, but some will be preparing meals. You could visit the kitchen and find out what they know about Cathy Goodheart."

"You think they'll share secrets?"

"Eliot kept his mistress under this roof up until a few days ago. I want to know Cathy's character. Find out if they liked her. Find out if she was only wanting to marry Eliot for his money. And inquire about Glen Stemple. I need to find out more about him."

"I'll offer to bake bread and ask for recipes to add to my collection," Lilibet said. "The kitchen is always the best place for gossip."

Meg looked around. "We've searched everything but the bed." She lifted the grass-filled mattress, and beneath the ropes was a trundle bed. She pulled it out. The covers had been tossed in place but not tucked. "They did leave recently."

"Who slept here?"

"No one mentioned a child back in London, but Eliot talked about his daughter, Anna. You would think Lord Dudlee would be happy to have a granddaughter."

"Not an illegitimate one," Lilibet said. "You saw

197

how Lady Dudlee treated me."

"That's the same woman who thinks naked statues demonstrate her good taste." She pushed the trundle back, but it wouldn't go all the way. She went to the other side and peered under the bed. "Look what I found."

She showed Lilibet a rag doll with hair of yarn and embroidered brown eyes and a red mouth. The gown was pink-and-white cotton. "Eliot said Anna lost her doll and cried for it."

"What are you going to do with it?"

She studied the doll. She needed to find out more about Cathy. "Return it."

Lilibet frowned. "You mean you want a servant to return it."

"No. I want to meet Cathy, and she won't be able to refuse me if I'm returning her daughter's doll."

"Do you think meeting the mistress of your future husband is a good idea?"

She needed a plan and quickly. "Cathy may be the key to our situation. I'll visit the Reverend Goodheart first. His behavior will give me a better idea of how he feels about his daughter."

"Owen will insist he accompany us," Lilibet warned.

"I know, but as long as I'm enthusiastic about the wedding, he won't stay too close. I hope."

They headed for the door. "Someone is coming," Lilibet warned.

Meg shoved aside her gown and slid the doll through an opening in her petticoat and into the top of the pannier. She pulled her gown forward and looked up as Eliot entered.

"What are you doing in here?"

"Isn't this to be my room?" Meg hoped her voice sounded nonchalant.

Eliot's mouth was set in a grim line. "After we are married."

"As this will be my future bedroom, I'm deciding whether to replace the rugs, draperies, and other items. I'll be looking at the other rooms and making a list of changes. I hope you don't object?"

Eliot looked around and sighed. "Do as you wish." He turned and left the room.

"Do as you wish?" Lilibet repeated. "What's wrong with the man?"

"He's in mourning for Cathy and Anna."

"They're not dead."

"They are to him." Meg was mourning Banner in a similar way. "He said Cathy wouldn't be his mistress after he married. She loves him too much to share him."

"Then he'll be faithful to you."

"He doesn't love me." Meg waved toward the adjoining room that belonged to Eliot. "I don't want a man to be physically faithful when his heart belongs to another."

"He could develop tender feelings for you."

"Love isn't something you can control. You see a man crossing a room, your eyes lock, and you miss a dance step. His voice rumbles across your heart and awakens every sense in your body. He nearly dies in a storm, and you thank God for sparing him. You rise every morning in anticipation of seeing his face and dream of him every night."

"Micah warned you not to fall in love with the captain."

Meg sniffled back tears before they fell. "I didn't

plan it. But my feelings are unimportant. He doesn't love me."

"Do people stop loving each other?"

"Mother did. But sometimes I wondered if she loved Father in the deepest part of her heart but refused to show it. I doubt I could be that strong and deny my true feelings."

They hurried across the hall to their room. Meg removed the doll, wrapped it in cloth, and placed it in her mother's trunk. "Come here, Lili."

She knelt beside her.

"Push here." A secret compartment opened. Inside were a few pieces of jewelry.

"I remember more in your mother's jewelry chest."

"She sold most of it to help others, but if something happens and you need to escape, I want you to take what's left and run away."

"But it belongs to you."

"And it's mine to share." She closed the compartment and locked the trunk. Meg went to the desk and removed a piece of paper. "I'll write a note to the Reverend Goodheart and ask for a meeting tomorrow."

"Are you telling Owen?"

"Yes, but I'll ask for a morning appointment. He hates to rise before noon. He won't be as observant if he's tired."

****

Like Meg had predicted, Owen grumbled the following morning as he took the seat opposite them in the carriage. "I don't see why your future husband can't go with you."

"He's busy. Besides, aren't you supposed to keep me from running away?"

He narrowed his gaze. "You don't like Eliot?"

"On the contrary, he will make the perfect husband." Meg waved her hand and sighed. "He allows me unlimited funds to spend on frivolities. He never questions my decisions. And he is most amiable. Why wouldn't I marry him?"

"Silly girls like you want to marry for love."

"My mother did that, and look what happened to her."

He pulled his hat down low on his brow and sneered. "I see your point. What about the captain? You chased after him aboard his ship."

She had flirted, but chased seemed a bit strong. How much did he know about their relationship? "The captain is a man women admire, but he doesn't marry them. He loves the sea." She worried she spoke the truth.

The carriage stopped in front of the Community Church, which was located two streets south of Main Street. Owen waited for them to step down as the driver assisted them. Meg had always been grateful she didn't have to touch the unpleasant man, but she realized he never offered to help.

The Reverend Thomas Goodheart and his wife stood on the stone steps to the church.

"Careful, Owen," Meg warned. "You may burst into flames for your sins when we enter."

"You need to learn to curb your caustic sense of humor. Some men do not find women like you funny."

The reverend greeted them, and introductions were exchanged. They followed him inside the foyer of the church and through an arched doorway to the sanctuary. Box pews lined the main aisle with walkways near the windows. A raised pulpit towered over the seats. He placed his hand on an oak table in the center of the dais. "This is where I conduct a wedding ceremony."

"The nuptials will take place May 28," Owen said.

"That won't give us enough time to post the banns," Thomas said. "You'll need a special license with such short notice."

"Lord Whittington obtained one in England, and Captain Youngblood delivered the documents to Mr. Richmond upon his arrival," Owen said. "I'm sailing this coming Saturday at one on the *Manchester*, and I'll need proof of the marriage before then."

"If the ceremony is in the morning, I can file the paperwork at the courthouse and obtain a copy with an official stamp."

"As long as it's ready before the ship leaves port," Owen said.

"Have you visited the other churches in town?" He addressed his question to Owen, but Meg answered.

"I have them on my schedule." Meg needed to find out more about the Goodhearts. "I'd like to walk the distance from the altar to the foyer."

"What do you need to do that for?" Owen turned to the reverend. "Women complicate everything."

"It's my wedding. You've rushed me enough." Meg counted the steps as she paced off the distance to the foyer of the church. "I also want to review the sermon and music as well as look at the room I'll be dressing in."

When Owen snorted, she asked, "How else will I make the best decision?"

"The anteroom next to the foyer is small but will allow you to prepare." Mrs. Goodheart led the way to a room off the entryway. Hooks lined the wall for coats, and shelves were built for storing clothing during the winter months. A table and chairs were in the center of the room.

Meg tried a door. "It's locked."

"That's a storage room," the reverend said. "I'm the only one with a key."

"I think this room will do." She took a seat at the table, and the others joined her. "I've chosen the music." She handed Mrs. Goodheart a list.

"I'm familiar with all of these hymns."

Owen removed a cheroot from a silver container.

"Go outside to smoke," Meg said. "I hate the smell of those nasty cigars."

He headed for the door. "I'll be waiting outside. Don't be long."

"Is Mr. O'Leary a relative?" the reverend asked after they were alone.

"He's my father's steward." Did others mistake him for a gentleman because of his fine clothes and arrogance?

"He seems concerned about the wedding being conducted quickly." The Reverend Goodheart lowered his gaze to her waist in an unspoken question.

Lilibet giggled.

Meg grasped the implication. "No, I'm not in a family way." She smoothed her skirt. "As you heard him say, Mr. O'Leary is in a hurry to leave and would like the marriage to be official before he sails. But what makes the marriage legal?"

"Once the marriage license is signed and registered at the courthouse, the marriage cannot be undone," the reverend said. "Are you worried someone may stop the wedding?"

"No, but the sooner Mr. O'Leary has his proof, the

sooner he'll leave Riverside." A plan was beginning to form in her mind. "When is the license signed during the ceremony?"

"I usually preach on the sanctity of marriage before a wedding, the congregation sings a hymn or two, and then the couple signs the license, church registry, and say their vows at the end. Finally, I announce the couple and present them to the congregation."

Meg mentally listed the series of events. "Can you have the license signed earlier?"

He frowned but nodded. "I can rearrange the ceremony to suit your needs."

Meg checked the latch by locking the door to the anteroom and then led the way into the foyer. "I think your church will do."

"Does Mr. Richmond know you plan to be married here?" he asked.

"He recommended your church." She ignored their looks of surprise. Did they think Eliot was throwing his illicit affair with their daughter in their faces?

"I think you should consider another church." He turned and headed up the aisle.

Mrs. Goodheart stayed with them. "I don't know if I should tell you this, but there is a reason the Reverend Goodheart objects to marrying you in this church."

"Because of Cathy and Eliot?" Meg asked.

Mrs. Goodheart placed her hand over her heart. "You know?"

"Yes. I overheard Eliot talking about Cathy and Anna." Meg kept her voice steady and nonjudgmental.

"I hope you understand." Mrs. Goodheart looked back toward the sanctuary. "He won't have anything to do with her."

"What about you?"

"I'm a woman. I know why she made her decision to…"

Meg needed their cooperation for the plan she was hatching. "She loves Eliot, and he loves her."

"It doesn't matter," Mrs. Goodheart said. "She's had a child out of wedlock, and the Reverend Goodheart had no choice but to disown her. I understand Eliot's parents will do the same to him if he refuses to marry you. I don't believe he will go against their wishes."

"Eliot won't defy his parents." Meg studied Mrs. Goodheart. "Are you a gossiping woman?"

"Oh no. And the women of this town know not to repeat anything about Cathy. I love my daughter and won't tolerate unkind words about her in my presence."

"I'm working on a plan where everyone can be happy." Meg took her hands and squeezed them. "I need you to keep the church available for Saturday. I'll be in touch once I can share the details."

Outside, Owen was smoking near their carriage. He threw his cigar to the ground. "I was about to fetch you."

"Niceties must be observed." Meg climbed inside and gave orders to the driver. "You can take us to the milliners."

The main thoroughfare through town was crowded with wagons, carriages, and pedestrians, and the driver slowed their carriage. Banner's ship wasn't the only one in port, and shoppers were eager to be first to view the newly arrived merchandise.

Owen looked around. "How long are you going to be?"

"As long as I need." Meg didn't hide her irritation. "I have a long list of tasks to accomplish in the days remaining before the wedding."

"Look there!" Owen pointed to the alley where they had come to a halt. "Isn't that the captain?"

Banner was knocking on the door to his second-floor lodging. A petite woman with blonde hair opened the door and signaled for him to enter.

Owen laughed as he studied Meg. "It must be true what they say about sailors. They have a mistress in every port or, in the captain's case, mistresses."

"Which is why I'm marrying Eliot," Meg said in a steady, barely controlled voice.

His smile turned sour, and he urged the driver forward.

Banner had told Eliot he would visit his rooms, so why was she worried? She knew Cathy Goodheart wasn't Banner's mistress. She wasn't as confident about Victoria.

Chapter Twenty

Banner had spent Monday morning meeting with buyers for his cargo and had calculated a nice profit when everything was sold. In the past he would have been pleased by his expanding wealth, but who would he share his good fortune with? He tried not to think of Meg. Why pine for someone he could never have?

He had given orders for the portion belonging to the Richmond family to be moved to their warehouses, and reviewed a copy of the manifest he would deliver with the letter from Lord Dudlee once Glen inspected the cargo. Something Meg had said gnawed at the back of his mind. Could Glen alter the manifest he gave Eliot to keep some of the shipment for himself? The only way to determine any discrepancies was to compare his copy with the one Eliot possessed. But he would be accusing Glen of a serious crime.

He was so deep in thought he almost missed the alley along the tailor's shop. He needed to retrieve some of his belongings from his lodging while temporarily living under Eliot's roof. He would need to move to his ship after the wedding. How could he sleep under the same roof, knowing his friend was bedding the woman he loved?

He climbed the steps to the second floor. Although he possessed a key to his own rooms, he knocked. Cathy opened the door and ushered him inside.

She was a pretty woman with golden curls and big blue eyes. Anna poked her head out from behind Cathy's skirt, a miniature of her mother except for Eliot's brown eyes. What man wouldn't want this child to be his granddaughter? Lord Dudlee was a fool.

"I'm sorry to take over your rooms, Captain Youngblood. I had nowhere else to go."

He shook himself free of his haunting thoughts. "I thought you reconciled with your mother."

"Yes, but she won't go against the Reverend Goodheart. He'd have an empty church if he didn't shun his sinful daughter." Cathy sniffled and pulled a handkerchief from her apron pocket to wipe away her tears.

"I'm sorry."

"It wasn't so bad when I lived with Eliot. He shielded me from the gossip of others, but now I'm on my own."

"No one visits you?"

"When I go to the market or run errands, a few people greet me. Glen Stemple helped me with some packages yesterday. He's remained a faithful acquaintance through all of this."

He regretted not reading the letters Meg had opened. Had she imagined a threat from Glen in order to avoid the marriage, or had the clerk poisoned Lord Dudlee's opinion of the woman before him? His hatred toward a woman as sweet and gentle as Cathy was unfathomable. "How long have you known Glen?"

She took a seat on the settee. "We met when he first arrived from England about six years ago. He attended Father's church. I was sixteen and impressed by his education and fine manners."

"Then he courted you?"

"Father wouldn't allow it until I was older. Then I had several callers, but Glen was the most steadfast."

He took a seat opposite her, and Anna patted his knee. He pulled her up onto his lap.

Cathy leaned toward them. "You don't have to hold her."

"She's all right." He pulled her against his chest and offered his watch for her to examine.

"She misses her father." She shook herself and dabbed at swollen eyes. "Glen introduced me to Eliot. He had only been in town a few weeks and was attending a spring dance. Eliot asked me to dance with him three times. Then he attended church and accepted an invitation to dinner from my parents. He never missed a service until…"

"How did Glen feel when your affections turned to Eliot?"

"He said nothing." She frowned. "My feelings for Glen were strictly friendship. Eliot was love. We were going to be married—"

"Until his father forbade it."

"Eliot was certain he would change his mind, but every time a letter arrived, Eliot would lock himself in his study and burn them."

"Then you never read any of the letters? You don't know what was written in them?"

"No." Her hands shook. "Eliot would be so despondent after reading one I didn't dare question him. Only when there was no hope did he tell me his father would disown him and he had signed the betrothal agreement. We prayed for a miracle, but when Lady Meg's arrival was imminent, he ordered the carriage to bring Anna and me here. He couldn't say good-bye, but I heard him sobbing behind the door of his study."

Her description matched the one of Eliot in his present condition. "You said Glen helped you with some packages. Was that the only time you've encountered him?"

Cathy frowned. "I've seen him three times since I've been living here. It's always in public. Either the market or on the street. Why do you ask?"

"I meant no insult. Please indulge my curiosity." He never bothered with romantic entanglements, but three chance encounters in such a short amount of time seemed high. Did Glen feel the same way as Cathy, that they were merely friends, or did he harbor stronger feelings? What if Meg was onto something? If Glen was in love with Cathy, he would have resented Eliot taking his place. But would he sabotage the relationship to the point of making Cathy an outcast and take advantage of a vulnerable woman? He didn't know the man well enough to determine if he was a threat.

He needed to finish his business. "I came to retrieve a trunk. I'm staying with Eliot until the…" He didn't need to remind Cathy of the wedding.

She began weeping. "I'm sorry to put you out." She dried her tears. "I've written my aunt in Philadelphia. She may allow me to live with her. She's elderly and needs a companion."

"You can stay here as long as you like. I have my ship, and I'll be working on my house this summer."

She forced a tentative smile. "I remember you sharing your ideas with Eliot." She paused, a sadness briefly marring her gentle features. "Have you finished your plans for the house?"

"I thought so, but Lady Meg pointed out the kitchen was too small and I should add more bedrooms. She's used to giving commands."

"That must be difficult for a captain."

"She's impossible." He looked up to see Cathy staring, a puzzled expression on her face.

"What is she like?"

She couldn't be talking about Meg. "Who?"

"The woman Eliot is going to marry. Is Lady Meg pretty?"

"She's beautiful." He spoke without thinking.

Cathy gasped, and a sob escaped her throat.

"Not as pretty as you, though." He would have to guard his opinion of Meg. What could he tell Cathy that would reassure her Meg was no threat? "Eliot barely acknowledges her. He misses you."

"Do you like Lady Meg?"

"She is the most headstrong and frustrating woman I have ever met." He bounced Anna on his knee. "She doesn't follow any of the normal rules of behavior in society. She possesses an unlimited level of curiosity and has no shame when it comes to personal matters."

Cathy stared at him with her brows knit together. A smile spread across her lips. "You're in love with her."

"Lady Meg?" His voice rose an octave, and Anna whimpered. He reassured the little girl she was safe. "I would be an idiot to fall in love with a woman who is planning to marry someone else."

Cathy sighed. "We're all idiots in love."

"I'll get over it." The words sounded hollow to his ears.

"Is she in love with you?"

"She's going forward with plans to marry Eliot."

A sadness marred her features. "Women have fewer choices than men."

"This woman doesn't worry about choices. If she wants something, she goes after it." She had kissed him, but he had rejected her. Why had he denied his true feelings for honor? He recalled the pain on her face and needed to change the topic. "Do you have any messages for Eliot?"

She rose and moved to a desk. "I wrote a letter. Will you deliver it?"

"Of course."

She handed him a folded and sealed paper and took Anna in her arms. "I should cut all ties with him. I need to leave town so I can forget him."

"What about Anna?" He patted her on the head. "Do you think Eliot is going to forget her?"

Cathy burst into tears. "Why does Lord Dudlee hate me so much?"

"That is a mystery." He put the letter in his coat pocket. If anyone could find out, it was Meg. She was tenacious when she wanted an answer. Should he help her? He went into the bedroom, retrieved his trunk, and bade farewell.

Banner hailed a carriage and traveled to Eliot's home. He was given the room across from Owen. He stopped a maid in the hallway. "Which room is Lady Meg and Lilibet staying in?"

"They're in the front room." The maid pointed. "She said she didn't like the morning sun."

Morning sun? The woman loved sunshine any time of the day. He walked to her door, turned, and stepped off the distance to the staircase. When he reached the foyer, he stepped off the distance to the study and looked at the ceiling. "I thought I heard creaking upstairs, you crafty spy."

The butler informed him the women were out with Owen and Eliot had gone for a ride. He hoped the mare knew her way home. In Eliot's present state of mind, he would forget how to return.

Banner wandered about the house. Cathy had left her delicate touch on everything. She preferred soft colors and lighter woods, which made each room larger and brighter in appearance. Banner had planned darker wood for paneling and trim in his home. He wondered what Meg would prefer. He shook himself. He couldn't ask her to decorate his house.

Eliot was the first to return and headed for his study, his clothes dusty from his ride. He poured a drink.

"None for me." Banner delivered Cathy's letter.

Eliot tore it open. A smile appeared on his face and then disappeared as he read the words. "This is her final message to me. She has accepted our fates and wishes me the best."

Banner excused himself as Eliot descended into depression. He closed the study door and turned to be greeted by Meg, Lilibet, and Owen as they entered the house. The ladies had packages in their hands and handed them to the maid.

"Is dinner ready?" Meg asked.

"Whenever you want it served, Lady Meg."

"As soon as our guest arrives."

She couldn't mean him. What other guest had she invited? Banner looked toward the door when someone knocked. The butler took Glen Stemple's hat.

"Welcome, Mr. Stemple." Meg extended her hand. "I'm so happy you could join us."

"Thank you for the invitation."

Meg had invited Glen. The woman was as bold and brazen as Black Sam Bellamy. Dinner could prove interesting.

The maid announced that dinner was ready.

"Please be seated at the table." Meg looked around. "Is Eliot in his study?"

"I'll get him," Banner volunteered.

Eliot sat at the head of the table with Owen to his right and Lilibet to his left. Meg sat at the opposite end with Banner and Glen.

Large bowls were placed in front of each person, and loaves of bread were sliced on a wooden board with containers of butter and honey at each end of the table.

Meg lifted a spoonful. "I'm not sure what the cook has prepared, but it smells delicious."

"Most meals in the colonies are stews." Banner took a spoonful. "This contains venison, onions, carrots, and peas. The Southern colonies ship food north until our gardens start producing. Then you'll have a variety of vegetables and fruits to choose from, and the woods provide wild meat of every kind along with the usual pork, beef, and mutton."

Meg took a tentative spoonful. "It's good."

He offered her a slice of bread. "It sops up the juices."

"It's delicious," Lilibet said. "I'll need to ask for the recipe."

"You'll have your book filled in no time." Meg turned her attention to the man on her left. "What do you enjoy eating, Mr. Stemple?"

"Anything I do not have to prepare myself." Glen had a trilling laugh as if he were going up and down the musical scale. "I'm grateful for your hospitality."

"Eliot said you dined with him weekly," Meg said. "We welcome any loyal employee of the Richmond family."

Loyal? Men thought beating a man would elicit a confession, but a pretty woman with a winning smile loosened tongues quicker than any torture. Banner watched an expert at work.

"Eliot said you carry out his business decisions," Meg continued.

"I'm but a humble clerk. I give Mr. Richmond weekly updates, but now that he is to be married, I may not call as often. I don't want to impose." He took another slice of bread and added honey to it.

"Don't change your habits for me," Meg said. "I'm sure your visits are important. Although I don't have an interest in any merchandise a woman can't wear and will probably have to excuse myself when you talk business."

To eavesdrop. Banner studied her angelic face. If Connecticut ever needed a spy, Meg would be a capable one.

Banner turned his attention to Glen. "I had my men unload Lord Dudlee's cargo and transport it to his warehouse. Your man said you were out when I delivered the manifest."

"I had some personal business," Glen said.

"I'm sure you'll find everything in order, but let me know if there are any discrepancies."

"Of course." Glen turned to Eliot. "And I will record the sales to the merchants who have been waiting to purchase the goods."

Eliot looked up from staring at his full bowl, his face a blank. "What?"

"Eat, Eliot," Banner reminded him.

Glen turned to Meg. "I heard the wedding is set for Saturday. Is that true?"

"I need to return to England as soon as possible," Owen interrupted.

"How are your wedding plans progressing?" Banner remarked to Meg.

"We visited the churches and a few shops today."

"We saw you entering a young woman's lodging while on Main Street, Captain," Owen said.

Banner scowled. "If I was visiting a woman, I would be careful not to slander her name."

"Since I did not know the woman, I cannot ruin her reputation," Owen said.

"I believe the residence belongs to the captain." Meg turned to Banner. "You did say you lived above the tailor's shop."

"You visited Cathy?"

Banner had expected the question from Eliot, but Glen was the one concerned.

"She is living at my residence," Banner said in a controlled voice.

"That is improper," Glen said.

"Only if I was living with her, which I am not. I'll be staying here, for now." Banner turned to face Meg. "You don't have any objections, do you?"

"Why would I? You're Eliot's friend, and he invited you. Will you be standing by him at the wedding?"

"Yes. I promised his father I would see that Eliot fulfils his oath." He reached into his pocket. "I almost forgot. I have a letter from Lord Dudlee." He handed it to Glen.

"Most likely instructions for what to buy and ship in

the next trip." He placed the letter in his coat pocket.

"You have a great deal of control, Mr. Stemple," Meg said. "I find I cannot wait to read any correspondence that crosses my path."

"Indeed," Banner said under his breath.

"I have a curiosity for all things." She smiled at Glen. "Do you handle all of Lord Dudlee's business?"

"Yes. I was employed by Lord Dudlee before Eliot arrived."

"It must have been difficult to relinquish your duties to Eliot."

"He only oversees my work," Glen said. "My duties have remained the same."

She tore her bread. "So you have no ambitions beyond being Eliot's clerk?"

His spoon paused in midair. "There are many opportunities for a man in this country. I may wish to marry someday and establish myself in my own business."

"Any young lady in mind?"

"No." He attempted a smile. "I'm busy taking care of the Richmonds' business interests."

She leaned forward. "I hope you consider Lilibet, then."

Lilibet choked on a spoonful of stew.

Glen reddened as he looked at Lilibet. "I'm honored."

Banner reviewed the conversation in his head while they ate dessert. Glen had talked of starting his own business and possibly marrying. Could he have meant Cathy? He was upset she was living in his rooms. He needed to do some digging.

Chapter Twenty-One

Meg needed to talk to Cathy to further her plan. She wore a simple gown of pale blue with a petticoat of dark blue. Lilibet wore a similar outfit with a soft stomacher and lacings. They both wore close-fitting caps with a ruffled edge to cover their hair.

"Did you find out anything from the servants?" Meg asked.

"Cathy was sweet and gentle, and they adored Anna. You will not be well received as a replacement," Lilibet warned.

"Then we need to do something about that."

"You're going to win the servants over?"

Meg laughed at her disbelief. "You're the one everyone loves. They keep me around because of you."

"That's not true, but you are an acquired taste." Lilibet failed to keep a straight face and laughed with her.

"I think I'm souring your sweet disposition." She tied her straw bonnet over her cap. "Are you ready to go shopping?"

Lilibet fumbled with the bow of her bonnet. "Are you planning to run off and leave me behind?"

"I would never abandon you to Owen's clutches, but I need you to keep him distracted so I can visit Cathy." She opened her trunk and removed the doll. She pulled back her skirt and hid the doll inside the side hoop.

"What if Cathy doesn't want to see you?"

"I'm hoping the doll convinces her to open the door." But would Cathy listen to her plans? And what would she do if she disagreed?

"How am I to keep Owen from following you?"

"I'm counting on him not wanting to sit in a milliner's shop, but he will want to watch the door and window. With my bonnet and cape on, he'll think you're me. With them off, he'll recognize your red hair."

Lilibet frowned as she opened the door. "Why am I always the decoy in your plans?"

"You've proven to be good at it." She gave her waist a squeeze as they walked down the hallway. "And duplicity works."

An hour later the carriage driver stopped in front of the printing office, and Owen ushered them out.

Meg looked around. "What are we doing here? The millinery is down the street."

"I want to have an announcement of your wedding in the local paper," Owen said. "You can make sure the names are spelled correctly."

She didn't like this development but saw no reason to argue against it. They crowded into the small space in front of the counter.

A clerk stepped forward. "How may I help you?"

"I'd like to put an announcement in the paper," Owen said.

He handed Owen a piece of torn paper from a large roll. "Write it out here."

Meg stared at another man in a soiled apron loading small metal rectangles stored in wooden cubbyholes. "What are you doing?"

"Setting type." The man looked up and smiled when

he saw them. "Well, hello, ladies. How may I help you?"

Lilibet blushed while Meg smiled back, aware her youth and beauty allowed her certain privileges when it came to men who were flattered by a woman's attention.

"Your work looks interesting. How do you set type?" Meg asked.

He brought over a wooden container that looked like an unfinished box. "This is a composing stick. I place the type from right to left."

Lilibet squinted. "Isn't that backward?"

"Yes, but when the type is inked and printed, it reads forward."

"What do you do when the stick is full?" Lilibet asked.

"I transfer the type to a galley." He pointed to a shallow wooden tray. "When I have a full page, it's locked into a frame and moved to the printing press. The brayer can ink an entire page. We print pamphlets, books, and newspapers."

"How often do you print a paper?" Owen asked.

"The *Riverside Review* is biweekly. It comes out on Wednesdays and Saturdays."

Owen paid the man. "I want this to appear in this Saturday's paper."

He read the announcement. "You want it to appear the day of the wedding?"

"Yes."

"We can do that." He laughed. "Let's hope the bridegroom doesn't get cold feet."

"Or the bride," Meg added.

Owen smiled in a scary self-satisfied way that made her shiver. "I'm here to make sure they don't."

She didn't have time to worry about him. She had

her own plans to put in motion. They walked along the shops, peering into windows as Owen followed. The driver of the carriage kept pace with them.

Meg paused at the tailor shop. "I wonder if I should buy something for Eliot."

"Aren't you enough?" Owen asked with a smirk.

"Handkerchiefs with his initials would be nice." Meg led the way inside. Owen examined a coat while she ordered the gift. "I'll pick it up Friday."

She glanced at the alley to the entrance of Banner's rooms. She couldn't tell if Cathy was home. Her plan would come to naught if she had gone out. They entered the milliner's shop, and two women looked up to stare at Owen.

Meg waved toward a bench where an older woman sat. "You're welcome to join us."

He snorted and looked across the street. "I'll wait in the tavern. But don't worry. I'll be watching you."

"How did you know he'd do that?" Lilibet whispered after he left.

"He's predictable. Like Father, he can't pass up an opportunity to drink, gamble, or flirt with pretty women."

They moved around the store, looking at gloves, fans, combs, and other small items displayed beneath glass cases. They passed the front windows to keep Owen satisfied they were inside. He stared at them through the window of the tavern until a serving woman diverted his attention.

A saleswoman approached them. "Is there something you are looking for?"

"Do you have any lace?" Meg asked.

"To trim a gown?"

"No, I'm getting married soon, and I need a veil."

A gasp escaped from her open mouth.

Meg satisfied her obvious curiosity. "Mr. Richmond will be paying for it."

She reddened. "Let me retrieve some samples from the back."

"Most brides don't wear veils," Lilibet whispered.

"This one will." She moved in front of the window and waited until Owen noticed her. Meg made an abrupt turn as if unwilling to be stared at. She motioned Lilibet to make an appearance.

The saleswoman brought out several lace samples. Meg quickly discarded those that were delicate and transparent. She found a design that was dense with an intricate pattern and held it up in front of Lilibet's face. "This might work."

"I can barely see through this," Lilibet complained.

"Precisely." She turned to the saleswoman. "Ma'am, is there a door to the back?"

"Do you need a necessary? There's one near the stream."

The outbuilding would make a good excuse if caught. "Will you be able to create a veil from this material? I want it to be attached to a straw bonnet that is covered with lace and dried flowers." She pointed to one on display with a large brim facing forward. "Like that one."

"But no one will be able to see your face," the woman remarked as she held the lace over her hand.

"I'm a woman of mystery," Meg said. "I need it by Friday."

"So soon?"

"Mr. Richmond will pay extra to have it done on

time."

She gathered the material. "I'll begin working on it immediately."

Meg pulled Lilibet to the back and handed over her bonnet and cloak. "Change outfits enough times to make Owen think we're both inside."

Lilibet bit her lip. "What happens if he comes inside looking for you?"

"Tell him I'm in the necessary. I won't be long." Meg grabbed a shawl and a large cloth bonnet to hide her face. "Add these items to my bill." She covered her head and draped the shawl over her shoulders. After removing the doll from her pocket, she went outside and walked along the back of the building to the corner. She kept her head down and dashed across the alley and up the steps to Banner's rooms.

A petite blonde woman answered her knock.

"Cathy Goodheart?"

She stared at Meg. "Do I know you?"

Meg showed her the doll. "I believe this belongs to your daughter. I mean no harm. May I please come in?"

She widened the doorway.

The wooden table, chairs, and bookcases were sturdy oak with a dark stain, but a few feminine touches had been added with a tablecloth and pillows in pastels that reminded her of the décor at Eliot's home. "You decorated Mr. Richmond's house."

"Yes. How did you know?"

A little girl squealed and wobbled toward her with her hands outstretched. "Babbee!"

Meg handed her the doll. "You have a beautiful daughter."

"Anna, what do you say?"

"Dank you." She hugged the doll and twisted from left to right in a joyful dance.

"I can't stay long," Meg warned. "I'm being watched."

"Watched? Why?" Cathy's voice trembled.

"His name is Owen. He was sent by my father to make sure I married Eliot."

"You're Lady Meg?" She stepped back, her hand covering her mouth. "I thought you were a servant. You shouldn't be here."

"Don't be afraid." She held out her hands. "I'm here as a friend."

Cathy sniffled. "Congratulations on your nuptials."

She reminded Meg of Lilibet, sweet and shy, and compassion filled her heart. "I don't want to marry him." She showed her the scars on her shoulder. "My father beat me so I would sign the contract."

"How awful, but I don't know how I can help you."

"But you would try." She was exactly like Lilibet.

Cathy shook her head. "Eliot won't go against his father's wishes, and Lord Dudlee hates me."

She needed to convince Cathy to trust her. "Yet you've never met Eliot's parents."

She motioned for Meg to sit at the table and sat opposite. "That's why I can't understand his hostility."

"I made a promise to Lord Dudlee to make Eliot happy."

"Then you keep that promise. If he's happy, I'll be content." Her face did not reflect her words.

"If I marry him, he'll be miserable, but I may have a plan." Meg reached across the table and touched her clasped hands. "There's a slim chance of it succeeding, but if you're willing to do what I say, it might work."

A tentative smile appeared. "What must I do?"

"First you have to know the risk. Owen wants the marriage to be official by Saturday before he sails back to England."

"I heard how quickly the wedding would take place."

"That works in our favor." Meg could feel Cathy's hands trembling beneath hers. "He won't think I have enough time to put a plan in action."

"You have a plan?"

"Stand up." She stood close. Cathy was a natural blonde, but Meg's hair had lightened to nearly the same shade. Their figures were similar, and with stays they could wear the same dress.

"I'm a few inches taller than you. If I wear flat shoes until Saturday and you wear heels down the aisle, Owen shouldn't notice the difference." She ran her idea of a decoy through her mind. "You'll be dressed as me standing at the altar."

"You want me to pretend to be you and marry Eliot?" Cathy frowned. "But everyone will recognize me."

"I purchased a thick veil. No one will be able to see your face."

"Does Eliot know?" Her voice betrayed excitement.

Meg shook her head and peered into her eyes. "You cannot tell Eliot anything."

She turned away. "He's not speaking to me."

Meg pulled her around to face her. "You don't understand. Eliot is the most miserable man right now, but if he had any hint that he was marrying you and not me, everyone would see the change in him. We must keep him in the dark and unhappy."

She pulled her arm from Meg's grasp. "But that's cruel."

Meg recalled Banner's words the first time they met. "Eliot must believe he's marrying me and keeping his promise to his parents even during the ceremony. That way they can't disown him. I'll be the guilty party and take full blame for the deception. In order for Eliot to be guiltless, he must be ignorant of the plan."

"Now I understand," Cathy said. "But who would agree to perform the ceremony, knowing it's a lie?"

Meg stared into her eyes. "I've talked with your parents. Eliot and you will sign the license at the beginning of the ceremony, and it will be sent to the courthouse to be filed. Then the marriage cannot be undone."

"But my father hates me." Cathy swiped at a tear. "As the leader of his church, he has to set an example of morality."

"Would that change if you were legally married to Eliot?"

"Is that why he agreed?" Cathy's expression changed to a tentative smile. "They would be overjoyed. It would legitimize Anna, and we could attend church."

Meg had to be honest. "Your mother is willing, and I think we can convince your father to do his part."

"He hasn't already?" She paced across the room. "How could you come here and give me hope when it could all be for nothing?"

"I needed to meet with you first to see if you were willing to carry out the plan."

Cathy grabbed her hands. "I will do anything to be Eliot's wife, but what if my father refuses?"

"I think he loves you and Anna enough for me to

persuade him." Meg gathered her shawl around her shoulders. "The hard part will be sneaking you into the church unseen."

"Mother can bring me. She has a closed carriage, and she'll have to be there early to prepare the church."

She examined her gown. "Wear something simple you can change out of quickly. I'll have the wedding clothes you'll need. But we must keep everyone else in the dark. Can you keep a secret?"

"If it means marrying the man I love, yes."

"That includes Captain Youngblood and Glen Stemple," Meg warned.

"Why?"

"They might stop our plan."

Cathy studied her. "I understand why the captain might want to stop you, but why would Mr. Stemple be concerned?"

What had Banner told her? Meg needed to focus. "How well do you know Glen Stemple?"

"He's an old friend. He introduced me to Eliot."

"And you fell in love with Eliot." Meg looked at Anna who was sitting on the floor playing with her doll. "And when did Lord Dudlee forbid the marriage?"

"Eliot proposed more than two years ago and wrote to his father for approval. He forbade the marriage immediately, but we thought he'd change his mind."

"I believe Glen wrote terrible lies about you to Eliot's father to make him think you were a fortune hunter and insincere in your feelings toward his son," Meg said. "That's why he forbade the marriage."

Her mouth dropped. "Why would Glen do that?"

"Could he be in love with you? Did he ever court you?"

"Briefly, but that was before Eliot. He can't possibly think I have feelings for him."

Meg shook her head. "I know of women who will lie to eliminate competition. Why not a man? With Eliot married to another, would you consider marrying Glen?"

"He spoke of taking care of me." She went pale. "He said I should marry a man worthy of me. I'll tell him to leave me alone."

"No," she shouted before regaining her composure. "You must go about your normal routine and act as you always have toward others. Don't say anything to anyone or hint that there is any hope of happiness, or it would ruin our plans. Do you understand how important it is that you treat Glen the way you always have?"

Cathy nodded. "I'll try."

"They can't become suspicious. No one must know we are allies."

She stared into her eyes. "You're my friend?"

"We both want the same thing. We want you to marry Eliot."

Cathy hugged her. "How will I know what to do?"

"If your parents agree to the plan, I'll send word to you through your mother."

"What if they don't agree?"

Cathy worried as much as Lilibet. "I'm the daughter of an earl. I'm used to getting what I want."

"If you can make this happen, my prayers will be answered." Cathy opened the door.

"Nothing against Eliot. He's a wonderful man, but he will only be in love with you, and I can't settle for that." She arranged the bonnet to shield her face and covered her shoulders and gown with the shawl. She hurried down the steps, across the alley, and into the back of the store.

Lilibet was frantic. "I didn't think you'd ever return."

Meg removed her disguise and exchanged it for her own cloak and bonnet. She was folding the shawl when Owen entered.

"What is taking so long?"

"I couldn't decide on this bonnet or that one." She clapped her hands. "I'll take both. I'm sure Eliot won't mind."

The shop girl boxed the head coverings and wrapped the shawl.

"I'll be back on Friday to pick up the bonnet and veil." She handed the boxes to Owen. "You can carry these."

He dropped them on the counter. "I'm not your servant. I'm not anyone's servant." His words were spoken so venomously she stepped back. Had Owen resented his station in life so much that he hated her? Was this part of the motive for forcing this marriage?

Lilibet gathered the boxes as Owen stormed out of the shop. "What's wrong with him?"

"He doesn't want to be a servant."

"His birth won't allow him to be a gentleman. He must know that."

"Knowing and accepting are extremely different," Meg said. "Do you resent being restricted by your place in society?"

"I once thought about being a lady like you, but after attending all those boring social events and listening to the vicious gossip in London, I'm happy to be a cook and your companion." She gasped and turned red. "Not that it's wrong for you."

Meg burst into laughter. "I wholeheartedly agree about London."

"I would think Owen would be content being a steward," Lilibet said. "It's a position of trust and authority most men in his situation would consider fortunate."

"Owen has loftier ambitions," Meg said. "And he's greedy. He could have taken the six hundred pounds Mr. Clifton invested, but he found out about my trust fund. That's why he's so desperate to have proof of my marriage."

Lilibet opened the shop door. "And he'll have that Saturday."

"Don't bet on it," Meg said as they joined Owen in the carriage.

Chapter Twenty-Two

Banner had spent the morning on his ship sorting through manifest statements so he could compare his to those Eliot had given him. He had expected resistance or the defense of a long-time employee, but Eliot was too depressed to question his intentions.

He'd examined a majority of the shipments, and nothing appeared to be suspicious. Had he fallen victim to female hysteria, or did Lady Meg have an overactive imagination? She loved stories of pirates and adventure. He would have to warn her to keep her fanciful ideas to herself.

His thoughts turned to a few fantasies of his own as he walked into town. One involved snatching Meg from the church and sailing off with her. Would she protest or be eternally grateful? While daydreaming, he headed for his rooms above the tailor's shop and turned down the alley before realizing his error.

The door to his rooms opened, and Cathy backed out, struggling with a wicker baby stroller.

"Hold on!" He dashed up the steps and lifted the small vehicle for transporting infants. It was empty. "Where's Anna?"

"I wait until the stroller is safely on the ground before I put her in it," Cathy said. "I have nightmares of it tumbling down the steps."

"I can imagine." He carried the stroller to the

ground.

Cathy brought out Anna and put her in the basket on wheels. "Did you come by for something?"

"No, I was walking down the street with my mind wandering and found myself standing at my old doorstep out of habit."

She studied him before speaking. "Will you watch the baby while I retrieve my basket? I'm on my way to the market."

Would she be able to shed light on the character of Glen Stemple? "May I join you?"

She blushed. "I would be honored, Captain."

As he tucked a blanket around Anna and her doll, he noticed a movement across the street. Someone backed into the shadows of the building and hastened down the alley. Was Eliot watching Cathy? The man was despondent, but would he risk meeting with her so close to his wedding day?

"I'm ready," Cathy sang out as she locked the door and descended the steps. Understanding why Eliot was in love with Cathy wasn't difficult. She was pretty in a delicate feminine way that made men practice their best manners and have a desire to protect her.

Outwardly, Meg displayed a calm demeanor, but her passionate responses to his kisses revealed an unexpected wild abandonment that threatened to overpower them. He'd hurt her by confessing their kisses were a mistake, but he couldn't risk touching her again and losing all control. She stirred fires that had only been embers before, and they could combust and destroy their lives. Acting on his feverish desires meant betraying Eliot's trust and losing the respect of others. He would never allow anyone to think of Meg as less than a lady.

"Where are you?" Cathy asked.

"What?"

"You are so deep in thought no wonder you turned up on my doorstep. Who are you thinking about?"

"Who? I'm not thinking of anyone." He needed to guard his feelings more carefully.

"Some woman has pricked your heart," Cathy said.

She was treading in dangerous waters. "My love is for the sea."

"Of course." She smiled in a way that made him suspicious. "Was it a quiet crossing?"

"We ran into a nor'easter."

"Your passengers must have been terrified." Cathy's voice was filled with fear.

"Most of them." If he hadn't ordered Issy to keep Meg below deck, she probably would have joined him at the helm. Her taking charge of undressing him after the storm was bad enough. If he hadn't been freezing, he might have…

"You're smiling, Captain. You tempt me to discover your secrets."

He frowned. "Why do women think men have mysteries to uncover?"

"Everyone has something to hide," she stammered. "You have known Lady Meg the longest. Is she a woman of her word? Do you trust her?"

Did he dare confide in her? She was too closely tied to Eliot. "Lady Meg is the most dishonest person I know, but only when she is trying to find out the truth."

Her brows came together in a frown. "I don't understand."

"Neither do I. The woman enjoys stories about pirates and reads other people's correspondence. She plots and schemes and confesses all of it without shame. But if I were in trouble, I'd want her by my side. She would make a formidable partner."

Cathy gasped as a man blocked their path. "Mr. Stemple."

Glen tipped his hat. "Cathy." He turned to Banner. "Captain." He looked toward the wagons and stalls set up in the square. "The market is busy today. Are you shopping?"

"Yes, I thought the baby would enjoy the nice weather." She looked at Anna. "The fresh air has put her to sleep."

"She's a beautiful child," Glen said. "Like her mother. I hope to have a couple of my own someday."

The compliment was intimate. Why hadn't he noticed Glen's behavior toward Cathy before?

She blushed but said nothing. Her fingers gripped the handle of her basket. "Why don't I leave you men to talk while I make my purchases?" She turned to Banner. "Would you mind watching Anna?"

"I will guard her with my life," Banner said.

"I won't be long," she promised. "I only need a few items."

Glen watched Cathy as she moved among the vendors and purchased bread and cheese. He turned to Banner. "What were you doing at Miss Goodheart's dwelling?"

The shadow had been Glen and not Eliot. "Those are my rooms."

"I don't like you visiting her."

Was Glen a threat to Cathy? "She's living under my roof and my protection. You don't need to worry about her."

Glen looked alarmed. "Did Cathy say something about me?"

Cathy never said a bad thing about anyone. She always looked on the bright side of every dilemma, hoping a problem would resolve itself. Meg lacked the same patience and went on a crusade to right a wrong or expose an enemy.

"No, but she asked me to deliver a letter to Eliot."

"I could have done that."

Would Glen have removed the wax seal on Cathy's letter? He had the opportunity to read Eliot's correspondence and counter it with his own. Had he overlooked something in reviewing the shipping records? "I've nearly sold all my cargo. How is business for the Richmond family?"

Glen's gaze was on Cathy as she made her rounds of the market, and he spoke without facing Banner. "I think they'll be pleased with the profits."

"Lord Dudlee mentioned calling Eliot back home after the wedding. Will you be able to handle the work here?"

"I don't see why not." He tossed back his head and trilled a few notes of laughter. "I handled all the tasks before he arrived."

"That's right." Cathy was buying eggs. "Too bad Lord Dudlee didn't approve of Cathy. I think they would have been happy together."

"You don't know Cathy as well as I do." Glen's voice was cold. "She wouldn't like England."

Banner watched his expression. "I'm glad to hear Cathy will remain. I may want to court her."

Glen's face turned red as he clenched his fists. "Why? A sea captain is hardly a fit husband for a woman like Cathy. You would be gone much of the time."

Banner adjusted the blanket on Anna. "I don't think Cathy will complain. I have land, and I'm building a house. Anna is such a sweet child. And Cathy has proven she can bear children. She can give me some fine strong sons."

"You shouldn't talk about Cathy that way." Glen growled the words through gritted teeth. "She's not a breeding mare."

Meg had mentioned a motive for spreading malicious gossip. If Glen was in love with Cathy, he wouldn't want Eliot to marry her. What had he written and included with his business reports to poison Lord Dudlee's mind against the marriage?

"I mean no disrespect," Banner apologized. "I plan to court Cathy properly. It's not like Eliot can object once he's married to Lady Meg."

"Cathy doesn't want you to court her." He relaxed his tense body. "You would remind her too much of Eliot."

"Do you think?"

"I'm sure of it. Besides, she'll need time to forget him." He nodded. "You should wait for Eliot to return to England. Then you would face no obstacles."

"That's a good idea." Was that his plan?

Cathy rejoined them, and they escorted her to his rooms. Glen stayed close, offering to carry the stroller.

"I have some books to retrieve." Banner took the stroller inside and closed the door before Glen could join them.

Cathy carried Anna into the bedroom.

He selected a few books from his collection and waited for her to return. "Has Mr. Stemple been bothering you?"

She looked startled. "I think he's concerned about my circumstances." She shrugged. "He's a friend."

"There's a strong lock on the door and no other way in." He had wanted to prevent any break-ins while he was away at sea.

"I don't think he would harm me."

She wouldn't think ill of anyone. "It's best if you take no chances."

Banner gathered the books and headed outside. He noted Glen talking to another man across the street. He had been waiting to see when he left.

As he walked to Eliot's house, he glanced back to see if Glen followed. He didn't see him. He deposited his books in his room and found Meg gliding down the hallway. Had she been waiting for him? "I owe you an apology."

She stared in surprise. "Men don't apologize."

Cathy would have said men *didn't* need to apologize. "I do when I'm wrong."

She claimed her bonnet from a peg in the foyer. "Let's go for a walk, and you can tell me why you're sorry."

Banner took his hat from the sideboard. "Where's Lilibet?"

"Learning how to make something called johnnycakes. She's filling the book Micah gave her with every recipe she can talk someone into sharing. I think she's determined to be a cook no matter what her mother thinks."

He looked around. "Don't you need a chaperone?"

"Owen or the man he hired is lurking about. He'll follow at a respectable distance."

This section of town had no footways, and the road was dusty, but Meg didn't complain. She had braved the two-month voyage and a nor'easter and now faced her impending wedding with valor. How could he help her?

She lifted her face to the sky. "The sun shines nearly every day here unlike London. I could enjoy living in Riverside."

"Eliot will have to return to England sometime."

"Let him."

He didn't know what to make of her remark, but her smile sent his heart racing like a ship in full sail.

She placed her arm through his. "So what are you apologizing about?"

He patted her hand. "I had an interesting encounter with Glen Stemple."

Her smile was sweet but laced with sarcasm. "The man who innocently corresponds with Lord Dudlee?"

"If you're going to be pompous, I won't apologize."

"Sorry." She bowed her head. "I will act contrite."

"Don't change for me. You thought he was writing ill of Cathy Goodheart to turn Lord Dudlee against her." He coughed. "I acted badly about you reading the letter written to him, but your suspicions may be correct."

"And how did you come to this conclusion?"

A hint of gloating coated her words, but he couldn't blame her. She had been right. "He's been watching my dwelling where Cathy is staying."

"The little weasel."

He laughed at her description. Her outspoken opinions were the reason he loved her. "He was defensive when I talked about courting Cathy."

"You're courting Cathy?"

Did a trace of worry strain her voice? "Glen bristled

more than you. But that proves he has a motive for preventing Cathy from marrying Eliot."

"He wants her for himself."

He stopped and studied her. "How do you know that?"

"I'm a woman. I was courted two years ago by a great many men. Those who were possessive didn't like losing."

Men competed for women. Not always for marriage. "He admits to courting her before Eliot came along. Now that he's cleared the path for himself, he doesn't want me invading his territory."

"What is he going to do about it?"

"He advised me to wait until you and Eliot return to England. Which may be sooner than expected if Glen writes more letters to Lord Dudlee."

"We would sail on your ship," Meg said. "He would eliminate all his competition."

"And could ask Cathy to be his wife."

Meg paused, staring into his face. "What about Anna?"

"You know about their baby?" He searched his memory. Had he mentioned the child?

"I found her doll in Cathy's old room."

"But she had a doll today in the stroller." The truth dawned on him. "You visited her?"

She shrugged and continued their walk. "Briefly."

"She didn't say anything about your visit when she spoke of you."

Meg looked surprised. "What did she say?"

He stopped walking so he could study her reaction. "She wanted to know if you were honest."

Her eyebrows arched above worried hazel eyes.

"What did you tell her?"

"I said I trusted you, but now I'm beginning to doubt my judgment." He snagged a loose curl and secured it behind her ear. "What are you up to?"

"I simply returned her child's doll. I was civil. Cathy said her family disowned her. Will Glen be able to support her and Anna?"

"He's paid a modest sum and doesn't appear to live above it." He reeled from the change in direction. The woman knew how to keep him off balance.

"My mother taught me to look at the money to find out whether someone was trustworthy. Did you look at the reports of cargo Glen claims he sold?"

"Against my better judgment I asked Eliot for his copies of the Richmond cargo he receives from Glen and compared them to my originals. I found no discrepancies."

She looked disappointed. "Why malign Cathy to the Richmonds and keep honest books? Don't a liar and a thief go hand in hand?"

"I think you need to stop accusing a man with Glen's good reputation of stealing funds." He began walking. "I'm wondering if you haven't accused Owen unfairly. You said the money for repairs was invested. Has he stolen anything from your father?"

"Not yet, but he's planning to do something. This quick marriage and my trust fund are tied together."

He wanted to dismiss her crazy notions. "Can you prove it?"

"Micah may find the proof. He's almost as determined as I am in uncovering the truth." She leaned close. "Are you sure Glen hasn't been stealing from Eliot?"

"There are too many safeguards. I have my manifest of the cargo. I give a copy of the Richmond cargo to Glen, and once he sells it, he gives the updated list with the profits to Eliot."

"Did you compare all of them?"

"I went back several years," he defended. "I will not give in to your suspicions. Glen Stemple is innocent of any wrongdoing. I have no reason to suspect him of anything devious."

He'd seen that determined look in her eyes before, and it did not bode well. He wanted to dismiss her suspicions as unfounded, but if she was right about Glen influencing Lord Dudlee's opinion of Cathy, could she be right about the cargo and money?

Chapter Twenty-Three

Meg needed the cooperation of the Goodhearts in order for her plan to succeed. But first she had to inform Eliot she had chosen the Community Church for the site of their nuptials. If she waited until Saturday to spring the location on him, he might balk. She knocked on his study door, which he kept shut most of the time.

"Come in," Eliot said in a dreary monotone.

She pitied him. The bright sunshine that had been Cathy and Anna were missing from his life. He kept the curtains drawn as if he didn't deserve warmth and light. He was bent over his desk and didn't look up until she coughed.

He looked surprised. "Lady Meg."

She sat opposite him. "I thought we should discuss the upcoming nuptials." She kept her voice light and cheerful. She had to convince him she wanted the marriage even if he did not. He wouldn't dishonor her by refusing to wed if she was willing. "I have my gown and veil, and I've decided on the church."

He looked worried, but she pressed on. "I talked to the Reverend Goodheart at the Community Church, and he is more than happy to conduct the service."

"He is?" Eliot's shock was evident in his high-pitched question.

She hoped the lie turned into the truth. "Yes. I have arranged to meet with him and his wife today and finalize the plans. I hope you approve." She wasn't giving him much choice. If he disapproved, he would have to admit Cathy was his mistress.

He rose and walked to the sideboard where he poured a drink. He downed it in a single gulp. The man could easily turn into a drunkard in his depressed state.

"Do you disapprove?"

He resumed his seat. "If the Reverend Goodheart approves of performing the marriage, I see no reason why I shouldn't."

"I have one more request," Meg said. "I'd like to have the betrothal agreement and special license to give to the reverend today so he'll have the official records."

He searched his desk and retrieved the documents and added some coins. "His fee."

She took them and stood. "I gave your parents my word I would make you happy, and I intend to fulfill that promise."

"You can try." He clutched his head in his hands and looked about to cry.

She quietly backed out of the room and closed the door.

She found Lilibet in the upstairs bedroom writing in her book of recipes.

"I can't believe there are so many new varieties of food to prepare. I hope I can remember everything the cook told me."

Meg lit a candle and placed the betrothal document in the fireplace. She set it on fire.

Lilibet dropped her book and ran across the room. "What are you burning?"

"Quiet," Meg warned. "It's the betrothal agreement."

Her mouth dropped open. "You're destroying it?"

She used the poker to burn any remaining sections and finish the demise of the document. "It's the only copy. Without it, I can't be held accountable for breaking the agreement."

"But what about your father and Lord Dudlee? They witnessed it."

"They're in England. Father can't disown me any more than he has, and I plan to write Lord Dudlee and inform him of my guilt. By the time he receives it, Cathy and Eliot will be legally wed, and the deception will be on my head alone. What's he going to do to me? There's no dowry to return, and plenty of people saw the scars on my back. I'm betting he will be happy to allow a woman to take the blame for any social scandal."

"What if the Reverend Goodheart doesn't agree to your scheme?"

"There's only one way to find out." She gathered her new bonnet and shawl and handed a straw hat to Lilibet.

They met Owen coming up the stairs.

"Where are you going?"

"Making arrangements for the wedding," Meg said. "Eliot agreed on the location, and we're going to the church to meet with the Reverend Goodheart now." She didn't wait for a reply as they hurried down the stairs.

Lilibet glanced back. "He's going to be furious if we leave without him."

"Is he coming down?"

"No, he's heading to his room."

"I need time alone with the Goodhearts." Before talking to Eliot, Meg had informed the coachman to have the carriage ready, and he was waiting in front of the house. Owen would have to saddle a horse or walk.

When they arrived at the church, Mrs. Goodheart was playing a hymn on the harpsichord but stopped when they entered.

"We've come to meet with you about the wedding," Meg said.

"We can talk in the reverend's office." She led them to a back room where the Reverend Goodheart sat behind a plain but sturdy desk. His Bible was open, and he hastily wrote on a piece of paper.

"I'm sorry to disturb you, but Eliot and I have agreed to have the wedding here with you officiating. I want to finalize the plans." She removed her cloak. Her gown was cut low in the back, and although her scars had faded since her beating, they still marred her flesh. She needed to gain their sympathy.

Mrs. Goodheart glanced at her back, gasped, then failed to comment.

"Oh, don't worry about those scars," Meg said. "My father believes if you spare the rod, you spoil the child."

Mrs. Goodheart took the chair next to hers. "He beat you?"

"I was defiant. I refused to marry Eliot."

"But you're marrying him now," the reverend said.

"I was a bit of a coward." She met his gaze. "He promised twenty lashes, and I agreed to the marriage when he reached eight."

Mrs. Goodheart placed her hand on her breast. "One would have been too many for me."

"I've always thought that Bible verse about beating a child was misinterpreted," Meg said. "They used a rod to direct the oxen in Biblical times. If you didn't teach the oxen to turn, you couldn't plow a field. They were useless. If that's the example, then the verse means if you don't teach children to be useful, their lives would be wasted."

"I like your interpretation better than your father's," Mrs. Goodheart said.

Meg glanced from Mrs. Goodheart to her husband. "I know you're both God-fearing people. I need you to swear you will not repeat, reveal, or react to anything I am about to say."

"I consider any confidence given to me a matter between us and God. What do you wish to confess?" the Reverend Goodheart asked in a lowered voice.

"I do not wish to marry Eliot, but as you see, my father forced me in order to gain a fortune after I walk down the aisle." She didn't need to tell them that Owen might be the one claiming the money.

"Your father is forcing this marriage because of greed?"

"He leads a useless life filled with debts." Meg removed the special license from her pocket. "My father obtained this marriage license so the wedding could take place immediately. As you heard, Mr. O'Leary is in a hurry and needs proof of the marriage."

"Which I will be happy to provide."

She leaned forward. "Do you love your daughter, Cathy?"

"We do not speak her name," the reverend said.

"I love her." Mrs. Goodheart turned to her husband, a determined expression on her face. "I will not abandon Cathy and Anna because some man refused to wed her."

"Eliot did not refuse to wed her," Meg said. "His father forbade the marriage."

"A righteous man would have married her, especially when she was in a delicate way because of him," he said.

"I won't judge." Meg pointed at the Bible on the desk. "I know he loves his father and honors him by not going against his wishes."

"We are commanded to honor our parents, but he disgraced my daughter," he said. "They have a child out of wedlock."

"I was born out of wedlock," Lilibet said. "Lord Whittington took advantage of my mother when she worked in his kitchen."

"I'm sorry." Mrs. Goodheart turned from Lilibet to Meg. "I thought she was your sister."

Meg took Lilibet's hand. "She is. My father took advantage of many women. Instead of firing Lilibet's mother, my own protected her, and she was raised with me and my brother, Micah."

"My mother loved me, and Lady Meg's mother loved me in spite of the circumstances of my conception," Lilibet said.

"So I should forgive my daughter for Eliot's sins?" His voice rose in anger. "Why didn't he convince his father to approve of the match?"

"Eliot pled his case more than once," Meg said. "He loves Cathy and would marry her if he didn't have to go against his father's wishes. I believe Lord Dudlee's opinion of Cathy was vilified by a local man."

"Who?" he shouted.

"Do you know Glen Stemple?" She had only one letter from Lord Dudlee to condemn the man, but Banner had said Glen was watching Cathy and was defensive when confronted. She had to be right.

"He works for Eliot and is a member of this congregation," he said. "In good standing."

"What was his relationship with Cathy before she met Eliot?"

"He asked my permission to court Cathy, but that ended when she met Eliot," he said. "She should have married Glen."

"Did Glen propose marriage?"

"Yes," Mrs. Goodheart said. "But she turned him down. She was hoping Eliot would marry her."

"Eliot never proposed?"

He cleared his throat. "Yes. I read the banns in church, but that was before Anna was born. When he received a letter stating his parents didn't approve, the wedding was delayed. Then Cathy began to show her pregnancy, and she moved in with him."

"She had no choice," Mrs. Goodheart said. "You threw her out of our home."

"She should have waited until her wedding night to give in to their lusts. She shamed the family."

Meg waited for his anger to recede. "I believe Glen wrote vicious comments about Cathy to Lord Dudlee. I can't prove it. I don't have any of the letters, but Lord Dudlee said he was saving Eliot from a woman who only wanted to improve her station with a title and wealth."

Mrs. Goodheart looked at her husband. "Cathy would never do that."

"Lord Dudlee has never met her and doesn't know anything about your daughter but what Glen has told him. He thinks Cathy has bewitched Eliot."

He stood and stared. "Why would Mr. Stemple lie about Cathy?"

"What is the tenth commandment?" Meg asked.

He didn't hesitate. "Thou shalt not covet."

"I think he wants Cathy for himself. I understand he

would call every week to share business news with Eliot but stayed for dinner. Since she has moved to rooms in town, he accidentally runs into her when she is out in public."

"I was with her once when he joined us," Mrs. Goodheart said. "He was extremely attentive."

"If I marry Eliot, would Glen be able to convince Cathy to marry him?"

Mrs. Goodheart nodded. "She's so unhappy she could easily be persuaded to accept any man's proposal."

Meg searched their faces. "Are you willing to allow Eliot and Cathy to be manipulated by a liar?"

"No, but what can we do?" Mrs. Goodheart asked.

"I'm here to correct the circumstances," Meg said. "I've seen how miserable both of them are. I promised Eliot's parents I would make him happy, and the way to do that is to have Eliot and Cathy wed. The problem is that Eliot cannot know he's marrying your daughter."

The reverend frowned. "Why not?"

She explained the reasons she had shared with Cathy. "If my plan succeeds, Eliot will keep his future inheritance, he'll be married to the woman he loves, and Anna will be legitimate."

He cleared his throat. "I could hold my granddaughter?"

"If we succeed. Everyone must believe the marriage will proceed as planned. No one must know the truth but us four and Cathy."

"How can I deceive Eliot into marrying Cathy when your name is part of the vows?" he protested.

"Because my name is Margaret Katherine."

Mrs. Goodheart gasped. "Her name is Mary Catherine."

"I believe it's divine intervention I was chosen to be Eliot's bride." Meg tapped on the Bible on his desk. "Glen Stemple has slandered your daughter's name to prevent her from marrying the man she loves, the father of her child. This is our chance to right a wrong."

The reverend took his wife's hand. "What must we do?"

"The marriage certificate must be signed by Eliot first, then Banner as his witness. Then Cathy will sign, and Lilibet will witness her signature. Her true signature. You sign last and send the license to the courthouse. You can fill the time with a sermon and hymns. Once the document is official, you said no one can challenge the legality of their marriage. You'll ask Eliot to say his vows and then Cathy."

Mrs. Goodheart shook her head. "Won't people recognize her?"

"I've purchased a thick veil, and she'll wear my dress." She turned to Mrs. Goodheart. "You bring Cathy to the church and have her wait in the storage closet. Owen may search the anteroom to make sure I can't escape. After he leaves the room, Cathy can unlock the door, and we'll make the switch."

"The door doesn't unlock from the inside." The Reverend Goodheart showed her a key. "And I need this to lock it."

"Then lock Cathy in, and when Owen is done, Cathy can kick the key out, and I can open the door."

Mrs. Goodheart looked worried. "Do you think your plan will work?"

"It's the only one I could think of that would make everyone happy," Meg said. "Have someone you trust register the license at the courthouse. Glen might challenge the marriage afterward."

The Reverend Goodheart considered her proposal. "What if Eliot refuses to sign, not realizing it is Cathy?"

"I'm counting on his sense of duty to go through with the ceremony."

He extended his hand. "Then I have a wedding to perform."

They finalized details and were walking down the aisle when Owen barged in. He was red in the face, and his hair stood up in uneven tufts. "You didn't wait. I had to walk here."

"We've finalized the wedding plans and are heading to the bakery to order desserts for the wedding dinner." She clapped her hands and squealed so loudly he covered his ears. "I can't wait to be married."

Chapter Twenty-Four

Banner joined Eliot in his study after dinner. Spending time with Meg had been difficult, especially with her and Lilibet talking about the upcoming wedding plans during the meal. He excused Meg's enthusiasm to her role as a bride. What woman didn't want to be the center of attention on her own special day? He hadn't given her a choice. He hadn't proposed marriage, and even if he had, why would she marry him instead of Eliot, who was a firstborn son? In his limited experience women valued titles, wealth, and position over love. But he had thought Meg was different.

The women had gone upstairs, and Owen had gone out on his nightly walk. Issy had followed Owen during the week and reported the steward spent several hours drinking and gambling with the locals at the Red Pony Tavern. But Owen wasn't taking any chances on Meg running away. Banner spotted a man smoking a cigar and watching the house from across the road.

Banner left the study window and poured a drink for Eliot, who leaned back in his chair and sighed. His friend looked on the outside like he felt on the inside. The wedding was two days away, and neither one of them wanted the event to occur.

"Lady Meg appears to have all the plans for your nuptials in hand, but are you ready for the wedding?"

Eliot's took a long drink before answering. "I can't

go through with it."

"Are you calling it off?" Did his voice betray hope?

"I can't defy my father." Eliot stared at him, desperation on his face. "Why don't you kidnap Lady Meg and elope?"

He'd dreamt something similar the night before. "Are you crazy?"

"I've noticed you have an interest in her. Did you not form any attachment while on the voyage?"

If only Eliot knew how intimate they had become. Banner needed to divert the conversation to a safer topic. "She drives me to distraction. She has the absurd idea that Mr. Stemple has been reducing the quantity of items on the manifest and selling them for himself. To satisfy her obsession, I compared past manifests of mine with yours."

Eliot looked confused. Unlike his father, he had no head for business. "Is that why you asked for them?"

Banner opened a packet. "I'm returning your manifests. I compared them to mine and found no discrepancies. Lady Meg has an overly active imagination."

Eliot removed a folded document from his desk. "Then I guess you don't want to compare the manifest Glen delivered earlier today."

A thump echoed from above. A mischievous imp was eavesdropping on their conversation.

"I have my current manifest." Banner removed it from his coat. "I might as well compare them. Can I use your study?"

"If you want to waste your time, go ahead." Eliot dropped the old manifests Banner had returned into a bottom drawer. "There is no reason Glen would cheat my father."

"How well do you know him?"

"He's been an employee of my father's company for years. But the only time we socialize is when he comes to dinner and discusses what he's sold and what Father wants him to buy."

"And it's Glen who delivers the manifest and any correspondence?"

"Yes, it saves me a trip to the dock." Eliot rose and poured another drink for himself. "You're wrong about Glen. Whenever he came to dinner, he brought Cathy a little gift to show his appreciation."

"And you didn't mind?"

"Few people called on Cathy after her father disowned her. I thought it was kind of him."

Meg's suspicions wouldn't stop bothering him. "Didn't Glen once court Cathy?"

"That was before I met her." Eliot resumed his seat. "She has no feelings for him."

"But he may have feelings for her."

"Everyone loved Cathy." He downed his drink and shrugged. "He never disrespected her. He would never jeopardize his position."

"I'm trying to figure out how your father became poisoned against Cathy." Banner stood and paced about the room. "Someone wrote to your father about her in unfavorable terms. He described a woman who was trying to deceive and bewitch you out of your title and wealth."

"Cathy isn't like that."

"Your father has never met her, so where did he gain that unflattering image?" Banner stopped in front of the desk. "I only delivered letters from you and Glen."

"He wrote business reports," Eliot said. "Glen thought the world of Cathy. He would never disparage her to my father."

"What if he's obsessed with her? Why visit every week when he could have sent his reports through a courier? Why the gifts? With every letter you wrote, Glen wrote one. When you talked of marrying her, he could have written your father to prevent it."

Eliot leaned back in his chair. "But we were living as man and wife."

Would Glen overlook her infidelity? "As long as he prevented the marriage, he had a chance to win her. Once you wed Lady Meg, he can comfort Cathy and restore her respectability as his wife."

Eliot buried his face in his hands. "That's best."

He hit his fist on the desk. "Are you insane? She loves you."

"I can't disobey my father. If not out of duty, then out of love."

"What if his objection is based on lies? Don't you want to convince him to change his mind?"

"I tried. Now it's too late." Eliot sobbed, and his shoulders shook.

If his friend had reconciled himself to the marriage, Banner had to do the same. He saw Eliot to his room and noted a light showed beneath the door to Meg's room. She was awake. Had she overheard everything he had discussed with Eliot? He hoped so.

He waited in the study, comparing the two manifests to pass the time. He expected the results to be the same as the previous lists, but something was wrong. He had his own manifest for goods he had sold in his coat and placed it next to the ones on the desk. Even though all the goods were accounted for, Glen had sold much of the cargo for less than what Banner had obtained for the same items. Had Meg been right? But instead of the number of items being different, the discrepancy was in the profits made from selling the same items. Would he need to apologize for doubting her?

He was startled by the front door opening and blew out the light.

Owen barged into the study and froze when he saw him. "I didn't know the room was occupied. Why are you sitting in the dark?"

"The flame went out." He relit the candle. "Must have been a draft."

"I'll leave you."

He lifted the manifest. "I was reviewing some paperwork for Eliot. He grew tired and went to bed. How may I help you?"

"I usually indulge in a little wine before retiring." Owen headed to the sideboard and lifted a decanter. "Do you care to join me?"

He nodded. "I won't refuse free drinks."

Owen offered him a glass. "To our generous host."

"You've made yourself at home in Riverside. I hear you enjoy the Red Pony Tavern most nights."

"They treat me with respect," Owen said as he took a seat opposite the desk from Banner.

Respect was important to the man. "I'm surprised you're in a hurry to return to London. It's hard to escape the brand of a natural child."

He bristled. "You should understand how it is. The rich feel they have a right to look down on you. I had no control over the circumstances of my birth. No more than you did as a second son."

"True, but I've done well with the cards I was dealt."

"And I plan to make the most of mine." Owen emptied his glass and left it on the desk. "To rich men who are foolish with their money." He rose. "I think I will retire. Two more days in this primitive town and my business will be concluded."

"I'll accompany you." Banner placed the crystal tumblers on the sideboard and snuffed the candlestick on the desk.

Moonlight filtering through the windows guided their steps to the second floor. He went to his room, waited fifteen minutes, and crept down the servants' staircase. The study was empty. Where was Meg? He sat in a chair in the dark corner. He had nearly dozed off when he heard a faint creak.

She slipped in like a soft breeze and sat at the desk, her back to him. She struck a flint and lit a candle she had brought. He had left the three manifests in plain view, and she aligned the copies side by side as she ran her finger down the figures. "I knew it."

"Interesting reading?"

Meg softly squealed as she turned to face him. "Banner."

He rose from his seat. "I nearly fell asleep waiting for you to appear."

She turned her attention to the papers. "You scared me."

He stood behind her, trapping the chair against the desk. She wore a nightgown and robe. Her hair was loose and fell in a cascade of soft curls. "I knew you'd come." He kneaded her shoulders with his fingertips. "Have you no shame? Don't you already know everything from eavesdropping from above?"

"If you would confide in me, I wouldn't have to spy." She groaned. "That feels good. I've been tense trying to deal with all these problems myself."

"What problems?"

"Glen Stemple. You said his manifest matched perfectly with Eliot's." She lifted the list of cargo from the desk. "The number of items matches what you recorded, but the dollar figures are lower than this one with many of the same goods." She lifted his manifest. "What is this?"

"That is my list of goods sold. I seem to be a much better businessman than Glen. I sold all my items at a higher profit than he did with Eliot's cargo." He sighed. "It doesn't matter. Eliot is reconciled to his fate. He's going to marry you to please his parents."

"And I must keep my promise."

"You're giving up?"

"We both know I must marry Eliot, but Glen should not go unpunished if he's been stealing from Lord Dudlee." She turned her attention to the manifest. "How do you prove he's a thief?"

A pain radiated in his chest. How could she give up? That went against everything he knew about her. "I was comparing the numbers when Owen returned home."

"Owen." She didn't hide her contempt. "He can't give up his vices for even a week, and he's added smoking those smelly cigars to drinking and gambling. The coach driver lost a week's pay to him."

"He drank a good portion of Eliot's wine before retiring."

"I heard you come upstairs, too."

He leaned close to her ear. "But you didn't hear me sneak back down using the servants' staircase."

She shook the papers. "Can he be arrested?"

"It's difficult. I'll have a couple of my men talk to the merchants who purchased cargo from Glen and ask them how much they paid. If their numbers are higher than the ones Glen reported, then he's pocketing the difference."

"Some of the differences are slight, but they would add up." She stood and walked toward the window before facing him. "Is there any chance Eliot will change his mind about the wedding?"

"Everyone in Eliot's life has taught him obedience, duty, and family honor. And he's afraid of being poor. His father did not teach him any of his business expertise, and he has shown no interest in learning any. The man has no skills to survive without his father's help."

"He's pampered, distraught, and unable to make the simplest decision," Meg said with a note of pity.

"He needs a woman in his life to guide him." Cathy had stayed by his side even when her parents disowned her. Her quiet strength had encouraged Eliot. But Meg expected more of a man. She could come to despise Eliot.

Meg stepped closer. "Eliot loves his father and wouldn't do anything to hurt him. And that's why the wedding must proceed."

"You're going through with it?" His voice rose in alarm.

"I promised Eliot's parents I would make him happy. I intend to keep my word." She waited for him to move aside. "Besides, Owen would drag me kicking and screaming up the aisle to make sure his plans were fulfilled."

He followed her through the doorway. "His plans? I thought this marriage was your father's idea."

Meg turned to look at him in the foyer. "I underestimated Owen. He stays in the shadows and watches for the most vulnerable time to strike." She fought back a sob. "And he shows no mercy."

He followed her up the stairs, and they parted on the landing. When he entered his room, he noticed an echo as his door latched. Did someone else close their door at nearly the same time?

Chapter Twenty-Five

Meg had spent a restless night, wondering if she should have confided in Banner. But if he told Eliot her plans, everything would be ruined. She could do nothing about Glen Stemple, but stealing from his employer supported her belief that he had interfered with Cathy and Eliot's happiness. She needed to right that wrong.

"Are you ready to go?" Lilibet asked as she gathered their belongings.

They needed to stop at the tailor's shop for the monogrammed handkerchiefs and the milliner's shop to pick up her bonnet and veil for the wedding tomorrow, but they had to wait until Owen awoke. He was in a foul mood and stared at her on the ride into town. It was unnerving, like a poisonous snake slithering upward to strike. Was he suspicious? She couldn't afford to underestimate him like her father had the past few years.

"I'll find the milliner," Lilibet volunteered when they entered the shop.

Owen grabbed Meg's arm and pulled her toward a curtain covering the opening to a side room for measuring and fitting gowns. "A word, Lady Meg."

She attempted to jerk free, but he held tight, his foul breath causing a wave of nausea. The man had skipped any personal hygiene.

"Have you forgotten my promise to take Lilibet back to London brothels where she'll suffer at the hands of dozens of men every night if you don't go through with the wedding?"

"I have every intention of proceeding with the nuptials." Her voice was cold. She wanted him to believe she had no choice.

"Then what were you doing with the captain last night? I saw you coming up the stairs together after I had retired. You were in your nightclothes."

"I wore a robe, and Captain Youngblood is an honorable man. He would not betray his friend, especially under his roof. He was born a gentleman and knows how to conduct himself like one."

"Even gentlemen have needs. What were you doing?"

She pulled her arm free from his grasp. "We had a business discussion."

"Business?" He laughed. "You must think I'm an idiot."

"It would be impolite to tell you what I think about you, but I'm telling the truth. Captain Youngblood discovered that Mr. Stemple reduced the amount of profits on goods listed on the manifest he gave to Eliot. He's pocketing the difference."

"Why would he show you and not Eliot?"

"He needs proof, which he has not yet obtained. Mr. Stemple is a trusted and loyal employee of the Richmond family. This betrayal will upset Eliot greatly. He does not need any distraction before the wedding. I asked Captain Youngblood not to reveal Stemple's betrayal until after the ceremony. Then the authorities can arrest and hang him."

"Hang?" Owen blanched.

"What punishment would you recommend for an

employee who betrays the man who has paid him a fair salary for years and discovers he is a thief?"

He loosened his cravat. "I still think there is something between you and the captain."

"Do you think I want to be married to a sailor, a man who has a mistress in every port? Eliot will provide me with wealth and the social position my mother would have wanted for me."

"She's getting the bonnet with the veil," Lilibet interrupted. She looked at Owen and stepped back. "Is something wrong?"

"No, Owen will wait outside." She waited for him to obey.

"Tomorrow will go as planned, or you'll both suffer my wrath." He hurried out the door.

"Too bad a runaway wagon didn't find him in its path," Meg said.

"What did he say?" Lilibet whispered.

Meg pulled her toward the closed curtain to the dressing room. "He caught me with Banner last night coming up the stairs from the study."

"Oh dear. What did you tell him?"

"I made an excuse, but he's still suspicious. I need some way for him to let down his guard. We can't have him watching us too closely tomorrow."

"You could tell Banner your plans."

"No, I can't. He's too honorable. He was upset I read the letters from Lord Dudlee. If he found out what I was plotting, he'd feel obligated to tell Eliot." She sighed. "And Eliot must be ignorant to be innocent in his father's eyes."

"But he kissed you," Lilibet said. "That must mean something."

"He regrets kissing me." A sob escaped her lips. "I'm afraid he may try something to stop the wedding, and we can't let him."

"You can't keep him from coming. He's standing by Eliot."

"It's Owen I'm more worried about," Meg said. "If only we could convince him that Banner has no interest in me."

"That would require another woman," Lilibet said.

"Would I do?" Victoria pushed open the curtain of the dressing room. "You should make sure no one is inside before conspiring so close. How may I help?"

Victoria was the last person Meg expected to volunteer. "You want to help me?"

"I enjoy gossip. It's the reason other women are drawn to me and also fear me."

"You can't repeat anything we've said," Meg begged. Victoria could ruin everything.

"What have you said? One of Mr. Richmond's employees may be cheating him. It's not uncommon. I'm more interested in why you don't want Mr. O'Leary to think there is anything romantic between you and the captain."

"There isn't," Meg said. "But he suspects something. I don't need the stress on my wedding day."

"So you need Mr. O'Leary to see the captain with another woman. Will I do?"

Meg barely knew Victoria, but she could distract Owen as well as Banner. She looked at Lilibet. "Do you think we should trust her?"

Lilibet shrugged. "I don't see how we have any choice."

"As long as you give me the details to whatever

you're plotting," Victoria said.

"I can't do that."

"After the ceremony," Victoria amended. "I'm sure whatever you are planning, it will cause an uproar. I want to be the one who has all the answers."

It was against her better judgment, but she needed Victoria. "Can you convince the captain to invite you to supper tonight? We need you to flirt with him and Mr. O'Leary."

She smiled in the soft seductive way that came naturally to some women. "I believe I can."

"Don't let him know it was my idea."

"Of course." She raised a single eyebrow. "What about after supper?"

Meg understood the innuendo and gulped. "That will be up to the captain."

****

Meg had spent the afternoon packing everything she and Lilibet would need for the wedding the next morning, and now they were dressing for supper. Meg wore a gown of pink satin and white underskirt with white ruffles along the edge of the overskirt and along the seam of the bodice. The lace-edged fichu modestly covered her breasts.

"I thought you might wear something more daring," Lilibet said.

"I want all eyes on Victoria tonight."

"Are you sure?" She echoed her worry.

"If she seduces Banner, it's my fault. I've thrown him into the lion's den, and it serves me right if he finds happiness elsewhere." She burst into tears.

Lilibet hugged her and handed her a handkerchief. "Stop, or everyone will know something is amiss."

Fear and apprehension beat a warning in her heart. Meg straightened her shoulders. "It wouldn't be *awful* being married to Eliot."

Lilibet stared at her, disbelief etched on her features.

A tear escaped. She swiped at it. "The plan has to work."

"What about Banner?"

"I can't think about him until after tomorrow. If I fail, I'll lose him. He's too honorable to make me his mistress."

"You wouldn't settle for that." Lilibet took her arm, and they walked down the stairs.

Voices drifted out of the parlor.

"Victoria must have arrived, or they would be in the study sharing drinks," Meg said.

The men rose as they entered. They had brought their glasses with them. Victoria was seated and wore a yellow satin gown cut daringly low. Any false movement and her perfectly displayed breasts would spill out of the limited barrier.

Meg moved to Eliot's side. She needed to make sure he didn't bolt before tomorrow's ceremony. "Are you looking forward to tomorrow?"

"Is everything ready?" Eliot asked in a shaky voice.

"Yes, I picked up everything I will need, and the maid pressed our dresses. We'll be leaving early to dress at the church."

"What church did you decide on?" Banner asked.

"The Community Church."

Banner choked on his drink.

Victoria patted him on the back.

Banner looked to Eliot, who was studying the liquor in his glass. "Can you change the location?"

"The Reverend Goodheart agreed to officiate, and Eliot approved the location," Meg said. "Everything is finalized. All you need to do is show up." She took Eliot's arm. "Your father would be disappointed if you left me standing alone at the altar."

"I will not humiliate you or my father," he promised.

She whispered and laughed with Eliot as if they were a couple in love, but when she turned to face the others, no one acknowledged her. They were listening to a story by Victoria. Even Lilibet seemed mesmerized by her voice. Meg waited until she finished before announcing supper. Both Owen and Banner offered their arm for Victoria. She chose Banner.

A surge of jealousy heated Meg's face before she caught Owen staring at her. She took Eliot's arm and pressed against it. "I'm looking forward to tomorrow. I have so many plans for the house."

Eliot made no reply as he seated her and took his own place at the head of the table. The supper consisted of leftovers from dinner with the servants serving soup first.

Victoria turned to Meg. "I hope you don't mind that Banner invited me to dinner."

"Your presence is always welcomed at our table." Her voice shook slightly as she buttered a thick slice of bread.

Owen leered at Victoria. "I only regret that I will be leaving tomorrow and will only enjoy your company tonight."

"Your departure is my loss." Victoria looked at Meg. "I must ask you how you were able to plan a wedding so quickly the next time I marry." She turned to Banner. "I heard a rumor you were building a house.

Does that mean you'll be seeking a wife soon?"

Banner had been lifting his spoon to his lips and froze.

Victoria laughed lightly. "Don't worry, Captain. I believe in long courtships."

Panic seized Meg. Had she fallen into a wiser woman's trap? Was Victoria using her to coax Banner into marriage? What was she going to do?

"I have yet to finalize plans for my home." Banner glanced in her direction. "Someone suggested a few changes."

"Your business ventures must be profitable to build a house," Victoria said.

"Not as much as your former husbands'."

"But I don't need a wealthy husband this time." She smiled as the soup bowls were removed.

Ham slices were served with mustard sauce. Victoria knew how to command attention as the men competed for her favors. She maintained a steady stream of conversation but focused on Banner, who sat to her right.

Meg was too inexperienced to battle for a man. She had never known one worth the fight until now. And her plan required her to sit passively while another woman doted on the man she loved.

Spice cake was served for dessert. Meg barely touched hers.

"It's getting late, and tomorrow will be a busy day for these two," Victoria said as she rose. She touched Banner's arm. "I hope you will escort me home."

"Of course." Banner bid everyone else good night.

"Would you mind if I accompanied you as far as the Red Pony Tavern?" Owen asked as they gathered in the foyer.

"The more the merrier." Victoria turned to Meg. "Thank you for a lovely evening. I hope everything turns out as you planned tomorrow."

Meg stood in the open doorway as Banner and Owen escorted Victoria to her carriage. A heaviness settled in her stomach, and she couldn't blame the meal. She was tempted to tell Banner to stay. She wanted to touch him and laugh at his witty remarks as Victoria had done. She wanted to ride in an open carriage with him in the darkness of the evening and kiss until their lips were swollen and bruised from passion. And so much more. But she fought every natural impulse and said nothing.

Eliot entered his study and closed the door without acknowledging her existence.

Meg climbed the stairs with Lilibet. Being married to Eliot would be like living with a corpse. "What have I done?"

"What do you mean?" Lilibet asked.

"Did you see how she flirted? I invited her tonight. She stole him right from under my nose."

"But you asked her to convince Owen that Banner wasn't interested in you."

"Until after the wedding. But this could be permanent. What if he marries her?"

"I don't think it will go that far."

Meg disagreed. Her heart ached within her chest as she undressed. She wanted to cry, but Eliot might hear her from below. Lilibet climbed into bed and was soon asleep, but Meg was restless. She sat in the chair by the window and stared out into the darkness, searching for a familiar figure to appear. A sob escaped, and she allowed the tears to silently flow.

Chapter Twenty-Six

Banner sat next to Victoria in her carriage with Owen opposite. How had he ended up in this predicament? When she had bumped into him earlier on the street, he couldn't say no to her when she hinted about joining him for supper. Then she had flirted and fawned over him as if they were more than casual acquaintances. He had no experience with a woman's manipulations and felt like a pawn on a chess board. But what was Victoria up to?

His thoughts drifted to Meg and the hurt look on her face when she stood in the doorway of Eliot's house when they departed. Tears had glistened in her eyes. But how could she judge him when she was going to marry Eliot tomorrow and expected him to escort his friend to the church and stand at the altar while they said their vows? He couldn't declare his true feelings while she was betrothed to Eliot, but didn't she know how he felt?

Owen's droning voice brought him back from daydreaming. He was attempting to impress Victoria by bragging about his acquaintances in London, dropping titles and names of men who barely tolerated Lord Whittington let alone his steward. Did Owen believe his own lies?

"I spent the season with the finest families in London," Owen said. "I've met many beautiful women, but none compare to you, Victoria."

She fanned herself even though the night air was cool. "You flatter me, Mr. O'Leary."

"My friends call me Owen. I hope you consider me one."

Banner didn't attempt to join the conversation. He recognized a braggart when he heard one. They were nearing the tavern Owen frequented.

Owen had fleeced several Red Pony Tavern patrons of their hard-earned money during his short visit, according to Issy. The men suspected Owen had cheated, but they knew he was leaving after the wedding and didn't call him out on it. He wouldn't be missed by the locals.

"Someday I hope to be a wealthy man and return to the colonies," Owen said.

"Where do you propose to obtain this fortune?" Banner interrupted. "I hope you're not planning on marrying a rich widow."

Victoria frowned at Banner. He was only trying to protect her.

"I have my own sources of income, but a wealthy wife would be a welcomed asset, especially one as beautiful as you." He exited the carriage and bowed over her hand. "You would be the belle of London on my arm. I hope you will be my companion tomorrow at the wedding."

"I would be happy to sit with you."

He grinned at Banner, tipped his hat, turned, and entered the tavern.

Banner and Victoria continued along the street and turned along a side road. Her home was the largest and most opulent in Riverside.

"I'm sorry if I overstepped," Banner apologized. "I

don't like Owen."

"He's an obnoxious oaf. His flattery fell on deaf ears."

"I'm glad. You've always struck me as a practical woman."

"Ouch." She patted his arm with her closed fan. "I'll ignore that comment because he's a dangerous threat to Lady Meg."

She had his full attention. "What do you mean?"

"Yesterday I overheard a conversation in the milliner's shop between Owen and Lady Meg. He threatened to take Lilibet back to London and sell her to a brothel if Meg didn't marry Eliot."

Owen would use Meg's love for Lilibet against her. "He'll be no threat after tomorrow."

"After she marries Eliot." Victoria bestowed a warm smile upon him. "I think we did an excellent job of convincing Owen you have no intention of eloping with Lady Meg."

He leaned back in the leather seat. "She made it perfectly clear she's going forward with the wedding."

"That was the reason she invited me to dinner."

Banner shook his head. "I invited you."

She laughed. "You think you invited me. Meg wanted me there tonight to convince Owen you had no interest in her." Her voice was animated. "I think we succeeded."

Were his feelings a game to women? "I'm not interested in the little hellion. She lies, she spies, and she has no shame. Her actions don't match her words. I have no idea what to think or do about her."

"How long have you been in love with her?"

"I'm not." He crossed his arms. "I told you how I

felt about her."

"I never have trouble keeping a man's interest, but tonight I struggled to keep yours. And she couldn't keep her eyes from you. If two people were ever madly in love, it was you and Lady Meg."

"And yet she marries another." He didn't disguise the disappointment in his voice. He thought he was a man who would never suffer heartache, but with the wedding so close, he was physically sick from thinking of losing her.

"I know it's difficult for a man, but let her take control," Victoria said. "She has a plan."

"She does?" A plan shouldn't have surprised him, but why did it require her to marry Eliot?

Victoria held up her hands. "I don't know what it is. But I'm sure if she needs you, she'll ask."

The carriage stopped outside her front door, and he helped her to the brick walk. "I might want to spend my time with a woman who knows how to treat a man."

"I treated my two husbands horribly. If you want to hurt her, then stay out all night. She's probably crying right now."

He searched her face in the light of the lamp hanging above the doorway. "How do you know?"

"When I was her age, I believed in romance. I gave myself to a man I loved. When he was done with me, he discarded me like garbage thrown in the river. I was devastated and wanted to die. Finally, I picked myself up and found my footing, but I never gave my heart in such a pure and powerful way again. Why do you think I marry rich, old men who appreciate me? Don't chip away at her love and think you can win it back. At some point her heart will break, and you will lose her."

"I already have. She's marrying Eliot."

"Why?"

"I don't know."

"Then you should ask her while you still have time."

Banner watched her go inside and proceeded down the street on foot. Eliot's home was on the other side of town, and he needed to think. He was in love with Meg, but he couldn't humiliate Eliot by running off with his bride the night before the wedding. Or could he? Was that what Meg wanted?

He entered the house and let his footsteps echo as he climbed the stairs. A door opened as he reached the landing.

Meg stood in the doorway in her nightgown. She sniffled. "Banner."

He walked toward her room, and she pulled him inside. It was dark, but moonlight streamed through the window. Lilibet was in bed, asleep.

"Did you bed her?"

He backed up against the door she had closed and searched for the handle. "What?"

"Did you make love to Victoria?" Her voice was urgent.

He almost lied. "No."

She stepped back into the moonlight, and tears glistened on her lashes. She'd been crying.

He remembered Victoria's warning. "I left her at her doorstep. She said you invited her to dinner tonight. She said you had a plan."

She threw her arms around his neck and kissed every inch of his face before focusing on his mouth.

His body instantly responded. He forced her away. "What are you doing?"

"I'm kissing you."

"What about Eliot?"

"I don't want to kiss Eliot." She pulled the tie from his hair and ran her fingers through the long locks. "You're much too neat for a man who's shared Victoria's bed."

Hadn't she heard him? "I didn't share it."

"I know, but Owen will be back soon, and he needs to think you are having an affair with Victoria."

"Why?" He recalled Victoria's words. "Has he threatened you—or Lilibet? I can deal with him."

Her warm hand touched his face. "I know, my brave pirate prince, but this battle requires subtle intrigue. Owen needs to believe he's succeeding in his plan."

"Isn't he?"

She unbuttoned his waistcoat and tugged his shirt free from his trousers.

"Easy," Banner warned as he glanced toward the bed. Wouldn't three be crowded? Whatever her plan, he was eager to comply. He kissed her, speaking the words of love through silent lips. His hands expressed his emotions, caressing her body as sighs and groans escaped her deepest center and stoked his own desires. He wanted to pleasure her, to drive her to the abyss of satisfaction, and take her over the waves of ecstasy. He nuzzled her neck and with his teeth undid the string holding her nightgown together. His mouth feasted on the silky flesh exposed as her gown fell away, and he took the fullness of her breast in his hand, teasing the nipple to a stiff peak before suckling. He wanted her beyond logic, beyond reason.

Meg tried to pull away. "What are you doing?"

He pressed her body against the door. "Making love

to you."

"We don't have time for that. Owen is due home."

"What does he have to do with this?" He pulled her against his arousal. He had never wanted a woman more and battled for patience and control. Discovery was the pathway to intimacy. How far they traveled on the journey of passion depended upon her. Was she willing to surrender her virginity? They could declare their feelings for one another in other ways.

She pushed against his chest and grabbed the opening of her gown. "That's enough."

He understood her initial shyness and wanted to reassure her. "I'll show you how to make love without going too far."

She grabbed a handful of his hair. "You're disheveled enough."

He continued to touch and kiss her.

"You need to go down the servant stairs, out the back door, and walk around the block. Wait for Owen to return from the tavern. Then return to the house. You need to sound happy. Sing a song." She groaned as his hands sought to pleasure her.

Sing a song? "What are you talking about?" Banner lifted his head and stared into her face. "I'm not going anywhere."

"You have to convince Owen you were with Victoria."

"Why?" He stared into her eyes, trying to comprehend the meaning behind her words.

She pressed her palms against his chest. "We can't let him interfere when I marry Eliot tomorrow."

"You're going through with the wedding?" The words were like cold water thrown on him. He removed his hands from her body and tucked his shirt into his trousers.

"Don't do that." She yanked it out.

"I don't know what game you're playing, but if you're going to marry Eliot tomorrow, I'm not going to bed you tonight. I won't betray Eliot for one night of pleasure."

"I don't want you to betray him." She placed her hands on his cheeks, framing his face. "Do you trust me?"

"I'd have to be stupid to trust you." He stared into her eyes. Tears glistened on her eyelashes. "Oh hell, why not? Yes."

She opened the door. "Make Owen believe you were with Victoria."

"One problem, my frustrating vixen. He's going to wonder why I didn't spend the night with her."

She stepped back, her brow furrowed. "You need an excuse for coming back." She gasped, and a smile lit her face. "Tell him you have to make sure Eliot is at the church on time. You can't do that from her bed."

Nothing she said made sense. "Are you going to be at the church?"

"Lilibet, Owen, and I will go early. I'm dressing in the anteroom."

He stepped into the hallway. "You're going through with this mockery?"

She glanced down the hallway before looking into his eyes. "You said you trusted me."

"You want me to stand by and watch you marry the man?"

She placed a hand on his chest. "You have to make sure Eliot goes through with the ceremony. He must sign the license. Can you do that for me?"

"Then you'll be legally married to him." He shook his head and threw up his arms. "If you want to marry him, who am I to stop you?"

"Wait." She pulled him toward her and kissed him, gripping his long hair in her fists. "You didn't look kissed enough."

He pressed her against the open door and kissed her long enough to brand her as his. Whatever her plan, it had better not include her marrying Eliot. He'd kill him and make Meg a widow if he had to. "You're mine."

"You were mine first." She framed his face with her hands and kissed him so slowly it was torturous. She glanced down the empty hall. "Go and make your appearance."

"Anything else?"

"Make sure Owen knows you had a good time." She closed her door.

The woman was crazy. He almost turned toward the main staircase but realized the servant stairs were the other way. He met no one in the kitchen and slipped out the door. He walked around the block, trying to make sense of what had happened. What was Meg up to, and why hadn't she confided in him? Didn't she trust him? So why did she ask him to trust her?

He heard Owen open the front door to the house and saw his hired man leave his post. He messed up his hair with his fingers to add to his disheveled appearance. Meg had kept his hair ribbon. He sang the chorus of a sea chanty like instructed. She couldn't blame him if her plan went awry. He was doing everything she asked.

Owen was seated in Eliot's study, sampling his wine.

Banner leaned against the open door. "Pour me a drink."

Owen didn't hide his surprise. "I didn't think you'd be back tonight."

Banner took the drink. "A man doesn't have to spend the night to enjoy the charms of a woman." He smirked. "Besides, I have a duty to make sure Eliot arrives at the church tomorrow. I can't do that from sweet Victoria's bed."

Owen lifted his glass. "To women who don't mind your absence in the morning."

He clinked his glass against Owen's. "And to the husbands who never know their wives weren't alone."

Owen resumed his seat. "I saw you and Lady Meg come up the stairs together last night and was worried you'd fallen for her charms. I wouldn't want you to do something foolish to prevent the marriage."

Meg had been right about Owen's suspicions. He needed to assure him his interests were elsewhere. "She's too high above my station. My brother has the title and a couple of heirs. Besides, I'm married to the sea. No woman wants a husband who is absent for months at a time. But they don't mind a visit from a lover."

"I'm glad you're on my side. I hate women who meddle in my business."

"I thought Lord Whittington was your business."

"Which is why I must return to England," Owen said. "Lord Whittington's debts will be paid, and Lord Dudlee will have ties to a noble family."

Banner put his empty glass on the sideboard. "Everyone will be happy."

Owen downed the remaining wine in his glass.

"Even Lady Meg. She'll have the weak but honorable Eliot Richmond heeding her every command. Too bad he doesn't know how to keep her in her place."

He ignored the insult to his friend. "Like with a whip to the back."

"She flaunts the scars, but it was the first time I saw her afraid." A thin smile betrayed his sadistic pleasure from the incident. Owen rose from his chair. "She gave in too easily. I would have liked to have seen the full twenty lashes, one for every year of her privileged life."

Banner balled his fists to keep from smashing one into Owen's face. "You'll lose a worthy opponent when you sail."

"She never truly bested me. She thinks I'm a lowly servant, but she doesn't realize that a little coin can bring respect to a man. A large amount can bring him great power."

Lady Meg had guessed his plans and sabotaged them. He schooled his features. When Owen returned to England, he'd find Lord Whittington sober and Micah guiding his father's finances. Seeing the look of disappointment on his face would almost be worth the trip. He bid him good night as Owen poured himself another drink.

Chapter Twenty-Seven

Meg had listened at the hole in the floor when Owen had returned. Banner had done what she asked. Owen was convinced the captain was no threat to the impending nuptials. She joined Lilibet in bed after listening for Banner's door to close, but all she could think about were the kisses she had shared with the man she loved. She welcomed his touch and wished he could have done more than tease the promise of pleasure from her body. What if something went wrong with her plan and she had to marry Eliot? Her body shook in revulsion as she thought of Eliot's hands on her. She tried to sleep, but she feared disaster, and her dreams turned into nightmares.

In the morning, Meg and Lilibet dressed in simple gowns and carried the last of the packages to the carriage.

Lilibet counted the boxes. "I think we have everything."

Owen looked tired and ragged as he stumbled out the door. "Why can't you dress here?"

"I don't want my gown to be wrinkled," Meg said. "It's my wedding day. You can afford to be gracious."

He ordered the servants to add his travel trunk to their belongings.

Meg waited for Lilibet to climb into the carriage. "You could stop here after the wedding."

Laura Freeman

"And backtrack? I'm going straight to the dock after the wedding." He sat across from them. "You better not try anything."

"Why wouldn't I want to marry Eliot? He's gentle, generous, and going to give me everything I want. I'd be a fool not to take advantage of him." Meg smiled. "Father was right to arrange this marriage."

"There's a bit of your father in you." Owen sneered, but his voice hinted of admiration.

"If he was a better opportunist, he wouldn't be in debt."

Owen leaned against the padded seat and closed his eyes. Meg didn't trust him to be asleep and talked about the hymns and flowers until they reached the church.

Lilibet climbed down out of the carriage and hurried inside while Meg directed the servants.

"Leave that one," Owen ordered as one of the men lifted his trunk.

Lilibet unpacked the gowns as Owen inspected the room. He tried the locked door to the storage room.

"As you see, there is no escape," Meg said. "You can stand guard outside while we dress."

"If I suspect any trickery on your part, I will invite myself in."

"I would expect nothing less from a man who isn't a gentleman." She closed the door and quietly latched the lock.

Lilibet knocked on the storage room door. "It's safe." A key appeared on the floor, and she unlocked the door. Cathy and Anna emerged from the dark space.

"You brought the baby?" Lilibet had a look of horror on her face.

"I'm sorry. I couldn't find anyone to watch her, and

282

Mother is playing the harpsichord for the ceremony."

One more thing that could go wrong. "Will she be quiet?"

"She's ready for a nap." Cathy arranged several blankets on the floor and placed Anna on them.

"We can stack the boxes and trunks around her in case Owen comes in," Lilibet suggested.

Cathy looked at them. "Owen? The man you spoke of?"

"The one intent on making me marry Eliot," Meg confirmed. "The man we have to fool."

Cathy looked worried. "How are we going to do that?"

"For now, help me dress, and I'll make an appearance to Owen in the foyer."

Lilibet handed the embroidered petticoat to Meg. "Do you think it'll work?"

"Even if we fool Owen, I'm more afraid of Banner trying to save me from a loveless marriage and whisking me away from the altar." That vision had been one of her nightmares.

Lilibet went pale. "Oh dear."

She grasped her arm. "Your job is to prevent that."

"How?" Lilibet's voice squeaked.

Meg had run out of ideas. "I don't know, but everyone standing at the altar is for the marriage even if they don't know it."

"Where will Owen be?"

"Probably guarding the main doors so I don't flee before the nuptials."

Meg's heart fluttered like a bird's wings, and she looked the part of a nervous bride as she dressed in the wedding gown made in London. The underskirt and center of the bodice were beige with gold embroidery near the hem. The overskirt was crème silk with white roses sewn in the fabric. Small ruffles began at the neckline, framed the wide bodice, and trailed in waves down the front of the skirt and along the hem. Larger ruffles accented the skirt. A large bow covered the bodice and was edged in gold trim. White lace peeked out from the wide sleeves at her elbows.

Her hair was pulled back with curls ending at her shoulders. "Fix Cathy's hair so it's the same length as mine while I make an appearance."

Meg stepped outside the room and glanced around. Owen was in the entrance talking with Victoria. He saw her and approached.

"Is Eliot here?"

"Captain Youngblood brought him and took him to the reverend's office," Owen said. "They appear to be sober."

"You look lovely, Lady Meg," Victoria said.

"Thank you, but Mrs. Goodheart was going to make a couple of bouquets for Lilibet and me." She looked around.

"I'll find her," Victoria volunteered. "We don't want you to worry about anything on your wedding day."

Meg turned to Owen. "Tell Victoria to leave the flowers on the table. Lilibet will retrieve them when we're ready to begin the ceremony."

"How soon will this spectacle begin?"

"Lilibet is dressing, and I need my veil. Entertain Victoria while you wait." She went back inside and leaned against the door. Her heart was beating too fast, but the first step was completed. Lilibet had changed into her own gown and helped her undress. They turned their attention to Cathy and dressed her in the wedding gown.

Meg glanced at the door. Owen wouldn't wait long, but if he was in a hurry to escort her up the aisle, he wouldn't have time to examine the bride too closely.

Cathy stroked the silk fabric. "I could never afford something so beautiful."

"Consider it my gift to you." Meg removed the ruby ring on her finger. "Put this on. Lord Dudlee gave it to me, and Owen will recognize it."

Meg helped Cathy slip her feet into high-heeled shoes. She stood in the flat shoes she had been wearing all week. "We're nearly the same height now. Owen shouldn't notice. Now the final touch."

They placed the bonnet on her head, which completely covered her hair except for a cascade of curls poking out in the back that matched the length of Meg's shorter hair.

Cathy pulled the veil down in front of her face. "I'm glad I know every inch of this church. I can barely see through this, but I should be able to find my way to the altar."

Meg walked around her. "My own brother would think you were me. Owen will escort you up the aisle, but barely touch his arm. We detest each other. As long as you don't speak, he won't know it's you."

"What if he asks a question?"

"Nod but don't answer," Meg said. "Remember, you're a nervous bride."

"I won't have to pretend that part," Cathy said. "What about when I say my vows?"

"Your father will speak your name softly, and you can whisper."

"He knows it will be me marrying Eliot?" Cathy's

voice revealed her disbelief.

Meg finished lacing her plain gown and took her hands. "Yes. He helped with the plans. He loves you."

Cathy sniffled.

Meg lifted the veil. "Don't cry." She handed her a handkerchief. "This is a happy day for you."

"How can I ever thank you?"

"Let's finish the ceremony before any congratulations." She fixed the veil so it covered Cathy's face and reviewed the sequence of events. "Remember to sign your real name, and Lilibet will witness it. Once the document is registered at the courthouse, the marriage is official. Your father will preach until the messenger returns. Then you'll say your vows. Finally, he'll pronounce you man and wife. And then you kiss and live happily ever after."

"What if Eliot doesn't sign?"

"I asked Banner to make sure he signs the license." Another thing that could go wrong.

Cathy hugged her. "Thank you." She turned her head toward Anna who grunted in her sleep.

"I'll take care of her. You get married." Meg signaled to Lilibet to open the door while she stayed hidden behind it.

Cathy made her way out.

"You can signal Mrs. Goodheart to begin playing the music," Lilibet said as she shut the door.

Meg closed her eyes and said a quick prayer. She quietly packed the trunk and waited for whatever disaster ruined her plans.

Chapter Twenty-Eight

Banner paced in the small room that served as the Reverend Thomas Goodheart's office. Eliot sat at the desk, looking like a man condemned to the block but dressed for a festive party. His suit was a dark-rose color with a vest in a pale shade of pink. Delicate lace poked out from the wide cuffed sleeves, and his cravat had been tied in an elegant bow at his neck. The clothes had been selected by his father and copied his peacock taste.

Banner had dressed in a dark-blue coat with a lighter-blue waistcoat, another gift from Lord Dudlee. They both wore white breeches and stockings with black buckled shoes. The shoes were new and uncomfortable.

Eliot had barely spoken two words since they arrived. Banner could find no words to encourage him.

"I can't go through with it." Eliot stood and moved toward the door. "I need to get out of here."

Banner blocked his path. "You can't leave Lady Meg at the altar."

"You marry her." His eyes held no humor. He meant every word.

Banner considered his proposal as an acceptable alternative, but Meg had asked him to trust her. She had asked one thing from him—to make sure Eliot signed the license and went through with the wedding. Was Meg playing a cruel joke upon him? If nothing stopped this farce, Eliot would be married to the woman he loved.

The Reverend Goodheart opened the door. "Gentlemen, it's time for the ceremony." He patted Eliot on the back. "Be of good cheer. All may turn out the way you want in the end."

"What do you mean?" Banner asked, but he refused to explain.

The reverend led them to the front of the church. The pews were filled with members of the church, town, and workers for the Richmond family. Glen Stemple sat in the front pew, an unnatural smile on his face. If Meg was correct, he had orchestrated Lord Dudlee's refusal for Eliot to wed Cathy. He wouldn't waste any time courting her.

Griffin was talking to the merchants who had purchased the same goods from Banner and the Richmond warehouse. Was Glen justified in recording less money for the items he sold, or was he reporting lower numbers and pocketing the difference? If they found him guilty of theft, he would be disgraced and couldn't bother Cathy from jail.

The music began, and everyone seated in the pews rose to their feet and turned toward the back of the church. Eliot remained facing forward, but Banner watched as Lilibet walked up the aisle, a small cluster of flowers in her hand and a nervous smile on her face. Meg and Owen followed. She bore herself proudly, but he couldn't see her face beneath the thick lace. Why had she chosen to hide her beauty?

Lilibet took the bouquet Meg had carried and stood across from Banner. Owen held his arm stiff with Meg's left hand resting lightly on top. The ruby ring stood out against her pale skin. Pale? Meg had acquired a tan to her skin while at sea. Had it faded already?

"Who gives this woman in marriage?"

"I do." Owen turned and marched to the back of the church where he sat next to Victoria in the last pew.

Did he think Meg would run away? He would knock Owen out of the way if she chose to run.

The Reverend Goodheart welcomed the guests and talked about marriage. He mentioned the legal bindings and produced the special license. Eliot was first. Meg had asked Banner to make sure he signed. It made no sense, but he had promised to trust her. He would keep his word no matter how events played out.

Eliot took the quill, dipped it in the inkwell, and paused above the blank line where the reverend pointed. The signature would seal his fate.

"Sign," Banner growled. He glanced toward Meg to see if she approved, but could see nothing behind the thick veil. Meg didn't even look his way. Did she realize what she was doing?

Eliot scratched his signature on the parchment. The Reverend Goodheart handed Banner the quill, and he witnessed Eliot's signature with his own. He had fulfilled his part. He silently cursed as Meg took the quill and scratched her name on the document. Lilibet stepped forward and witnessed the signature with her own.

The reverend signed his name and sprinkled pounce on the ink to dry it. He handed the document to a man standing near the pulpit. "Take this to the courthouse and bring back proof the marriage has been registered."

Banner's heart sank. The legal portion of the ceremony was completed. Meg had made a fool of him. Only Eliot's need for a friend kept him in place instead of bolting for the door and his ship.

The church registry was opened with all the

marriages and christenings listed inside. Again, Eliot signed his name. Banner wasn't required to witness it, and The Reverend Goodheart handed the quill to Meg, who signed her name in the same row. He handed the book to a lad who carried it to his office.

A hymn was sung, and the reverend began a sermon from I Corinthians about love. Banner shifted on his feet, his shoes pinching his toes. Would he ever get to the vows and end this travesty?

The courier returned and handed the Reverend Goodheart a document with a seal and ribbon attached. The marriage was legal.

The reverend began a prayer. After everyone repeated, "Amen," he smiled at the couple. How could he be happy? Eliot was not marrying his daughter. She and Anna would forever be ostracized. What sort of father took joy in that?

The Reverend Goodheart began the vows. "Dearly beloved, we are gathered together here in the sight of God, and in the face of this congregation, to join together this man and this woman in holy matrimony. Wilt thou, Eliot Isaac, have this woman to be thy wedded wife, to live together after God's ordinance in the holy estate of matrimony?"

Banner nudged Eliot when he hesitated.

"I do."

The reverend turned to Meg. "Wilt thou, Mary Catherine, have this man to be thy wedded husband, to live together after God's ordinance in the holy estate of matrimony?"

Mary Catherine? Her name was Margaret Katherine. The reverend had spoken her name too softly for those in the audience to hear the error. Even Eliot seemed to have missed it. Banner looked at the woman beside Eliot more closely. The veil disguised her face, but he had studied her figure for two months. The waist was thicker, and even with heels, she was too short to be Meg. The women had switched places. He glanced toward the back of the church. Owen was fawning over Victoria, unaware of the trick. Meg must be in the anteroom. The corner of his mouth twitched. The woman was a genius and a sadistic beauty. She had tortured him without any hint of her plan.

"I do."

The voice did not belong to Meg. Eliot recognized it as well and turned.

"Steady, man," Banner warned.

"Do you have a ring?"

Banner handed the ring to the reverend who talked about the symbol of love. He handed the gold band to Eliot, who took Cathy's hand.

"Repeat after me. With this ring I thee wed."

Eliot said the words and slid the gold band onto her finger in front of the ruby ring.

"I now pronounce you man and wife," the Reverend Goodheart announced. "You may kiss your bride."

Eliot lifted the veil and stared at Cathy.

"Don't you want to kiss me?" Her soft voice teased him.

A smile returned to his face after a long absence. He pulled her into his arms and complied. A cheer rang out from the crowd.

Banner released a breath. Why had Meg kept the deception a secret? Owen was the obvious reason, but she could have told him and Eliot. He looked at the change in his friend. His entire countenance had transformed at the sight of Cathy. If Eliot had known Cathy was to be his bride, he would have revealed the secret by his exuberant behavior.

Banner was in love with a lying, devious, scheming woman who had left him feeling both furious and frantic. He recalled the curves of her body beneath his hands. Meg would keep boredom out of their marriage in and outside the bedroom.

"What God has brought together, let no man put asunder," the Reverend Goodheart announced. "I present to you Mr. and Mrs. Eliot Richmond."

They turned as everyone applauded. The clapping subsided, silence taking over as the identity of the bride became apparent.

"Cathy!" Glen shouted as he jumped up from his pew seat and pushed others out of the way to reach the bride. "You can't marry him!"

Eliot stepped between Cathy and Glen. "She's my wife."

"No. You were betrothed to Lady Meg." Glen looked around at the crowd. "You broke the agreement. Lord Dudlee will have this marriage annulled."

"The marriage has been officially registered," the Reverend Goodheart said. "It cannot be undone."

Glen clenched his teeth as he pointed at Eliot. "I've waited too long to make her mine after you stole her."

"I never belonged to you," Cathy said, clutching Eliot's arm. "I never agreed to marry you."

Glen reached for the bride. "I love you, Cathy. I always have."

Cathy pressed against her husband. "I've always loved Eliot."

"That doesn't matter. Women don't know what's

best for them." Glen glared at Eliot. "She'll come to love me when I provide for her and give her my name. Unlike you."

Eliot's spine stiffened. "She has my name now."

"And how will you provide for her?" Glen's voice rose in rage. "Lord Dudlee will cut you off."

"Not when he finds out you're the one who has been poisoning him against Cathy with your lies," Banner said.

"He believes me," Glen said. "He'll think Cathy tricked Eliot into marrying her."

"He thought he was marrying Lady Meg. His father can't disown him for obediently going through with the wedding." Eliot was innocent of any duplicity. Meg was brilliant.

Glen lunged at Eliot, but Banner anticipated his move and blocked him with one arm while striking him with his fist. Glen collapsed to the floor.

"I could have done that," Eliot said.

Banner rubbed the knuckles of his hand. "I'm fulfilling my role to guarantee your happiness on your wedding day."

Griffin had made his way up the aisle with the town magistrate and had watched the drama with the other guests. He pointed at Glen's prostrate form. "You were right, Captain. He's been changing the figures in the ledgers to reflect a lower sale price and keeping the difference. Several merchants confirmed the price they paid was higher than the one he recorded."

Banner turned to Eliot. "Your clerk stole from you by lying about profits."

The town magistrate stepped forward. "Do you want him arrested, sir?"

"Yes," Eliot said. "I'll deal with him tomorrow." He looked at Cathy. "I'll be busy tonight."

Chapter Twenty-Nine

Meg leaned against the door to hear what was going on in the church. The ceremony should be over, but men were shouting in the distance. One of them was Banner. What had happened?

Anna was awake and sat up, looking around the room. "Mama?" Her lip trembled, and a fat tear slid down her cheek.

Meg searched the blankets the little girl had been nestled in and found her doll. "Don't cry. Here's your baby."

Anna hugged the doll but sniffled. "Mama?"

Meg lifted her into her arms and placed her onto her hip. "Let's go find her." Eliot and Cathy had to be legally wed by now.

She unlocked the door and cautiously opened it.

Owen was standing in the arched opening to the sanctuary and turned. His eyes widened in surprise before a snarl came to his lips. He strode toward her before she could react. He jerked open the door. "Don't think your little trick changes anything." He snatched Anna from her arms.

Meg reached for the child. "Give her back!"

He withdrew a knife from his coat pocket and held it against the little girl's throat. "Come with me quietly, or she dies."

"Don't hurt her." Meg tried to reach for Anna, but

Owen backstepped, leading them toward the door. She surveyed the crowd of people inside the sanctuary of the church, but they were standing, and their attention was focused on the front. She couldn't see Banner or Lilibet over their heads.

"Lady Meg!" Victoria's declaration was drowned out by the cheers of the congregation as she stepped toward them.

Owen waved his knife. "Sit down, Victoria, or I may have to mar that beautiful face."

She met Meg's gaze briefly but obeyed.

He returned the blade to the baby's throat and motioned for Meg to leave the church.

"I'll do what you want, but put the knife down," Meg begged. "She's a baby and doesn't understand. She may jerk, and you'll cut her accidentally."

"Or intentionally." He followed her down the stone steps. "Let's go."

A boy stood outside with broadsheets in his hand. "Latest news including the wedding."

Meg stopped. "The wedding?"

"Buy us each copies," Owen ordered as a crooked smile creased his face.

Meg searched her pocket for coins and bought two copies from the boy.

Owen grabbed one of the broadsheets. She read hers. On the back page was the announcement of the marriage between the honorable Eliot Richmond and Lady Meg Culbertson of Whittington Manor. It contained the information Owen had provided earlier in the week to the printer's office. They had set the type before the event so the paper could be sold this morning.

She shook the paper at Owen. "But this is wrong.

I'm not married."

"It doesn't matter." He folded his copy and placed it in his pocket. "Do you think I didn't have a plan if somehow you didn't marry Eliot? They'll print the correct announcement in next week's edition, but with this written public acknowledgment, I won't need a letter from the Reverend Goodheart to prove your marriage."

With the newsprint record, he could convince Peter Clifton she had wed. He could claim her trust. She had underestimated Owen, again.

The driver jumped down from the carriage they had arrived in and opened the door. Owen tossed Anna inside, who wailed at the mistreatment.

Meg jumped in and pulled the little girl into her arms.

"Take us to the docks and hurry," Owen ordered as he joined them.

"The docks?" Meg asked.

"I told you I was sailing on the *Manchester*. She'll arrive in London before any news about Eliot and Cathy's marriage reaches anyone."

He sneered in a way that made her stomach churn. She heard her name and leaned out the window. Victoria was running toward her, but the carriage was too far away for her to catch them.

"You don't need Anna now. Leave her with Victoria."

"As long as I have this child, you'll do as I say." He looked with disgust at the sobbing girl. "Shut her up."

Meg hugged Anna and cooed comforting words to her as the carriage passed through town without slowing. She couldn't jump, especially with a baby. Her hope remained with Victoria who would tell Banner of their plight. She stroked Anna's hair until her sobs turned to sniffles.

Owen stared at her, his eyes cold. "How did you get everyone to agree to your deception?"

She saw no reason to lie. "Eliot and Banner didn't know."

"I don't believe you. The man wanted to marry the reverend's daughter."

"But you would have noticed the change in him if he had any hope of marrying the woman he loved."

"And what role did Captain Youngblood play in your plan?"

"I only asked him to make sure Eliot said his vows and didn't bolt from the church. He thought I was the bride."

He relaxed against the seat. "I could have sworn you were smitten with each other."

She prayed Banner loved her and came for her, but surprise would aid him. She snorted. "You saw how he acted with Victoria. Men are fools when it comes to women."

"She's a beautiful lady. I would have claimed her if I had more time."

She forgot to hide her disdain. "You threatened to cut her face, the exact thing you praise."

"Women need to submit." He leaned forward, hate in his eyes. "A lesson you would do well to learn."

She remained silent until the carriage stopped at the dock. Owen grabbed Anna before Meg could stop him. He stepped down with the girl tucked under his arm like a package.

"Ow, hurtin' me," Anna protested.

The driver lowered Owen's trunk to the ground.

"The *Manchester* is at the end of the pier."

"Have someone deliver my trunk."

The driver motioned to a stocky man standing nearby and told him to carry the trunk down to the ship.

Meg remained seated inside, determined to protect the baby. "I'll go with you if you leave Anna in the carriage."

"Get out," he ordered.

"Lord Dudlee will not forgive you for hurting his granddaughter. He'll hunt you down and see you hang for murder."

Owen's pale skin reddened. "If you swear to do as I say, I'll leave her behind."

Did he think she held herself to honor oaths like men? "I swear." Meg exited the carriage but stood near the door. "Put her inside."

He plopped her on the floorboard.

Meg lifted her to the corner of the seat and placed her doll in her hands. "You'll see your mama and papa soon." She left the broadsheet on the seat. It wasn't much of a clue, but Banner might understand the danger she faced.

Owen tugged on her arm. "You're wasting time."

"Stay here, honey." Meg stroked the child's cheek. She stepped back and looked at the driver. "Take the carriage to Eliot Richmond's home."

"You don't leave until we're aboard the *Manchester*." Owen gripped her arm so tightly she winced.

"Yes, sir." He must have heard enough to know Owen meant the child harm. He stepped between them and the carriage door and gave her a slight nod. The look on his face reassured her he would keep Anna safe.

Owen pulled Meg along the pier. He kept his free hand in his pocket where he hid his knife. "You do anything to cause trouble, and Lord Dudlee won't have to worry about any granddaughter. I'll go back and slit the little girl's throat."

The sailors paused to give her an appreciative glance or a nod of their heads as she passed. She smiled and made sure they would remember her. Banner had been far away in the front of the church. How long would it take for him to know of her kidnapping? Would he arrive in time?

"Keep your mouth shut," Owen warned as he pushed her forward up the gangplank. His trunk had been deposited on the deck, and the stocky man waited to be paid. Owen handed him a coin.

He grunted his displeasure and left.

"Welcome aboard, I'm Captain Germaine." An older man with a short white beard greeted them. "I was almost ready to sail without you." He looked at her. "I was unaware there would be another passenger. Will you need another cabin?"

"Another room won't be necessary. I'm Owen O'Leary, and this is my sister, Lilibet. She decided to return home with me."

Lilibet? What game was Owen playing?

"There's a bunk and the barest necessities in the cabin, Mr. O'Leary. Will your sister be comfortable?"

"As well as can be expected for someone in her poor state of mind," Owen said. "She's heartbroken. Jilted by her lover. I'll have to keep a close eye on her."

"Please do," the captain said. "We wouldn't want anything unfortunate to happen."

"My thoughts exactly."

Meg opened her mouth to argue Owen's lies, but he squeezed her arm.

"Come along, Lilibet. You'll forget that worthless rake soon enough. Hopefully, no one will hear of this scandal in London, and you'll marry soon and put an end to the gossip."

"I'll get your trunk." A sailor's gaze met Meg's, and he gave her a slight nod. It was Issy. He had told her he would be returning on the first ship to England to spend time with his family. "This way."

Issy led them to a small cabin beneath the quarterdeck. He dropped the trunk near the lower bunk.

Owen looked around. "Not much space. I hope I won't have to share. Especially with my sister in the room."

"Three of the crew were assigned to this cabin, but we'll find other accommodations. The space is yours and your sister's." Issy looked at the hooks in the ceiling beams. "I'll be back shortly, sir."

Meg felt the ship shift beneath her feet and listened as the crew shouted orders to cast off the lines and unfurl the sails. The canvas snapped with the filling of the wind, and the boards creaked with movement against the water. They were leaving and soon would be out at sea. A dread chilled her heart. What if Banner couldn't rescue her? What if she failed to escape? But Issy was her ally. She needed to learn Owen's schemes and counter them with her own plans.

"Why are you calling me Lilibet?"

"Because Lady Meg married Eliot." He removed the broadsheet from his coat pocket. "None of the crew were at the wedding, but I will confirm it occurred with this."

"Then what do you need me for?"

A knock interrupted them.

He patted the pocket containing his knife. "Not a word." He returned the wedding announcement to his coat and opened the door.

Issy had tugged his cap low on his face, but Owen never paid attention to underlings. He had barely noticed any of the sailors on the *Gabriella* except to order them about or complain.

Issy carried in a length of rope and a couple of blankets. "I thought this would give your sister some privacy. Will you take the top bunk or the bottom one?"

"Bottom." Owen leaned against the wall as the ship moved. "Neither one of us enjoys sea travel. We'll take all our meals in our room, and bring an extra slop bucket."

Issy strung the rope from hooks in the ceiling beams and tossed the blankets over it to form a cloth wall across the top bunk. He turned and bowed toward Owen. "I hope you reconsider joining the officers. Captain Germaine enjoys having company with his meals."

"Give him our regrets." Owen closed the door. "Don't waste time making plans to escape. That's the last time you'll have any interaction with the crew."

She needed to bide her time. Issy could only do so much to help her, and Banner would need time to gather men and supplies. It could be days or weeks before he reached her. "What are your plans for me, or should I say Lilibet?"

He moved a chair in front of the door and sat. "You brought this on yourself. You should have married Eliot."

"Eliot married the woman he loved."

"I knew you would try to escape the marriage. You

were clever to wait until the last minute to enact your ploy, but did you think your deception at the altar would affect me?" He removed the broadsheet from his pocket and locked it in his trunk. "Now I need to be the first to reach London and collect my money before anyone hears the truth about the wedding."

"You mean *Father's* money."

"Do you think I worked for dear old Father all these years for the pittance he doled out? I was his son, and he treated me like a lackey. When Father broke his leg, I seized my opportunity to gain more control over the family finances." He removed his knife from his pocket. "I stopped making repairs and kept Father drunk so he wouldn't notice how decrepit his properties had become."

She normally wouldn't show any interest in Owen's schemes, but he was drooling, eager to share. "Since I can't stop you, why don't you enlighten me on how Father's poverty is going to make you rich?"

He waved the knife in the air. "The fool can't add a column of numbers twice and come up with the same number. He trusts me implicitly, so it was easy to manipulate the books and transfer unspent funds into investments I could access. I was accumulating a tidy sum when your mother noticed that the expenses for repairs listed in the ledger were never completed."

She stared into his soulless eyes. How could this monster be related to her? Tears stung her eyes. "You killed my mother?"

"I never touched her, but I followed her to Cornhill Street. She was going to visit the family solicitor. I spooked a horse pulling a cart. My intention was to scare her, but fate had other plans."

"What you did wasn't an accident. You murdered her." She raised her hands and rushed forward to strike him.

He moved quicker and spun her around, capturing her with his free arm. He placed the blade of the knife at her throat. "What do you want your fate to be?"

She stood frozen, the cold steel against her skin. "Why didn't you take what you had stolen and leave?"

He shoved her toward the bunks and took his seat. "I would have gone last year with a few hundred pounds, but Mr. Clifton asked me about your trust fund. Do you know your grandfather invested money for you?"

"No," she lied.

"A sizeable amount had grown over the years, much larger than the money I had planned to take. Only there was a condition. You had to wait until after your twenty-first birthday to collect it. But if you married before then, your father would receive the funds. Or should I say, I'll receive the funds when I show Mr. Clifton the article proving you've married the honorable Eliot Richmond."

She looked toward his locked trunk. "Did Father know anything about the trust fund?"

"At one time, but I made sure Mr. Clifton only dealt with me." He leaned back in his chair and used the tip of his blade to clean under his dirty nails. "I needed to find a husband for you quickly, and Lord Dudlee and his gossiping wife made it widely known they were looking for a titled woman to marry their son. It didn't take much to convince your father the match was advantageous."

She recalled the beating. "And he convinced me."

"He's easily manipulated when he's drunk. I honestly think he was shocked and appalled by his behavior once he was sober enough to realize what he had done to you."

"You don't need to defend him," she spat the words. "I don't mind you robbing him, but Micah is his rightful heir. Have you left him anything?"

"He has a good education and a title. That's more than I had."

"Father sent you to school and gave you a job."

"A servant's job," he sneered. "I was his son. His firstborn. But English law doesn't allow a bastard to inherit. You don't know how it feels to be an outcast. I'm only taking what I deserve."

She needed to know how far he would go. "But I'm alive and unmarried. What keeps me from telling Mr. Clifton the truth?"

A crooked smile emerged on his lips. "I've already laid the groundwork for your suicide. Poor Lilibet is despondent over a lost love," he mocked. "She wouldn't be the first woman to fling herself into deadly cold waters to escape scandal. After you're gone, I will tell Captain Germaine that you discovered you were with child and chose to die quickly rather than face the shame of immorality."

Meg backed against the post supporting the bunks. He planned to murder her, but when? "How long before I take the long swim in the sea?"

"I always admired how you used humor to hide your fear." He bared his crooked yellow teeth. "The time of your death depends on you. If you behave, I'll wait and allow your depressed mental state to grow. If you misbehave, I'll dump your body overboard during the night and make your excuses."

His words terrified her because he could do exactly what he threatened. "Won't the captain report my death?"

"You mean Lilibet's death." He chuckled as he stood and took a step toward her. "Her mother will mourn, but by the time Lord Whittington realizes you were the real victim, I'll be long gone with enough money to live like a lord."

"You'll hang!"

"No body, no proof." He stabbed the knife in quick jerks in her direction. "Get up on the bunk."

She was too scared to move.

He grabbed her wrist and pulled her toward the trunk. He poked the blade into her back. "Up."

She climbed to the top bunk and pulled the blankets along the rope.

Owen stopped her from completely closing the opening. "That's far enough." He cut off the extra length of rope dangling below the knot Issy had tied and stabbed the end of the knife into the wood of the bunk. He grabbed her hand, made a loop around her wrist, and tightened the rope, cutting into her skin.

She screamed, but he slapped her hard. She tasted blood on her lip.

"I shouldn't have told you my plans, but I enjoyed the look of horror on your face. I hate women who don't scare easily. Tell me something funny, Lady Meg. Make a joke."

She was frightened enough of the madman to remain silent.

He looped the end around the bed rail between the rope supports and wrapped the other end of the rope around her other wrist and secured her to the bed frame so she could barely move except to lie on her side.

Owen removed a handkerchief from his pocket.

"Open up." When she refused, he squeezed her cheeks to make her comply and shoved the linen cloth into her mouth.

He moved to the end of the bed, removed her shoes, and tossed them on the floor. She gasped and struggled as he raised her petticoat. His hand slid up her stocking and tugged on the garter tie.

She tried to work the handkerchief out of her mouth with her tongue so she could scream.

He pulled her stocking off and tied it around her face to secure the gag in her mouth. "That's how I like my women. Silent."

He patted her bruised cheek. "Be a good girl, and I may share my food when they bring it." The ropes on the bunk below creaked as he lay down.

He could have all her food if it made him sick and aided her escape. She studied the knots Owen had tied. After supper, after he had fallen asleep, she could begin the job of untying the rope.

Hurry, Banner, she prayed.

Chapter Thirty

Banner guarded Glen until the magistrate had him in custody. The congregation surged forward to congratulate Eliot and Cathy. He fought against the crowd and searched for Meg.

Victoria appeared in the back, standing on a pew and waving her arms. He pressed toward her, ignoring the complaints from those moving in the opposite direction.

When he was close, she pointed outside. "He's taken them."

Fear gripped his heart. "Who?"

"Mr. O'Leary! He had a knife to the baby's throat. He forced Meg to go with him." She pointed to a gap where a coach was missing in the line of carriages.

Griffin and Lilibet had followed Banner down the aisle. They gathered on the lawn where a boy was selling broadsheets.

"Announcement of the wedding today." He waved a paper.

Banner grabbed a broadsheet and realized what the announcement meant. "Owen has his proof." He tossed the boy a coin.

"Thank you, sir. You're most generous."

"He was leaving on the *Manchester* today," Lilibet said. "When does it sail?"

"One." He looked at his timepiece. It was ten minutes after, but the ship could still be docked. "I'll go after Meg and Anna."

"I have a horse," Griffin said. "Take it. I'll follow in a carriage."

"You can take mine," Victoria said.

"Gather as many of the crew as you can," Banner shouted as he mounted the horse. "The *Manchester* may have sailed."

As he rode toward the harbor, a driver of a carriage waved him down. "Are you looking for Lady Meg and a little girl?"

"Yes." He jumped from his horse and yanked open the carriage door. Anna was sitting on the seat, shredding a piece of paper. She looked up and smiled.

He turned to the driver. "Where's Lady Meg?"

"Mr. O'Leary took her aboard the *Manchester*. I overheard him threatening to kill the child if she didn't obey. She told me to take the child to the Richmond house."

"Her parents will be there," he said. "Tell them what happened."

The *Manchester* was gone when he reached the harbor, but the *Gabriella* was tied up at the dock. He boarded his ship and called for Duffy.

"Captain, I had your trunks stowed in your cabin."

He had sent his belongings to the ship, anticipating Eliot's wedding night. "Any crew aboard?"

"A few. What's wrong, Captain?"

"Owen has taken Lady Meg on the *Manchester*. I need a crew to go after them."

"Some of our men signed on for the *Endeavor's* crew," Duffy said. "She's sailing to China."

"I'll talk to the captain. Load fresh water and food for a week's voyage. When Griffin arrives, tell him to go to the harbormaster's office and obtain the course coordinates for the *Manchester*."

"Aye, sir," Duffy said. "We'll find her."

Banner didn't answer. He'd never been more afraid in his life. Why had Owen taken her? If she returned to England, Lord Whittington and Lord Dudlee would know the wedding never occurred. That left one alternative. Bodies were never recovered from the ocean.

He boarded the *Endeavor* and sought out the captain. "I'll pay double wages for a week's voyage."

"We sail in a week."

"I need to reach the *Manchester*." He explained the kidnapping.

"Talk to the crew," the captain said. "It's a two-year voyage, and a delay of a day or two won't matter."

Banner stood on the quarterdeck and pleaded his case to the crew gathered below. "I'll pay every man who can raise a sail double the wages and have you back in time to board the *Endeavor*."

"The money is incentive enough, but what's in it for you, Captain? Why do you want to rescue Lady Meg?"

He recognized the man as one of the deckhands who had sailed on the *Gabriella* from England.

"You know the answer. I love her."

"I wanted to hear you say it." He raised his hat into the air. "I'll help you and challenge every man here who has ever loved a woman to join us."

The others voiced their allegiance.

The crew and supplies were on board in time to take advantage of the last of the ebbing tide. Banner gave the order to cast off the mooring lines and raise the sails. He loaded all the canvas, knowing he would need the full wind to reach the *Manchester* before Owen harmed Meg.

Banner stood at the helm until nightfall, his eyes straining the horizon for any sign of another ship.

"You're dead on your feet, Captain," Griffin said. "Get some sleep. I'll let you know if we spot anything."

Banner was too exhausted to argue. "I may not be a religious man, but I've seen too many wonders in the world not to believe in God. I've been praying since we left the dock."

"The men are saying their prayers, too."

Banner was up at dawn to search for a ship.

"Sails on the starboard side!" a man perched in the rigging called out.

Banner grabbed his spyglass and searched the horizon. The top sails were visible. He prayed it was the *Manchester*. He closed the distance and confirmed her identity. "Signal for her to take in her sails. We're coming alongside."

When they were closer, he ordered the sails on the *Gabriella* furled and came abreast of the other ship. He handed the helm over to Griffin.

Banner stood on the starboard side, his foot on the rail as he searched for Meg. "Do you have a woman aboard named Lady Meg?"

"No," Captain Germaine answered. "We have a woman named Lilibet. She's traveling with her brother."

"She's the one I'm searching for," Banner shouted. "I'm coming aboard."

"We're not close enough for you to cross," Duffy warned.

He had slept in his wedding attire and removed the coat and waistcoat. "Then I'll swim."

"We'll lower a boat." Duffy ordered the men to prepare the longboat.

Chapter Thirty-One

Meg had waited for Owen to fall asleep. He had lowered her gag and removed his wet handkerchief when the food arrived, and untied one hand so she could eat a slice of bread with butter on it.

Owen ate both meals and threw them up in the slop bucket.

Meg used the distraction to loosen the knots on her other hand. When Owen recovered, he raised the stocking over her mouth, forgetting the handkerchief she hid beneath her skirt, and retied her free hand.

"Go to sleep." He plopped on his bed and groaned.

Night had fallen, and Meg listened to Owen snoring below. All those hours learning to tie and untie knots allowed her to free one hand from the rail. She lowered her gag and worked on the other wrist until both hands were free.

She tied bowline knots into the rope ends so she could slip her wrist into the loops if Owen woke and checked to see if she was tied. She kept her stocking tied around her neck so she could replace it as well and removed her other stocking in case she had a chance to run.

Owen had left a lit lantern hanging from the ceiling beam that provided light as she quietly searched the bunk for anything that might aid her. She slid the cover off the cubbyhole and found a pen, ink, and a small journal inside from the previous occupant. If she didn't escape, she wanted her family to know what had happened. She uscd her knife from her pocket to cut a few sheets out of the journal and dipped the quill into the tin inkwell.

Meg finished her final note. In her message to Aunt Felicity and Micah, she explained what had happened and how Owen was using a broadsheet to prove she had wed Eliot. She proclaimed her love and told them Lilibet was safe in Connecticut in spite of what anyone might say from the ship. She, most likely, was dead, her body lost at sea.

She wrote Lord Dudlee and explained how Glen had poisoned him against Cathy. She praised his new daughter-in-law and granddaughter and confessed her deception of Eliot, begging him not to disown his son.

Her letter to Banner was filled with how much she loved him and had hoped for a life together. She carefully folded each letter and addressed the outsides.

She placed her letters inside the cubbyhole and closed the lid. Issy, hopefully, would find them and deliver them. She had been up most of the night and was tired. Should she place her hands into the rope in case Owen surprised her? She faced the open side of the bunk, and the ship made an abrupt turn. Before she could brace herself, she rolled against the wall. She listened as the command for taking in the sails was given. Were they approaching a storm?

She strained to hear above Owen's obnoxious snoring. A ship! It had to be Banner and the *Gabriella.* Now was the time to escape. She scooted to the end of the bed and dropped to the trunk. She crept to the door. When she lifted the latch, Owen awoke.

"What are you doing?"

She yanked on the door and made a dash to escape.

Owen caught up to her as her bare feet reached the open deck. He grabbed her skirt, which tore as she pulled away. She screamed, but he held tight to the fabric.

"Ignore my demented sister." Owen looked around at the crew staring at them. "Go back to your work."

"You don't give the orders," Captain Germaine said. "Release the woman."

Owen waved his knife in the air. "Get back."

"Let her go!" Banner shouted from the deck of his ship, nearly abreast of the *Manchester*.

Meg struggled against Owen's grip, searching for the small knife in the pocket beneath her skirt. She slashed at Owen's hand holding her captive. Blood spurted from the wound.

He cursed and released her.

She dashed for the rail. "Banner! You came for me."

He stepped to the opening for the gangplank. "Always."

She felt hands on her back pushing her forward over the rail. She searched for a hold and found none. Meg fell, her body dropping toward the water. She was a good swimmer and had dived from a short cliff, but this distance was going to take the breath out of her if she didn't spear the water. She raised her hands over her head and straightened her body as she hit the surface.

The cold struck her numb, and she didn't know how far she had sunk beneath the surface. Her eyes opened to a murky darkness. Which way was up? She swam toward the light above, kicking as her wet petticoat tangled in her legs.

She felt something stroke her bare leg. Was it a shark? She kicked, trying to put distance between herself and the creature. Her head broke through the surface, and she gulped down mouthfuls of air to fill her empty lungs.

Another head surfaced. It was Banner. He blew out sea water from his lips in the bouncing waves. "You kicked me."

"I thought you were a shark." She threw her arms around his neck as tears mixed with the salt water dripping from her hair and face. "I was afraid you wouldn't come. I heard the men shouting about another ship and escaped, but Owen was right behind me." Her body trembled. "He was going to kill me."

His arms held her tightly. "I have you now." His voice was reassuring.

She searched his face for any hint of anger. "You forgive me for not telling you about my plan?"

"The plan where you don't marry Eliot?" A wide grin creased his face. "I'm overjoyed." He kissed her, and she showed him how grateful she was he had come for her.

Men whistled and clapped above them. She pulled away long enough to catch her breath. "What about Anna? I told the driver to take her home."

He brushed wet hair back from her face. "I passed him on the road. She's reunited with her parents by now."

"Get out of there, you fool lovers, before the ships smash into you," Griffin shouted.

The ships had moved perilously close, and sailors were using pikes to push against the other ship to maintain distance.

Captain Germaine lowered a swing chair, and Banner helped her sit on the narrow plank. He climbed a rope dropped over the side of the ship and reached the deck as her feet touched the boards.

She charged Owen, her hands balled into fists. "You forgot I could swim. You should have waited until dark to knock me overboard. Your plan to tell everyone Lilibet killed herself failed."

Owen waved his knife and backed up toward the stern cabins. He looked around at the crew. "You can't believe anything she says. She's insane."

"You're the one mad. I'll have you arrested for your crimes," Meg said.

A queer expression brightened his face. He dropped his knife to the deck and spread his arms wide. "For what? I haven't broken any laws."

How could he pretend to be innocent? "You kidnapped me!"

"I have a letter from your father giving me the right of guardianship until you marry." He pointed at her and smirked. "Are you married?"

She pointed to the rail. "You pushed me overboard."

"You tripped and fell over the railing. I tried to catch you." Owen turned to Captain Germaine. "Anything she says will be a hysterical woman's word against mine."

"Liar!" Meg looked at the men on the deck. "Everyone saw you shove me."

Banner put his arm around her and whispered in her ear, "Can you prove he's done anything worth hanging?"

She relaxed against his chest, the problem evident to both of them. "He was going to take my trust money."

He stroked her cheek. "But he hasn't."

She pointed as she recalled Owen's confession. "He's responsible for my mother's death."

"You can't prove I had anything to do with that." He jabbed his finger toward Banner. "You can have Lady

Meg. Let me sail to England."

"So you can rob me of my trust fund?" Meg broke her silence. "Micah and I found out about your plans, and he's taken over management of Father's finances. Your plan was never going to succeed."

"You knew!" Owen lunged, his hands outstretched as he reached for her neck.

Banner moved swiftly, driving his fist into Owen's face. He crumbled to the deck.

"I wanted to hit him." Meg kicked Owen's leg with her bare foot. "Can I at least keelhaul him?"

"Keelhauling?" He chuckled. "I'm going to ignore your bloodthirst because you're angry, and I love you."

She stared at his face. "What did you say?"

"Clean the water out of your ears, darling. I've been in love with you since the first time I saw you, dancing like an angel on clouds. I was never going to forget your face, your smile, or the sound of your laughter. Then I discovered you were promised to Eliot. You made my world into a hell on Earth."

"But you have to go through a nor'easter to appreciate the calm." Meg smoothed the wet fabric of his shirt, outlining the hard muscles of his chest beneath. "When you fall in love, you have to expect a few storms."

He kissed her. "I love you, my darling schemer."

"And I love you, my honorable sea captain." She nodded toward Owen sprawled on the deck. "What are we going to do about him?"

A glint showed in his eyes. "Do you trust me?"

"That's not fair." She pouted as she considered his words. "Yes, I trust you with my heart, my body, and my soul."

317

"I borrowed crew members from the *Endeavor*, which is leaving for a two-year voyage to China. They could use an extra man."

Owen at sea for two years? A smile tugged on the corners of her mouth. "And Owen loves sailing." She flung her arms around his neck and kissed him with all the joy he brought into her life. She pulled away, nibbling on his bottom lip before speaking. "And you think I'm wicked."

"My mother would have envied you."

"Envied?"

He twirled her in his arms. "For all the adventures we'll share."

"My mother would have approved of you," Meg said. "A romantic who isn't afraid to break a few rules."

"You're a bad influence, my love. Our children will be hellions on land and sea." He turned to his crew. "Take him aboard the *Gabriella* and throw him in irons."

They placed a gangplank across the narrow gap between the ships and claimed Owen.

"Shall I fetch his trunk?" Issy asked.

"Issy!" Banner shouted.

Issy offered Meg a blanket, and Banner arranged it around her shoulders.

"I've been keeping an eye on Lady Meg, sir. I didn't expect her to make her escape while I was furling sails."

"Bring his trunk, and you'll find three letters in the cubbyhole of my bunk," Meg said.

Issy returned with the trunk and handed it over to one of Banner's crew. He gave her the letters. She handed the one addressed for Lord Dudlee to Captain Germaine. "Can you deliver this when you reach London?"

"You wrote letters?" Banner asked.

"While Owen slept. I was afraid he would end my life before you arrived. One is to Aunt Felicity and Micah so they would know what happened. I'll need to add a few lines so they know I'm alive and will be collecting my trust fund." She handed him a letter. "This one is for you. It's a beautiful declaration of love. If I had perished, it would have brought tears to your eyes."

He stroked a wet tendril from her face. "I'm glad you can laugh about it now. I'll read it when we're alone."

She pointed to the letter in Captain Germaine's hand. "I wrote to Lord Dudlee and took full blame for Eliot's marriage to Cathy. I also told him how Glen lied. I think he'll approve of the couple once he reads my explanation."

"Why didn't you trust me and tell me about your plans?"

She placed her palm against his cheek. "I wanted to tell you, but you kept talking about loyalty and honor. You would have felt obligated to tell Eliot, and that would have ruined everything. If Eliot knew he was marrying Cathy and not me, he would have been grinning from ear to ear, standing at the altar. How did he look?"

Banner's chest rumbled with laughter. "Like a man sentenced to the gallows."

"Good." She opened her blanket and pressed against him. "How did you look?"

"You had me fooled until I saw that the woman's hand resting on Owen's arm was pale." He examined her hand. "The sun has not had time to fade from your skin."

"I will have plenty of sun on my voyage to

England."

He looked hurt. "You're staying on the *Manchester*?"

"No, but before we sail on the *Gabriella*, I think we should marry," Meg said. "You show up at the church on July 18, and I'll walk down the aisle."

"July 18? I don't care about your trust fund."

She nuzzled his neck and whispered in his ear, "You will when I tell you how much is in it."

He pulled back and gazed into her eyes. "I don't need it or want it. You spend it on whatever your heart desires. I only ask one thing." He kissed her with enough passion to leave her wanting more. "When you walk down the aisle, promise me you won't wear a veil."

A word about the author…

Laura Freeman was a reporter for sixteen years for local papers and the Gannett national papers in Northeast Ohio. She won the Press Club of Cleveland's Ohio Excellence in Journalism award twice and the Ohio Newspaper Association award several times. Her novels include historical romances Impending Love and War, Impending Love and Death, Impending Love and Lies, Impending Love and Capture, Impending Love and Madness, Impending Love and Promise, a holiday novella Tackling Molasses Crinkles, crime mystery Raining Tears, and mystery Tangling a Web of Deceit.

~*~

Find Laura online at:
https://twitter.com/laurafreeman_rp
https://www.facebook.com/laura.freeman.5648
https://authorfreeman.wordpress.com/